Doorways

Doorways

A Bermuda Jones Casefile

by Robert Enright

URBANE
Publications

urbanepublications.com

First published in Great Britain in 2016
by Urbane Publications Ltd
Suite 3, Brown Europe House, 33/34 Gleaming Wood Drive,
Chatham, Kent ME5 8RZ
Copyright © Robert Enright, 2016

A CIP catalogue record for this book is available
from the British Library.

ISBN 978-1-911129-57-8
EPUB 978-1-911129-58-5
MOBI 978-1-911129-59-2

Design and Typeset by Michelle Morgan

Cover by Julie Martin

Printed and bound by CPI Group (UK) Ltd, Croydon, CR0 4YY

urbanepublications.com

For Ford Dainty and John Baker,
Gone but never forgotten.

1

The flashing blue lights erupted from the top of the police car, illuminating the front of the magnificent Cartwright Manor. The huge, stone structure stood with an overbearing grandeur, the large, solid pillars of the front door cast in intermittent blasts of blue. The smooth stone reached three floors high, the wall segregated in perfect symmetry by the door-sized windows.

The drive to Eversley had been fairly straight forward, the dreaded M25 that linked him from Hertfordshire to Hampshire was quieter in the middle of the night, instead of the usual stop-starts. The streets of Eversley were quiet, quaint little streets lined with small, neat houses. A few country pubs that would undoubtedly have been full of locals earlier in the evening. On the outskirts of the town, Cartwright Manor sat in the centre of twenty acres. As he passed through the grand, iron gate and slowly cruised up the gravel path that cut through the vast, neatly trimmed lawn, Franklyn 'Bermuda' Jones whistled in admiration.

Casting his green eyes over the immaculate grounds, he slowly rolled his car to a stop, the engine cutting out with a gentle purr.

Two police officers stood fifty feet away, arms folded across their stab proof vests, watching as the car door swung open. The chill of the wind slapped Bermuda across his stubble covered face and threw his light brown hair into disarray. With the moon hidden by thick, spring clouds, the only lights were those emanating from the downstairs of the house and the nearby police car.

Bermuda added his own, cupping his hand around his zippo lighter as the flame flickered, touching the end of his cigarette and casting smoke into the air.

He flicked it, the metal lid clapping shut.

'Chilly night, huh?' Bermuda's London accent filtered through the smoke.

As always, Argyle had met him at their destination. Partnered for over three years, Bermuda had become accustomed to Argyle's ability to beat him to the scene of the 'crime'. Although Bermuda stood six feet tall, his partner towered over him by another eight inches. His muscular arms hung from his shoulders, exposed by the sleeveless armoured plate he wore over his colossal torso. His armoured legs stood firmly together and Bermuda was always impressed with the authority that Argyle's stance commanded. He on the other hand, in his jeans, shirt and long, black jacket, looked unquestionably human.

Argyle's grey, pupiless eyes, which sat deep in his dark face, betrayed his humanity. Not that it would be a problem. Especially as only Bermuda could see him.

'I do not surrender any thoughts or feelings towards elements.' Argyle's response was firm, his voice carrying a low bass. Bermuda nodded, taking another puff on his cigarette. He looked up at Argyle.

'I bet it's a hoarder.'

'We should assess the situation before reaching conclusions.'

'Yeah, yeah. I know. And we will.' Bermuda took another drag, smoke being snatched from the end of his cigarette by the whipping wind. 'But I bet you ten quid it's a hoarder.'

'I have never understood your kind's obsession with monetary gain.' Argyle shook his head as he spoke, his words emphasising his disappointment. Bermuda looked towards the officers, their impatience obvious. A smile crept across his handsome face.

'Let's go see what the fuzz thinks.' He pushed himself off from the car and took a final hit of nicotine before carelessly flicking the butt of the cigarette into the darkness. He slapped Argyle on the back, his hand a few inches from the long, razor sharp blade of the sword that hung there. Argyle was a fine swordsman and had saved Bermuda's life on a number of occasions with it. Argyle's second weapon; the 'Retriever', was fastened securely around his powerful forearm.

Bermuda's own weapon hung from the latch on his belt, hidden by his long coat. His footsteps echoed as the gravel crunched beneath his feet. Argyle walked silently beside him.

'So what's the situation?' Bermuda asked him, scanning the grounds again. He dipped a hand into his pocket and returned shaking a small box of mints.

'The woman's husband has vanished. Along with their canine companion. Their maid and a home help worker have also vanished within the last few days. Their relatives have stated that this was their last known location.' The two police officers stepped forward, getting themselves prepared as Bermuda approached.

'How old is the woman?' Bermuda asked, two mints rattling in his mouth.

'Mrs Cartwright is eighty-two-years old, a veteran of your people.' Argyle spoke, his voice firm and authoritative.

'You can just say old, Argyle.' Bermuda smirked, hoping to extract a reaction.

'Would seem strange for such an elderly person to be able to remove that many people.'

'Well strange is why we are here, big man.' Bermuda approached the two police officers, both of whom looked at him with caution. The shorter officer, mid-forties, thinning black hair and a shirt about to burst at the mid-section, spoke first.

'You ok there, fella?' He looked at his partner and smiled. 'Having a nice old chat were you?'

'Just getting updated on the situation,' Bermuda retorted, accustomed to the idea that people thought he was crazy. He looked up at Argyle and raised his eyebrows. The policemen followed his gaze, saw nothing and readied themselves as if Bermuda was about to attack.

'Is she inside?'

'Hold on now.' The younger officer, tall and muscular, reached out and put his palm into Bermuda's firm chest. 'We got a call about some 'specialist' coming down.'

Bermuda sighed to himself, and whipped his hand to the back pocket of his jeans. He pulled out the thin, leather wallet and flicked it open.

'Bermuda Jones, BTCO.' The two men squinted, trying to read the small print. The plastic card, covered by a sheet of clear plastic, bore his face and details pertaining to the organisation. The short officer scoffed and look up at him.

'BTCO? Never heard of it,' he said, almost mockingly.

'You wouldn't have.'

Bermuda stepped through and once again the young officer stepped in his way. Bermuda smiled at him politely.

'Sounds like a load of nonsense to me.'

'Could you please let me through? I have a job to do.' Bermuda held his stare.

'Well as far as I can see, that woman in there has something to do with the disappearance of three people. She doesn't need a BCOT, or whatever it's called, intervention. She needs to be taken in for questioning.'

As if he didn't even hear it, Bermuda once again smiled politely, the wind snatching up his hair and tugging it in multiple directions.

'Please let me through, Officer.'

The young officer glared at Bermuda, who politely waited. The elder officer stood to the side, a voice crackling through on the radio. Instantly his attitude changed and he pulled the other officer out of Bermuda's path. As they argued, Bermuda walked slowly towards the large, semi-circular steps that led up to thick, wooden doors. They were open, the brightly lit hallway welcoming him with a warm glow. Argyle followed, his colossal frame just fitting through. The entrance to the house was as grand as the structure itself, the hallway stretching out towards a broad staircase that split in two directions, wrapping back around the wall underneath the high ceiling, from which an expensive chandelier hung. The walls were lined with large artworks, their value not worth guessing. In the far corner stood a suit of armour, the metal shining.

Bermuda popped a mint into his mouth and then walked through the open door to the right, entering an elegantly decorated living room. An oak table sat near the magnificent bay window, shutting out the world with its drawn curtains. A soft rug welcomed Bermuda as he strolled in, locking his eyes on the elderly woman who sat on the sofa, a roaring fire crackling in front of her. Above the fireplace was a large painting, depicting what Bermuda imagined was Lord William Cartwright, the missing husband. Stood in his hunting gear, he emanated wealth and nobility.

Argyle walked calmly to the centre of the room, past a small cabinet which housed several expensive looking liqueurs. He stood powerfully, his short, black beard lining his strong jaw. Bermuda crunched the remnants of his mint and approached the sofa.

'Mrs Cartwright?' He offered, his tone friendly. The old lady turned, her wrinkled face forcing a welcoming smile. Her eyes were red, the turmoil of the evening apparent. Bermuda calmly removed his jacket and placed it over the back of the chair. He checked his watch, pulling his shirt back to reveal a heavily tattooed forearm.

'Please. Call me Eleanor.'

'Eleanor. Nice to meet you. I'm Bermuda Jones from the BTCO.'

'The what now?' She looked at him, puzzled.

'The BTCO. We deal with rather exceptional cases and believe that your husband is one such case.'

'My poor William. Where has he gone?' Bermuda had no doubts in his mind that she was innocent. Her grief for her husband was genuine. In the last three years he'd experienced plenty of it.

'That is what we are here to find out.' Bermuda ran his hand through his hair, sweeping it into a side parting. 'When did you realise your husband was missing?'

'It was, now let me see, a little before lunch time. I realised that Cordelia, our maid, was missing and it was almost time for lunch. Poor Willy, he went upstairs to the function room to find her and he didn't come back.'

'And Cordelia, she was in the function room?' Bermuda flashed his eyes to Argyle, who was already staring up at the ceiling. A grandfather clock ticked loudly in the background, battling the crackles of the fire for dominance.

'Yes. It is mine and Willy's diamond anniversary this Saturday and we are having a party. Oh it will be lovely, our families and friends all together. It doesn't happen enough nowadays, sadly.'

'So the last time you were aware of their presence, it was in the function room?' She nodded, sniffling slightly. 'I have also been informed of a home help missing also?'

'Laura? She didn't turn up today. I heard Bailey barking in the function room and asked her to tend to him. He stopped barking so I assumed she went home.'

'Bailey is your dog, right?' Bermuda looked back up at the painting above the fire, the flames illuminating the German Shephard that stood proudly by its master. 'Is he also missing?'

'He is...' Eleanor's voice cracked and she began sobbing again. Bermuda gave her a moment, beckoning Argyle over.

'I say we check out this room. We'll probably find our little guest there.'

Argyle nodded in agreement and Bermuda stood up, whipping his coat around and sliding his arms in. Eleanor looked up from the tissue she was dabbing her eyes with. 'Where are you going?'

'Mrs Cartwright, could you show me to the function room, please?' He slowly helped her to her feet. She nodded and with the help of her cane, hobbled towards the hallway. The blue lights burst through the windows from outside as she lowered herself into her stair lift. As it hummed to life and she slowly began her ascent, Bermuda walked briskly up the curved steps, following them to the landing on the right. A few white, solid doors aligned the wall, all closed with their contents kept secret. He popped another mint into his mouth as he scanned the art on the wall.

'This way, dear.'

He followed, approaching a double set of the doors at the end of the hall. Bermuda pulled the doors open and stepped over the threshold. Eleanor followed and switched on the lights, pride flowing from her at the tastefully decorated room. The wood floor shimmered with polish, the antique tables set neatly around the sides of the room. Blue lights flickered through the large windows.

'Is Bermuda your real name?' She asked as she ambled in. She turned back, suddenly worried by the look of concern on Bermuda's face.

Bermuda took in what he saw. It wasn't the fine art or the expensive furniture, or the mental image of a wealthy family enjoying their time together. What he saw was what he feared he would. A few feet off the ground on the far wall, was William Cartwright. He was trapped in the brick as if he had been built into the wall and then painted over, cocooned by the Other they were there to tackle. Although he wasn't moving, Bermuda knew there was a strong chance that the man was still alive.

Bermuda sighed, looking around and noticing Cordelia, her face twisted in pain as she also faded into the brickwork. Laura and Bailey completed the collection. It was all too familiar. Whilst Eleanor Cartwright wept for the disappearance of her husband and had concerns about her helpers, they were but a few feet away. But she couldn't see them. All she saw was a pristine room that was empty without the infectious sound of family and friends.

She didn't have 'The Knack'.

Bermuda was born with it, the ability to see The Otherside and what is truly around us. A parallel world, whose inhabitants predominantly look human, but survive on a very different set of needs. Many of them are harmless, drifting seamlessly into the shadows and corners of our world. They live peacefully, out of the sight of the regular inhabitants of our planet. But as with all species, there are a few who require more than peace to survive.

That is why the BTCO, the Behind The Curtain Organisation, were formed. Every agent has 'The Knack' and every agent has a 'Neither', an Other who has defected to our side. As the world goes about its business, the BTCO are monitoring Other activity, ensuring that the unknown co-existence is maintained. The world behind the curtain.

And now, in a stately home in north east Hampshire, Bermuda stood seeing what the rest of the world couldn't. His fist clenched, angry not just at the actions of the intruder, but what his life had become. This curse of vision, inflicted from birth, and the burden it placed on him, to risk his life case by case due to an ability he had never asked for.

As he pulled his lips into a thin line, Eleanor broke the silence.

'What is wrong?' Her voice was interspersed with sniffles.

Argyle entered the room, standing beside and looming over the oblivious resident. He scanned the room, seeing the handiwork of one of his fellow Others.

'It is a hoarder,' Argyle stated, his voice tinged with disappointment.

'Told you,' Bermuda replied, his hand shuffling inside his pocket.

'Told who, dear?' Eleanor asked.

'Never mind.'

'What is that you have there?'

'This?' Bermuda removed his hand from his jacket pocket and revealed a metal spinning top. The small object, glistening in the light, had intricate carvings down all four sides. Words inscribed with such precise detail, it required magnification to be read. 'This will draw our little friend out.'

'What friend?' Eleanor said in frustration, feeling as if she was part of half a conversation. Bermuda ignored her and walked slowly into the centre of the room, peering round at the pained expressions of the captive. As he did, Eleanor slammed her cane against the floor, the thud echoing around the large room. 'MR JONES!'

He turned, her wrinkled face fraught with anger. He looked to Argyle, who took a few steps towards the clearly agitated Eleanor.

'Ma'am, you may want to leave the room for this.'

'I am not going anywhere. Who are you talking to? And what is that in your hand?' She took a few steps towards Bermuda.

'Argyle, hold her.' Bermuda didn't turn as he spoke.

With a mighty hand, Argyle reached out and clutched the old lady by the shoulder. She stopped dead in her tracks, unable to move, despite her best efforts.

'I can't move!' She yelled in frustration. 'What is going on?'

Bermuda leant down, placing the point of the spinning top against the floor. His fingers grasped the small, engraved handle of the spinning top and he balanced it, ready to spin. He glanced back at her.

'Argyle, make sure she is fine.'

'Who is Argyle? What is going on?' She angrily bellowed, her arms struggling in what she could only see as thin air. Argyle, with his hand still firmly clasped to her, took a few steps to shield her from the door. 'What the hell are you doing?

Bermuda smiled at her.

'You might want to cover your ears.'

Before she could respond, Bermuda twisted the top and released his grip. The metal frantically twisted on the floor, drilling against the wood. Instantly, every window in the room shattered with a large crash, shards of glass spraying across the room like a sandstorm. The wind whistled in and the doors flew open, rocking their hinges to breaking point. The lights flickered, shrouding the stolen bodies within the wall in stop-start darkness. Eleanor watched in horror, her instinct to run hindered by her inability to move. Argyle stood ready, his other hand, the wrist clad in thick metal, clenched.

A horrifying scream echoed through the house.

Suddenly, the rapid noise of thudding rattled through the floorboards, the sound emanating from the room beneath. It grew louder as it made its way up the stairs, the impact rocking the staircase. Bermuda turned to face the door, his eyes closed as he took a deep breath. Behind him, the cold air blew in on another gust of wind.

The metal top continued to spin.

The loud banging approached the broken doors at speed and Bermuda opened his eyes.

'Hello, handsome.'

Jet black eyes peered back as the Other raced through the doorway. Running on all fours like a beast of prey, it was almost completely black, its back covered in gothic looking spikes where shards of its spine had pierced its otherworldly skin. Hanging from its open mouth were long, sharp teeth that mirrored the claws framing its monstrous hands.

As it bound towards Bermuda, he slipped his coat to the side to reveal his weapon, a tomahawk, which he whipped up from the latch with a quick spin. The hoarder raced towards him and leapt as Bermuda dropped to the ground and swung up.

The screech of pain shot through the house, cracking the window panes. Outside, the two officers were quickly calling for backup, panic- stricken at the carnage they could see from the driveway below.

The hoarder latched onto the wall, a gaping wound across its chest, and crawled across the stored body of William Cartwright. His wife looked on in despair, seeing only Bermuda rolling on the floor. She watched as he got to his feet, spinning the wooden handle of the small axe, the head made of a material she had never seen.

Otherworldly.

The hoarder was clearly feral; one of the more beast-like Others that had escaped to our side. It roared again at Bermuda, its thick claws clattering against the wall as it raced around the room.

'Are you ready, Argyle?' Bermuda yelled, spinning on the spot to keep the beast in his eye line.

'Ready.' Argyle raised his arm, the metal band around his wrist aimed straight at the monster. Resting atop it was a thick spike, attached to a metal chain that disappeared within it. The Retriever.

The Other bounded off the wall to the floor and then leapt again at Bermuda, its mighty claws cutting through the air. Bermuda spun to his left, dropping to one knee and swung his tomahawk. The metal, forged on the Otherside, ripped through the back of the hoarder's leg. It roared again in agony, falling to the floor and shaking the room on impact.

Eleanor stood completely still thanks to Argyle. Without hesitation, Argyle shot the Retriever, the sharp metal racing off his arm with marksman-like precision. The spike burst through the damaged leg, ripping out the other side and spraying grey blood across the floor. Instantly, the spike opened out into four sections, hooking back around and locking itself inside the leg of the hoarder.

It mustered a whimper of anguish before finally relenting, rolling onto its side in resignation. Bermuda stood, latching his tomahawk back to his belt before taking careful steps towards the defeated visitor. As suspected, attached to the front of its stomach was a small, blue rock known as a Latch Stone. Found on the Otherside, it allowed the Other who possessed it to combine itself with our world. To latch onto it.

When in possession, the Other can physically interact with humans, an ability that the BTCO only wanted reserved for its

Neithers. Without one, Argyle would not have been able to protect Eleanor, who stood in complete confusion. The wind howled through the shattered windows, causing the broken doors to creak on stressed hinges.

The glass crunched under Bermuda's feet as he took his final steps before reaching down and removing the stone with a hard tug. Instantly, all four inhabitants of the wall fell to the ground, their captivity over. As their bodies crashed against the hard, wooden floor, Eleanor screamed in horror. Out of nowhere, her husband and dog had returned to her. From thin air.

With confused steps, she shuffled through the glass to the elderly man on the floor, proof that the painting above the fireplace was a few years old. He slowly began to stir, a wrinkled hand reached up to cradle a head that was frosted with white hair. Laura and Cordelia were both starting to stir, the confusion of their disappearance evident in their movements. Bailey sprung to life first, bounding towards Eleanor who carefully accepted his welcome.

'Banish him.' Bermuda said to Argyle and watched intently. Argyle bowed down to one knee and held a small relic above the fallen Other. He muttered words of a distant language, a speech that Bermuda knew he would never understand. The blades retracted into the spike and slid automatically back up the chain before returning to rest on Argyle's wrist.

The fallen Other turned slowly, emitting a slow, painful groan as it slowly began to disappear, a small trail of black smoke rising from its chest and into the open relic in Argyle's grip. The beast on the floor finally disappeared as the last trail of smoke filtered in. Argyle snapped the lid shut and attached it to the grand belt that wrapped around his waist. It would be deposited when he returned to HQ.

'Let's go home, Argyle,' Bermuda smiled, his trainers crunching the glass. His partner nodded, his face etched with a slight sadness that always accompanied a banishment. Sometimes Bermuda mused that Argyle was more human than anyone else on earth.

As they crossed the threshold of the door, Eleanor yelled out to them, 'Thank you. Thank you so much.'

Bermuda turned back and smiled, the old lady was kneeling beside her husband, cradling him as he came to. Bailey circled them excitedly, his tongue hanging out of his mouth as he panted. Laura had gotten to her feet and was bent over and helping Cordelia. Bermuda nodded to Eleanor, whose face, splashed with tears of happiness, returned one in kind.

The front steps and driveway of the house were littered with the odd shard of glass, the windows at the front of the building had cracked or broken. Instantly, the two officers strode towards him, their faces a mixture of anger, fear and confusion. The younger, brasher one took the lead.

'What the hell happened in there?' He demanded angrily, pointing towards the large home. Bermuda just kept walking, his head down and the gravel scraping. The elder policeman hurriedly walked towards the door of the house, speaking rapidly into his radio.

'Hey, I asked you a question!'

Bermuda reached his car and then turned back, the wind sweeping the hair from his forehead.

'I found them.'

He swung open the door and dropped into the driver's seat, as the young officer looked round in bewilderment at the emergence of Laura and Cordelia from the house. His colleague gently helped them down the steps and the young officer took one last, cautious look at Bermuda before jogging over to assist. Bermuda turned the key and the engine roared into life as Argyle approached the car. After clicking in his seatbelt, Bermuda pressed the button and his window slid down with a faint hum.

'You owe me a tenner.' He smiled upwards at Argyle, who responded with a less than impressed look. Bermuda smirked as the window began to climb again. 'I'll stick it on the tab.'

With a small spray of gravel, he drove off back down the driveway and into the night.

2

The large, red bus slowly rattled to a stop, shuddering at some poor brake work from the driver. Jess Lambert jolted from her drunken doze, startled by the sudden jerk. She looked out of the window on the upper deck at the streets below, her eyes fuzzy with the final strands of sleep clutching at her. It took a few moments before she realised that she still had a few more stops, the 343 bus making its final route of the night towards Peckham in south-east London.

Dressed in a tight fitting red dress, she adjusted on her seat and rested her head against the glass. Scanning the bus, she saw an old man, his hands firmly clasping a carrier bag that swung between his legs. Further down sat a young lad, no more than twenty, who was fast asleep. She could almost see the alcoholic aroma wafting from him.

She sighed, closing her eyes again and smiled.

The launch party for a new designer perfume she had attended was a step in the right direction. Employed as one of the show models, she was actually starting to feel like she could have a career in modelling. She was approached at eighteen, when she was attending University to gain a degree in English. With flowing blond hair that cascaded down her defined face, she was aware that she garnered a lot of attention. Whilst doing small modelling jobs to help pay her way through University, she signed up with Vision, a fast-rising talent agency in London as soon as she graduated. Now, aged twenty-six, she was starting to make a name for herself, performing at catwalk shows and launch parties for some high profile clients.

She sighed, regretting the few extra cocktails she had drank at the after party, but the excitement of mixing with TV personalities and musicians overwhelmed her. Rubbing shoulders with the rich and famous of London was why she moved to the city after graduation, the chance to live a life of luxury that teaching wouldn't have brought her.

Her phone buzzed in her designer handbag, a warning that her battery was critically low. She also had a message, sent at just after midnight from her best friend, Sophie Summers.

Sorry Jess, had to leave. God that guy was a dick!! Enjoy the rest of the party and don't do anything too naughty. ;) xx

She smiled. She had met Sophie on her first day at Vision and they bonded straight away. The same age as her, Sophie wasn't as tall as Jess but she was strikingly beautiful. Her dark, flowing hair was offset by her piercing brown eyes that were tinged with flecks of green. Her cheek bones were sharp and rested above gorgeous dimples when she flashed her beaming smile. Jess thought of her previous best friends and how they had almost turned their noses up at her pursuing a modelling career. Not Sophie.

Sophie went with her to auditions and attended all of her

events. Jess did likewise, offsetting the quieter periods of work by temping in local offices. Their two bedroom flat, which sat on the third floor of a building surrounded by a gorgeous courtyard of fresh flowers and well-kept trees, was slightly more expensive than she would have liked to pay. But now, especially with this recent modelling contract, she was beginning to enjoy a more lavish lifestyle. Jess then cursed herself for being prudent, knowing a cab journey, although more expensive, would have meant she would be home already. Old habits die hard.

She sat up straight and her fingers began clicking on the screen of her phone and within a few moments a message was wending its way to her best friend.

Haha. I want to hear all about it. Just about to get off the bus so will be home soon xx

She smiled, but then shuffled uncomfortably on her seat. Another message was sent to Sophie.

Really need to pee! :(

As soon as the message sent, her screen flickered to black and she was greeted with a no power icon. She tutted and dropped her phone into her bag. She ran a hand through her hair, making a note to wash it in the morning.

The bus turned a corner and drove down Peckham High Street, all of the shops dark and the shutters down. A few drunk civilians wondered aimlessly up the street, their footsteps anything but synchronized. The occasional car sped past in the opposite direction, headlights interrupting her half sleep. She opened them, realised where they were and then pressed the button. A shrill ding echoed through the bus, notifying the driver of her exit at the next stop.

She took a final look around the bus; the old man had left at a previous stop without her realising. The young drunkard had slid further down his seat, waiting to be woken when the bus came to its final destination however many roads beyond his stop. The bus slowly pulled into the kerb just beyond Peckham Rye station and she carefully stepped up, her feet and calves killing her from the heels she had cruelly strapped to her feet.

The doors hissed and opened as Jess waved her thanks and stepped off, the briskness of the spring night catching her by surprise. She fished her cardigan from her bag and wrapped it around her, the effect minimal.

The road was dead quiet; the only noise was the reducing hum of the buses engine as it disappeared further up the road. A few lamp posts illuminated the street, their light striking the roofs of the cars that lined the pavement. Jess wrapped her arms around her chest and began walking, her head down as the spring breeze whipped by. Her heels clopped against the pavement as she took extra special care to navigate the crooked concrete, the night's worth of alcohol suddenly hitting her. She stopped briefly outside a grand house, the wall providing perfect support as she hunched over, feeling the impending burst of vomit on its way. She composed herself, resisting the need to throw up, at least until she got home, and turned left into a small side street.

It was another ten minutes to Garland House where Soph would undoubtedly greet her with a cup of tea, toast and stories of the TV Star that she ditched at the party. She willed herself to get home quicker and then stopped as she noticed a small walkway that cut through two blocks of flats. Both buildings were over four stories high and as she tried to peer through the darkness, she could just make out the street lights at the other end. As she squinted, she was sure she could see the front gates of Garland House.

She looked around; there was nobody about. It was almost two thirty in the morning and over two hours since Sophie had sent her message. She wanted to get home to the warmth of her flat and the safety of her best friend – this made her mind up for her.

She was completely unaware of the two, jet black eyes that were staring at her, willing her to enter the dark tunnel before her. The piercing stare that was urging her to step in and be one with the shadows.

As the wind blew her long, blonde hair behind her, she took a deep breath and stepped into the alleyway, hoping to be home soon.

■ ▮ ▎

He had sat and watched the world go by for hours. Watching as people walked through the streets, all convinced that their existence was linked to some sort of importance. All certain that the world would miss them, and so ironically oblivious to the insignificance of their miserable lives.

The cars, powered by a resource that was destroying their world, whizzed by. Humans, all wanting to see and experience the world without even a thought of the cost. That was what angered him most.

The arrogance of man.

A whole planet, an entire world, which they felt was their birth right to conquer. Foolish people. An abhorrent race.

As he sat on the wall of the large home, he watched as the family walked through the gates. The male, with his fading hair and large stomach, eagerly encouraged a young boy as he wobbled on a bike.

They soon disappeared from sight, which he found pleasing.

More instances of human interaction, all blindly walking past him, none of them aware of the power or danger his very attendance demanded. His dark, black eyes stared out, watching everything he despised. They sat in his sharp, marble-like face. His skin, a faded grey, clung tightly to his other-worldly skull. Three large scars ran down one cheek, the physical reminders of the torture he suffered. The branding of an apparent 'traitor'. His escape from The Otherside was marvellous, ripping free of their shackles and leaving a trail of bodies all the way to the gates.

He had removed the guard's heads as he passed through, a final gesture of contempt for the world that tried to lock him away. He shook the memory from his mind, his white hair swaying as it hung shabbily to the bottom of his neck.

Soon the sun retreated and the world became more familiar, the shadows painting themselves over the street with an aggressive beauty. He saw a few of his own kind, Others who had been granted asylum on this side of the gate. They filtered past pathetically, none of them daring to make eye contact with him.

He smiled, his razor sharp teeth coming together like a broken zip. The Otherside knew who he was and if Earth had any idea, if the humans could see him, then they would run too.

That time was fast approaching.

He reached a grey hand into the inside of his black suit, the blazer frayed at the edges from wear and tear. His long, spindly fingers wrapped round the Latch Stone that hung from his neck. His sharp nails dug into his skin, its thickness absorbing the pain.

Suddenly his head turned, the sound of high heels clicking against the pavement echoing throughout the street. He saw her and instantly knew she would be the one. He was in the correct place, as he had been for all of the others, and he watched as the blonde woman carefully walked down the street.

Another puny human, intoxicated on a needless beverage that rendered them even more useless and pathetic. There would be some of them who would shed tears, but they should be thanking him for his work. His eradication of the vile stains of humanity. She leant over near a wall; he could see her back arching as she took deep breaths.

He sat, strumming his long nails against the brick that he rested his hand upon. He knew she couldn't see him as she slowly turned the corner, her focus on just keeping herself standing.

He pushed himself up off the wall and lifted his top hat that had sat next to him the entire time. As jet black as his suit, he dusted some lint from the brim and then rested it atop his shabby hair. He took a few slow steps towards her, his eyes sparkling with anticipation as he reached into his pocket and pulled out the crudely carved device.

Another one for his collection.

He could almost feel her; how good it would be when she belonged to him.

She stopped still.

For a second he thought she had seen him, her eyes focused dead ahead of her where he stood. She then glanced towards the small alleyway, the dark tunnel where they would become one.

Where she would be his.

He readied himself, his hand grasping the sharp edges of his device as he prepared to snare her. He relished the anticipation of the inevitable screaming and panic as she fought against a force she could not see. A smile spread across his face, jagged teeth lit up by the fading lamp post above.

She willingly turned and walked into the alleyway. He watched with delight as she stumbled between the two buildings, her handbag swinging from her arm. It was all too easy.

The previous eight had all been easy; the human race had no way of stopping what he was becoming. But this was being served up on a platter. As she disappeared into the shadow, her footsteps echoed and bounced off the surrounding walls. With a calm quickness, he followed her into the black. She wouldn't emerge from the other end.

3

'Help me!'

Bermuda sat up in his bed in a cold sweat, the final words of the dream still echoing in his mind, clinging to him like a bad smell. He took a few deep breaths, his eyes scanning the room rapidly before he collapsed backwards. His damp hair hit an equally damp pillow. The dream was always the same, had been for the last two years, and he knew there wouldn't be a shrink in the world who would be able to decipher it. There wouldn't be one brave enough.

He opened his eyes again and stared up at the ceiling of his bedroom, four separate dream catchers swung gently above him. Hand woven in various parts of the world, they did more than just decorate the room. They kept him safe while he slept, the patterns that hung over him repelling the Others that wanted him dead.

He didn't know exactly what it was about the embroidered designs that fended them off, but he wasn't going to complain. Having killed a number of their kind, he understood the Otherside's want for revenge. As they rocked slowly above him, he cursed them for not protecting him from nightmares.

He sat up again, the duvet falling off to reveal his toned body, acquired by a frequent training routine and fighting practice with Argyle. His defined muscles however were hard to see, due to the tattooed scribe that covered his body from the neck down. Incantations and symbols that, over the years, had proven effective in warding off Others and their weaponry. Sweat dribbled down the words etched into the skin of his spine.

The little girl's voice still haunted from the dream and he sighed as he swung his legs to the floor. Perched on the edge of his bed, he stared towards the window; the spring sun was cutting through the blind in segregated strips. He slid the bedside drawer open and pulled out a small envelope. Feeling his heart sink. he slid out the photograph, immediately regretting a decision that would ruin the rest of his day. Staring back at him was a six year old girl, her blonde hair framing her freckled face. Baby blue eyes and a smile that wrenched every string of his heart.

His Chloe.

A small tear ran from his eye, weaving across his stubbled cheek. He wiped it away with the back of his hand before planting a kiss on the beloved image. It went back into the drawer. Back where it would be safe, where the Otherside wouldn't find it. Bermuda missed her deeply.

As the beads of water hammered from the shower head and drenched his ink covered frame, he closed his eyes. Bowing his head to let the water filter through his hair, he cursed the world for what it had done to him. Everything about his life had been ruined; the childhood that was trimmed with visions of evil; the odd looks; the words of anger from his mother who refused to believe in monsters.

The world that had declared him certifiably insane and locked him away in a hospital for three months.

The wife he had loved, who had left and remarried.

The daughter he refused to see.

All because he was born with the ability to see the truth. 'The Knack' is a rare gift, bestowed upon only a few people throughout the world. Those who can see beyond the usual parameters of our planet.

To The Otherside.

Bermuda punched the tiles that ran around the shower cubicle, unsure if the impact broke a knuckle or not. As he shook the pain away, he switched off the shower and stepped out. Reaching out for the towel, he caught a glimpse of himself in the mirror.

He knew he looked like a mad man.

But when the world tells you that you are crazy, but can't see the truth, it's better to step away than speak up. That is what the BTCO does. They quietly exist, maintaining the balance and treaty between our side and the other. Bermuda had tried to stay within the realms of a 'normal' life, but it didn't work. His ex-wife, Angela, tried her hardest to understand. But when you are the only one in the room who can see the demon hanging from the ceiling, you tend to become the only person in the room.

The BTCO found him not long after he 'escaped' from The London Institute of Mental Health, a hospital for those suffering with mental illness. He knew he didn't belong in there, but he was declared insane by three separate psychiatrists and locked away for three months. Three months of padded cells, judgemental looks and incorrect diagnosis. Then one day, as he lay on his bed staring up at the whiteness of his room, a hole emerged in the wall. Burning through like a match through paper, it appeared from nowhere, revealing a dusty world filled with dark smoke and furious winds.

There was no life worth living through there. But his life in the padded cell was worse.

Saying goodbye to the world that had turned its back on him, he stepped through. His body exited our world with the intention of never returning.

But he did.

The only person to cross to the Otherside and return. He hadn't wanted too, but Bermuda recalled the chase. The fiery red eyes that latched onto him as he ran for survival. The hole in the wall that he fell through, emerging on a dusty alleyway in Tiradent, Morocco. Lost in another continent with nothing but his white, institution-issued clothes; it took only a matter of hours before the BTCO found him. An organisation built and ran by some of the most powerful men and Others, with a reach that crosses two worlds, can always find needles in haystacks.

They wanted to recruit him with the promise of clearing his record.

He wanted to hold his daughter again.

He didn't realise that the cost of his curse would be so expensive.

KNOCK! KNOCK! KNOCK!

Bermuda snapped back from his wretched memory and looked around the room. He was sat on his bed, streaks of sunlight cutting across the unmade duvet. He had half-dressed, his jeans tightly fitting his legs as he pushed himself up.

KNOCK! KNOCK!

A fist pounded the front door of his spacious, two bedroom flat.

'Give me a sec!' He yelled out from his bedroom, the front door to the flat further down the hall. With a sigh, he pulled a plain, white t-shirt over his head and straightened it as he exited the room. He wandered down the hallway, passing the kitchen and living room, both decorated with a simplistic eye. The furniture was expensive, the sofa showing signs of age. The BTCO may have hoisted him from a normal life of insanity, but at least it paid well.

KNOCK! KNOCK!

'Jesus!' Bermuda exclaimed as he forcibly pulled the door open to be greeted by the stern face of Argyle. 'Oh, hey Argyle.'

Bermuda turned and pottered back down the hall, turning into the kitchen and flicking the switch on the coffee maker. It gently rattled as it started boiling. A quick shuffle of hands and a flick of a lighter and Bermuda puffed smoke out towards the open window. The grey, toxic cloud filtered out into the beautiful sky beyond.

Argyle strode in powerfully, his pristine armour glimmering in the rays of sun that broke through the window pain. Combined with the smoke that was filling the world, the vision before Bermuda was dream-like.

'Coffee?' Bermuda nodded towards the machine, brown liquid falling into his comical mug about disliking Mondays.

'Your need for such stimulating sustenance will result in ill health.' Argyle spoke calmly, his grey eyes offering sympathy to his partner.

'So no, then?'

Argyle shook his head. Bermuda grinned and reached out for the mug, taking a sip of the piping hot beverage before recoiling slightly. Steam rose from the cup, replacing the smoke that he stubbed out in the ashtray. He exhaled, blinking the remnants of sleep from his eyes and focusing on the imposing figure of his friend.

'Haven't seen you in a while, big man,' he offered with a smile.

'It has been eleven days since the Cartwright case.'

'Ah yeah. How did that all pan out?' Bermuda took another sip of his coffee.

'The humans have restored to normal life, however the maid has sought other employment. This was all in the report that was filed.'

'Oh yeah, I definitely read that.' Bermuda arched his eyebrows in sarcasm. 'Did the banishment go okay? Any hiccups?'

Argyle shook his head. Bermuda could see the discomfort it caused him; the knowledge that he was effectively deporting his own kind back to such a vicious world obviously hurt Argyle. Bermuda could appreciate how hard he tried to conceal it and thought better than to ask any more questions.

'Are you ready?' Argyle asked, changing the subject and taking a few steps towards the door. His mighty sword shimmered in the light streaming through the window. Bermuda chortled as he finished his coffee.

'And here I was thinking you had popped by for a social visit.' He shoved the empty mug into the sink, the porcelain rattling against a crowd of unwashed plates and cutlery. He walked past Argyle and back down the hallway to his bedroom. Quickly tossing the duvet back over to half make the bed, he threw on some socks and trainers, before pulling a hoody over his toned arms. He returned to the front door, where an impatient Argyle stood with his arms folded and a look of disappointment on his face.

'You should dress more formally. There is nobility in an agreed uniform.'

'Argyle, you may like dressing like a World of Warcraft reject, but I like to be comfortable when I work.'

'What is this world you speak of?' The question was genuine.

'Never mind.'

Bermuda and Argyle exited the flat, the door slamming behind them. They made their way to the stairwell, casually descending them.

'So what's the story?'

'A young lady went missing after a party last night.'

'Went missing or got lucky?' Bermuda asked cheekily, then frowned as he realised it had been over four months since he had last experienced any intimacy.

'She went missing on her way back from a celebration last night. Her friend is concerned as to her whereabouts.'

'Is she not just drunk and passed out on someone's couch?' Bermuda asked, turning back to his partner. A middle-aged mother crossed them on the stairs, the two of them stepping to the side. She glared at Bermuda with a curious eye, concerned at the man talking to himself.

He was used to it.

'She contacted her friend when near home and then never showed.' They reached the bottom of the stairs, the double doors opening to welcome them both into the glorious sunshine. It felt like the start of a wonderful and welcome summer. Without a cloud to cover it, the blue sky shone with a powerful glow. A few birds swooped by and the only noise was the distant hum of traffic.

'So where are we going?' Bermuda asked, walking towards his car, the locks retreating at the push of a button.

'The young lady's last known location was Peckham.'

Bermuda stopped walking, the car key hanging from his hand. He turned and looked at Argyle, disappointment etched across his handsome face.

'So I may as well get the train.' He shook his head and began walking towards Bushey High Street; the local train station a fifteen minute commute by foot. He lit another cigarette, walking briskly.

'The police have attended the scene and are awaiting our arrival.'

'I'm sure they can't wait.' Another cloud of smoke floated away behind them. 'If this turns out to be a general kidnapping, I am going to be very upset.'

'The woman was taken from a place where it is physically impossible for a human to disappear. There is evidence to show her entering the alley but not returning.'

'I see.' Bermuda finally registered some interest.

'There are no doors or exits through the alleyway. They have footage of her entering but not exiting. No one else is shown to be in the vicinity.'

'Interesting.' Bermuda finished his cigarette and the two of them walked in silence, the world only seeing one. Bermuda began to speculate the cause, knowing now why this case had been assigned to him.

The same as the Cartwright case.

His reputation, beyond his capabilities that surpassed any agent, was for finding people who vanished from the world. The people who disappeared with no trace or reason. It was how he had earnt his nickname, a name that sent shudders of fear and loathing through the Otherside in equal measure.

They stopped outside of the station and Bermuda shuffled around in his pockets as he checked the time board. The electronic screen, faded and in need of replacement, fuzzily showed he had five minutes before the next fast train to London Euston. Despite living in Hertfordshire, the train links meant he could get to central London within thirty minutes. His hands returned with a box of mints, two of which quickly found their demise in his mouth.

'I take it you're not getting on?' Bermuda lazily asked.

'I will meet you there,' Argyle stated firmly, nodding to underline his point. Bermuda didn't quite know how, but Argyle always appeared at the places they needed to be. As if his means of travel were outside the confines of our world.

Bermuda took a deep breath and took a few steps forward. He stopped at the station door, turning back to smile at the armoured warrior before him.

'Time to go to work.'

4

The London sun beamed down on the streets of Peckham, casting its warm blanket across the concrete landscape. The roads were lined by impressive houses, all set back beyond thick steps. Trees were rising from the earth in symmetrical patterns down both curbs, the only green in a vast grey world. Peckham itself had changed over the years; a younger, trendier crowd had arrived, replacing the bad reputation with a slew of pop-up bars and pretentious coffee shops. Young men and women, all on the edge of the current trends, meandered through the streets; all of them wearing outfits that made Bermuda shake his head in bemusement.

As he gently puffed on his cigarette, he smiled at a gorgeous woman who crossed his path. She sheepishly returned it, scurrying through the doors of the station and away from his life forever. Rows of shops greeted him, the doors bursting open with different cultures and conversations. Afro-Caribbean hair salons, Asian food markets, Italian Restaurants all greeted him, as if the world had decided to squash every nation onto a few, overly packed streets.

He walked to a peculiar soundtrack, every open door presenting a different song, each shop trying to outdo the previous. His own personal medley.

He continued down the street, away from the multi-cultural hustle and bustle, turning towards the residential area, immediately seeing a small crowd of the fashionable locals, their interests peaked. He sighed, flicking his cigarette and fishing for his mints as he approached them.

'Excuse me, please,' he said firmly. A few heads turned, trimmed with beards or stylish haircuts. He felt very out of place. 'I need to get through.'

'Can't get through, mate. The police have blocked it off.'

'I'm with the police,' Bermuda lied, presenting his BTCO badge. He flicked it back before the obstructive local could read it.

'Oh, right. What's going on?'

'That's a police matter. Now, if you don't mind.'

Bermuda held back his smile as the crowd parted, impressed with his faux authority. He strode through them; a strip of Police tape ran from lamppost to lamppost, fluttering gently in the warm breeze. It read: 'Do Not Cross'.

Bermuda ducked under and crossed into the crime scene, a police car with its lights still flashing was parked across the road, blocking off traffic at either side, another one at the other end of the street. A large van was also parked nearby, with Scene of Crime Officers (SOCOs) scattered around the area, their white suits making them look like ghosts in a low budget horror movie. PC Daniel Carter, a burly officer with scruffy black hair, took a few steps towards Bermuda.

'Sir, please return to the other side of the tape immediately.' He reached out a meaty hand, pressing it against Bermuda's chest. 'This is a crime scene.'

'I believe you're expecting me,' Bermuda responded, flipping open his badge for the officer. With squinted eyes, Carter tried to make sense of it.

'Oh, are you the specialist we were told is on his way?'

'The very same.' He smiled warmly at the cumbersome PC before him. 'What's the situation?'

'A young lady has gone missing.' He flicked open his notebook with large, clumsy fingers. 'Jessica Lambert. She didn't return home from a party last night.'

'Maybe she is still partying?' Bermuda winked, knowing his charm worked on most people. The officer smiled.

'Well her friend and housemate, a Sophie Summers, said she was almost home when her battery died so we have reason to believe she was in the area.'

'Any signs of a struggle? Or of her even being here?' Bermuda asked, scanning the area for anything that the regular police couldn't see. Nothing out of the ordinary.

'We have her on CCTV going into the alleyway, she lives just at the other end, at Garland House, but she doesn't come out the other side.'

'And you have CCTV on both sides?'

'Yep.'

'Maybe someone was waiting inside the alleyway?'

'We have eyes on that right now, but from what we can tell so far, no one was seen going in and waiting.'

Bermuda stroked his chin, thinking. 'So she just vanished?'

'Either that or she is playing a damn good game of hide and seek.' The officer chuckled at his own joke, before casting a cautious eye towards the ever-growing crowd of people. Argyle stood, straight and proud, his eyes taking everything in. Bermuda spoke again to the young, friendly officer.

'I'm going to need to see the alleyway.'

'Sorry, what organisation are you from again?'

'The BTCO. The commanding officer here should be expecting me. I need to see that alleyway.'

Officer Carter looked around, clearly searching for his superior. Bermuda cast his gaze in the same direction. An elder looking officer was standing at the mouth of the alleyway, his arms folded and a stern look across a world weary face as a SOCO explained the situation.

'Wait here,' Carter said firmly, striding powerfully towards the two of them. Bermuda looked around; everything he could see was of this world. No secrets just for him.

'That is the location of her disappearance,' Argyle's voice boomed next to him, making him jump slightly. 'Through that archway into the dark path beyond.'

Bermuda nodded in agreement, impatient as he watched the Sergeant shake his head and remonstrate a point to his subordinate. Carter slowly walked back towards them; his face told them their answer.

'Sorry sir, but you can't go in. The Sergeant isn't convinced that your presence is needed.'

'I'm sure they would have called ahead.'

'They did.' Carter sighed. 'However, the Sarge said he has never heard of your organisation and this is his crime scene so if you don't mind...'

'This is ridiculous!' Bermuda exclaimed, storming passed the apologetic officer towards the alleyway. As Carter yelled out for him to stop, Sergeant Kevin Milton stepped forward.

'What the hell do you think you are doing? I said I didn't want you on this crime scene so you either step back across that goddamn tape, or you will be driven back in handcuffs.'

Bermuda flipped his badge open.

'Sir, I am Agent Jones from the BTCO. My superiors called to say I would be here.'

'Never heard of it in my thirteen years on the force,' Milton replied with an irritating smugness. He slapped the leather badge closed in Bermuda's hand, their eyes locked, daring the other one to break. 'You are not getting on my crime scene so I suggest you fuck off back to your little BTCO and tell them the real police are handling this.'

Bermuda held the man's stare, the Sergeant limbering up as if expecting trouble. An excited whisper spread through the spectators and Bermuda felt a strong grip wrap around his elbow. He looked up at a sorrowful Carter, who motioned that he was to leave. Bermuda smirked at the Sergeant.

'I'll go. No need to have your lap dog here put his hands on me.'

Ignoring the insult, Milton motioned for Carter to release his hold, an order that was followed immediately. Bermuda straightened his sleeve and turned, walking back towards the crowd. His pathway was cut short by the invisible wall named Argyle.

'We have a job to do.' His words came through as a threat.

'I know, big man.' Carter turned in confusion as Bermuda spoke to no one. 'I need some help here.'

'What do you require?' Argyle stood straight, ready to work.

'I need a distraction.'

'How?' Argyle asked, watching as Officer Carter strode to his partner and began to slowly push him towards the edge of the police cordon. Bermuda, obligingly walking with the young officer, looked back over his shoulder.

'Improvise.'

As Carter roughly battled with Bermuda who was now

resisting his dismissal, Argyle scanned the area, his eyes running over the world that he was still learning. With noble purpose, he approached the police car, the blue lights reflecting powerfully off of his chest plate. One final glance to see Bermuda still struggling and Argyle bent forward and threw his hands under the side of the car. With a grunt of discomfort, he pushed himself upwards.

'OH MY GOD!'

'WHAT THE HELL?'

'JESUS FUCKING CHRIST!'

The wild screams of the crowd caused Carter to loosen his grip of the unwanted guest and realised their reason when he followed their horrified eyes.

His police car was tipping onto its side.

Forgetting Bermuda completely, Carter jogged over to the vehicle, his face turning a ghostly pale as he watched the two tonne machine begin to rise. He was soon joined by a perplexed Milton and the SOCO's. A flickering of flashes, like fireflies at twilight, filled the crowd as they looked to capture the moment on their phones.

'What the hell is happening?' Milton asked, failing to disguise the panic in his voice.

'I have no idea, sir,' Carter replied, his voice shaking as the car continued to tip, slowly rocking further onto two wheels.

'How is it doing that?' One of the SOCOs asked, his voice muffled by his face mask.

'Grab that side, quick,' Carter said, taking charge of the situation and reaching up to grab the car. Even with a firm grip and his impressive body weight, the car didn't budge. The other SOCO grabbed the side of the bonnet, trying to help pull it down. Between the two of them, Argyle stood, his arms rippling and shaking as he continued to push the car upwards. He glanced over his shoulder towards the cordoned area.

Bermuda was gone.

He slowly began to lower the car, the crowd gasping at the anomaly they had witnessed. Videos of it would be on the news later, members of the crowd eager to sell their footage. The internet would have a field day.

As the officers began to calm down, returning the car to its rightful place with all four wheels touching the ground, Argyle looked towards the entrance to the alleyway.

It was clear.

Bermuda needed more time.

As the officers congratulated themselves for resolving the issue, Argyle slowly walked to the other side of the vehicle. Taking a deep breath, he leant forward and sent everyone into another frenzy.

■ ▮ ▎

Bermuda ducked under the police tape and entered the small, darkened alleyway. The two buildings stood either side of it, shielding the walkway from the sun. Two long strips of concrete framed the cut through, not a door or exit in sight. His footsteps let off a small echo as he hurriedly walked, wanting to take as much of it in as he could. It was only a matter of time, amongst the furore outside, that they would notice he had gone missing.

His eyes searched one side of the wall, flicking through lines of graffiti that scrawled over it like the tattoo's across his body.

Nothing. Not one thing in the alleyway that could give him so much as a clue as to what happened to this poor girl. He looked at the small police cordon that was set up next to the wall, a few markings to ensure nobody ventured near.

As he approached, he saw a leather handbag, open with some

of its contents spilling to the side. A switched off phone, a makeup mirror – nothing that would indicate what had happened.

'Where did you go?' He asked, out loud.

About to leave, his vision danced over the wall and something caught his attention. He very slowly walked towards it, squinting with concentration. Amongst the obscene graffiti and art work, was a mark. A symmetrical engraving that looked as though it had been burnt into the brick itself. With a cautious hand, he reached out to run his finger through the groove. As the tip hit the course brick, he felt a small shudder through his body. A spectre of something else.

Something Other.

As his fingers ran along the coarseness of the imprint, he could feel something reaching out, a horrible feeling like a magnetic pull coursing from the brick. With a fretful frown, he retracted his hand quickly. It was becoming stronger, the nagging suspicion that he was being slowly pulled across to their side once again.

It terrified him.

He looked around quickly, the inevitable arrest reaching ever closer. His hand dipped into the back pocket of his jeans and retrieved his notepad. With a click, the pen hit the pad and he sketched down the marking, ensuring that the strange, twelve-sided shape was captured accurately. He took one final glance of the alleyway before jogging back to the entrance.

Argyle had ended his merry chase, although the crowd of people were still alive with excitement, crazy rumours of what they had witnessed spreading like wildfire. As he ducked under the tape, Bermuda was immediately confronted by an irate Sergeant Milton.

'Where the hell have you been?'

Bermuda slowly tucked the notepad into his pocket, ensuring it didn't get confiscated.

'I was just leaving and I think I took a wrong turn.'

'I don't know what the hell you are up to, but I swear to god, if I see you on my crime scene one more time, I'll arrest you myself. Understood?'

'Completely. I have everything I need anyway.'

'Right then.' Milton folded his broad arms across his chest, trying hard to convey his authority. 'Fuck off.'

'Ditto.' Bermuda flashed him an irritating grin and then sharply made a turn towards the excited gathering.

'You really should treat these men with respect.' Argyle's voice drowned out the noise of the afternoon as they approached the cordon.

'I have nothing but respect for them. But that guy was arsehole.'

'Did you find anything?' Argyle asked, following carefully behind Bermuda as they walked between the groups of excited pedestrians, all of them hoping for another phenomenon. Bermuda stepped out from them, into the beaming sun and looked up towards the sky. The warmth struck his face and he smiled, sliding a cigarette between his lips and flicking his lighter.

'I think so, big man,' he responded. He patted the back pocket of his jeans, turned on his heels and began making his way towards the station.

'Where are we going?' Argyle followed a few steps behind his partner. Bermuda blew a cloud of smoke into the breeze, appreciating Argyle's enthusiasm. Although not human, Bermuda trusted him more than anyone else.

'By the way, well done on the distraction. Very dramatic.'

'I did not intend to cause such a commotion.' Argyle's reply was tinged with apology.

They turned off the main road, following the walkway towards the other side of the alleyway. Already ahead of them, Bermuda could see the flashing lights of the police car; the officers carefully watched it in fear having seen Argyle's handiwork earlier. He chuckled to himself, wondering if Argyle would lift that car just to scare them all again. Argyle brought him back with a question.

'What are we doing here? The superior officer asked you to leave.'

'I have left. We are not going to the crime scene.' Bermuda didn't look back as he spoke, crossing the road quickly to avoid the gathering crowd on this side of the alleyway. Word was spreading fast of a missing person and magical, floating cars. Two white vans marked with TV logos stopped halfway up the road, teams of people scurrying out with recording equipment. Bermuda shook his head, knowing that they would never be able to report on the actual truth. Everything they would spout, regardless of how real it would seem, was all a fabrication. Scientists would speculate that a gravitational shift was responsible for Argyle's act of strength and loyalty. The Police will plead with the public to help them find Jess.

No one would know the truth.

A world wrapped safely in cotton wool.

A few more feet and Bermuda stopped at the gated gardens of Garland House, casting his gaze up at the large, white pebbled building that was segregated into flats. A few residents leant from their windows, watching the people below move around like excitable ants.

'Then what are we doing here? Argyle's question was edged with frustration. Bermuda stopped at the metal entrance way and turned back, his eyes sparkling with excitement.

'We are going to find out what the hell is going on.'

Argyle nodded and the two of them entered the grounds, marching towards the large front door that shimmered in the sunlight.

5

Sophie Summers jolted in a sudden panic as the intercom rasped through the hallway of her flat. Sat on the cream sofa in the spacious living room, she had drawn her knees to her chest and wrapped her arms around them. She wanted to fold up, hide away from a world that had stolen her best friend.

Her brown eyes stung from crying, her make up smudged and trailing dark streaks down her striking cheekbones. Her dark hair, usually flowing to her shoulders, was scruffily tied up in a lopsided ponytail; the stress of the day hung from her like wet clothes.

Her best friend was missing.

She had waited hours earlier, knowing Jessica was a few minutes from walking through the door. They were going to sit, maybe open another bottle of wine and excitedly discuss their careers. Like Jess, Sophie was also beginning to climb the model ladder, having just shot the autumn collection for a high street brand's soon to be released catalogue.

They had so much to discuss. So much to look forward to.

Now she was gone.

A few tears silently perched on the lids of her sore eyes, before hurling themselves down the well-worn paths of the others.

The intercom rasped again and she slowly approached it, stepping into the hallway lined with canvas paintings of European cities. She stopped in front of a watercolour depicting Amsterdam, as she reached a delicate hand up to the machine.

'Hello?' She sniffled, holding down the speech button.

'Hello. Miss Summers?'

The voice wasn't familiar.

'Who is this?' She asked, terrified by a strange voice on a day of stranger events.

'Ma'am, I am Agent Franklyn Jones. I'm here to interview you in regards to the disappearance of Jessica Lambert.'

Sophie reached out and pressed her hand against the wall for support. Her head bowed over as she struggled for breath, hearing a stranger talk of her friend's sudden vanishing brought over a new wave of sadness. She clung to the air that left her and steadied herself.

'Come in,' she said, trying to sound in control. She unlocked the building's entrance remotely and waited patiently. Nervously, she dabbed at her cheeks with a tissue, wiping away the evidence of heartbreak. Trying to arrange her hair into a more respectable state, she peered through the peep hole of her front door as she heard footsteps approaching.

The man was younger than he sounded, his light brown hair swept to the side in a neat parting. His face, handsome and lined with stubble, housed two green eyes that were looking around with interest. He was attractive and she scorned herself for even noticing given the circumstances.

He reached out with a toned arm and gently rapped on the door.

'Who is it?' She called out, second guessing her decision to let someone this close to her when she felt so vulnerable.

'Agent Jones. We just spoke a moment ago.' The words filtered through the thick door to her, a slight confusion wrapped around them. Sophie slowly opened the door, the light from the hall cutting through until the chain pulled. Her eyes flickered through the gap, nervously searching the strange man in front of her.

'Can I see some ID?' Her words shook slightly despite her best efforts. With a friendly and handsome smile, the man dipped his hand into his back pocket and produced a leather case. Flipping it open, she read the credentials that ran next to his photo. Her nose scrunched, revealing cute dimples that made him smile.

'Is there a problem, Miss Summers?' His words were calming.

'What is the BTCO?' She looked back to his face as he snapped shut the ID and returned it to its denim prison.

'It's a specialist unit. I have a few questions I need to ask you about your friend. I am happy to do this by phone or in the hallway if you like?'

'No, please. Come in.' She closed the door and rattled the chain free before welcoming him in. 'I'm just a little scared.'

'Understandable. Thank you.' Bermuda smiled at her as he stepped across a pink welcome mat, the word 'Welcome' embroidered in red roses. She slowly shuffled down the hallway; her figure dancing with such a natural fluidity, Bermuda couldn't help but watch her, until a disgruntled grunt from Argyle caused him to respectfully avert his gaze. She disappeared into the living room and as Bermuda entered, she was already curled up on the sofa, a thin, blue blanket wrapped around her legs. He smiled and took a seat opposite. Between them, a glass coffee table covered in tear stained tissues. Argyle took his stand in the corner, although she would never know.

'Ok, Miss Summers, if you could....'

'Sophie,' she insisted, forcing a smile through her apparent turmoil.

'Sophie,' he replied with one of his own. 'If you could tell me what you remember of last night that would be great.'

'Ok. I mean it was a standard party, really. Alcohol, some drugs...' Her eyes flickered to Bermuda in a panic. 'Not that we did any.'

'Don't worry about it. I couldn't give a damn if you did or not.' Sophie stared at him sceptically. 'Please continue.'

'Well, I got talking to this guy. Mark Rammage?' She looked at Bermuda expectantly. His eyes remained vacant. 'Plays one of the lead roles on Casualty?'

'Is that a TV show?' Bermuda asked, entirely genuine.

'Err, yeah. Anyway, I agreed to go back to his and then he started to get a little bit too full on in the cab. I mean, I'm not a prude but there is a time and a place.'

'Sounds like a classy guy,' Bermuda quipped, looking around the room. Argyle remained statuesque in the corner.

'Well anyways, he got out of the cab at his and I asked the driver to bring me back here. He yelled after me, called me a 'fucking bitch', but to be honest, the guy is a dickhead. Completely up himself.'

'Interesting. What can you tell me about your friend?'

He suddenly realised why she was relaying the pointless story of the TV star. The pain of her friends disappearance exploded forward, her face wrenching into complete discomfort. Her beautiful, dark eyes swelling under the weight of more tears. She raised a tissue, dabbing at the makeup stains as she spoke with broken words.

'She sent me a message saying she was on the bus. Honestly... that girl never gave up the night bus. She was frugal...and...and...'

'Take your time,' Bermuda said comfortingly, leaning forward on his chair.

'She was almost home and she said she really needed the toilet. Then that was it. I got worried after about half an hour as it is not far from the bus stop.'

'The one outside the station?' Bermuda asked. She nodded.

'When I reported it to the police they said they would look into it. I told them about the alleyway we sometimes cut through; it's just across the road there.' She motioned to the window with a flick of her head.

'I've been down there already.'

'What was all the commotion? I heard a lot of screaming?'

'Oh, nothing,' Bermuda replied dismissively, flashing a careful glance in Argyle's direction. 'Please continue.'

'That was it really. They checked the CCTV and said they saw her go through, so she was off the bus.' Sophie began to well up again, the tissue returning to battle the army of tears escaping from her eyes. 'She was so close to home.'

As Sophie buried her face into the tissues once more, Bermuda slowly pushed himself off his chair and carefully made his way towards her. Perching on the edge of the coffee table, he reached out and took her hand. Their eyes locked, hers shimmering through the wetness.

'I will find her,' Bermuda promised. She wiped her eyes.

'You don't look like a policeman.'

'I'm not.' He patted the top of her hand and stood up, throwing a glance at Argyle. He nodded for them to leave and the large warrior slowly began his journey to the door.

'What do you mean? You showed me your badge,' Sophie remarked, a tinge of paranoia creeping through her words.

'I'm something else.'

Bermuda stepped towards the door, his pathway blocked by the frightened resident as she leapt to her feet. He looked down at her, her delicate face lined with black streaks and her eyes decorated with confusion. Her voice reduced to a whisper, the strain of the day sapping her energy with every passing moment.

'I don't understand.'

'I work for a specialist agency. That's all you need to know.' He reached for his wallet, pulling it from the pocket of his jeans. 'I think something has happened to your friend that cannot be explained right now.'

'Like what? Oh god, do you think it's bad?' The tears returned, arching from the corner of her eyes and diving towards the soft carpet.

'I don't know. But I will find out.'

He gently reached out and rubbed her shoulder, offering her a warm smile. She looked down at his wrist, noticing the black etchings that emblazoned his skin. With his other hand, he removed a small card from his wallet, handing it to her.

'You call me if you need anything, ok?'

She nodded, looking at the card with an arched eyebrow.

'Bermuda? I thought your name was Franklyn?'

'It is. It's a dumb nickname that seems to have stuck.' He nodded a goodbye and made his way to the door, pulling it open with a turn of the handle. Unbeknownst to Sophie, Argyle ventured over the threshold first and Bermuda began to follow.

'Why do they call you that?' She called out. He stopped, turning to take in her beauty one last time.

'People go missing. And when they do, they call me.' They shared one last glance; he could see a blanket of reassurance start to gently wrap itself over her shoulders. She mustered a smile, the first genuine one since he had arrived. The beauty of her face sent a small flutter through Bermuda, reminding him that the world had denied him actual beauty and replaced it with a curse of darkness.

'Call me if you need to talk.'

'I will.' She looked down at the tightly grasped card and then back to him, her eyes reaching out with a desperate plea. 'Please find my friend?'

With a silent promise, Bermuda closed the door behind him, setting off with his partner to do just that.

■ ■ ▮

'Two pints of Doombar, please.'

The barman nodded, flipping the pint glass in his hand before gripping the mighty pump, the thick ale calmly dribbling out into the glass. Bermuda grasped the ten pound note in his hand, the coarseness rubbing against his skin. The day had been a long one; the case was clear yet he had no leads apart from a bizarre twelve-sided shape in his note pad. The young woman was missing, deleted from the world without a trace.

He needed a beer.

The Royal Oak sat across Watford Heath, a small green surrounded by semi-detached houses and was fairly busy. With many of the locals popping in for a first drink before commencing a heavier night in the town, the place was alive with conversation and laughter, all accompanied with quiet backing music. Bermuda had been regularly attending the pub since he moved to the area, appreciating the aesthetics of the building. Hard wooden floors with smartly arranged tables and a low ceiling with large, wooden beams running from wall to wall. The staff always had a smile and the selection of drinks was always appealing.

The young barman placed the two pints in front of him at the bar and then returned a few coins after Bermuda paid him. Taking a sip from his own drink, Bermuda carried them both from the bar, back out the door to the benched area that ran alongside the quaint building. Sitting on the second bench was his best friend, Brett Archer, lighting a cigarette and gratefully accepting the beverage.

'Cheers, mate,' Brett said, taking a large swig of the dark, brown ale. Bermuda nodded, taking the seat opposite on the wooden bench and held his glass up.

'Cheers.'

They both sipped, taking in the rich flavours before setting them down on the table between them, the course wood having seen better days. Bermuda slipped a cigarette between his lips, lighting it with a flick of his lighter. Opposite him, Brett tied his long brown hair into a messy ponytail, and smiling through his thick, dark beard.

'So, what's happening, BJ?' He asked, taking another swig.

'Don't call me BJ, man. I'd rather not be named after a blow job.'

'Fair enough,' Brett chuckled. 'So, why the beer? Shit day?'

'Long day. New case and to be honest with you, mate, I haven't got a clue what is going on,' Bermuda responded, rubbing the bridge of his nose in frustration.

'You never do. But you always figure it out, right?'

Despite his friend's positivity, Bermuda could only muster a small shrug before tipping half of his pint down his throat. They had been doing this for years, ever since they met at Derby University sixteen years ago. Fresh faced and with the world at their feet, Bermuda's studies were increasingly interrupted by his curse. It was near impossible to concentrate in a lecture when he could see that dark, slithering beast wrapping itself around the lectern.

It was more difficult to make friends when people thought you were crazy. Everyone except Brett, who not only believed him but did his level best to understand. An accomplished guitar player with a rasping singing voice, Brett was the lead vocalist in the thrash metal band – Frozen Death Call – and after some moderate success in the early Noughties, he was struggling to hold on to past glories. With a solid following in Europe, he spent most of his time performing in non-glamorous towns in Hungary or Slovakia.

Bermuda envied him however, seeing his genuine joy and love for what he did for a living. The freedom and enjoyment he got out of life.

He loved Brett, yet hated him at the same time.

With the glass almost emptied in front of him, Brett broke the silence and brought Bermuda back to the table.

'So wait, did you see Argyle today?'

Bermuda nodded.

'Awesome. How is he?' Brett asked enthusiastically.

'Same as ever. Pretty sure he was created without a sense of humour.' Bermuda finished his pint. 'Although, he did lift a police car to buy me some time on the crime scene, which was pretty cool.'

'Hold on, he lifted a car? Like, off the ground?'

'Yep.' Bermuda confirmed.

'That guy is a fucking legend!' Brett exclaimed before finishing the last of his pint. He pushed himself off the bench and disappeared through the low door way into the pub. Before Bermuda could even light his next cigarette, he had returned, two full pints in his grasp. The foam toppled over the rim and down his fingers as he placed them down, plonking himself opposite and stealing a cigarette from his friend.

'So, how's the band?' Bermuda asked, trying to take his mind off of the alleyway. The twelve-sided shape that made no sense. The constant feeling of something dark, reaching out from somewhere darker.

'Not too bad, thanks.' The words accompanied a large cloud of smoke. 'Got a few gigs in Helsinki at the end of the month. You should come along. Might do you good.'

Bermuda stared at his fresh pint, his fingers dancing through the foam ring the pint glass had imprinted on wooden surface. He frayed the ring into sharp edges, recreating the bizarre symbol he had seen in the alleyway.

None of the words got through to him.

'You ok?' Brett asked, concerned as he stubbed the cigarette into the ashtray on the table, the glass graveyard for the recently smoked.

'Sorry man. I'm a bit distracted.'

'The case?'

'Yeah. Some girl has gone missing and...I dunno...it just doesn't seem to add up right now.' Bermuda looked at the symbol, the foam dribbling and blurring the crude shape that he had sloppily recreated from memory.

'Where did she go missing?' Brett asked, interested and slyly slipping another cigarette from Bermuda's box.

'Right by her house. I spoke with her flat mate. She was really scared.'

'Hot?' Brett asked, boyishly pumping out smoke rings.

'She was actually. Not that it's important, but she was gorgeous. Why? What has that got to do with anything?'

Brett chuckled and took a long sip of his Doombar.

'Because it's about time you got yourself some action.'

Bermuda laughed, shaking his head at his inappropriate yet slightly accurate friend.

'It was hardly the time or the place. Plus, she would need to have some severe problems to see anything in a guy like me.'

'Hey now. You're not the worst looking guy in the world. I mean, you're no Brett Archer....'

'Thank fuck for that.'

The two friends laughed, clicking their glasses together and letting the tension of the day slip away from them. A few more mouthfuls and Bermuda was back at the bar, handing over more money in the relieving race for inebriation. He returned merrily, the effects of the alcohol starting to lighten his mood and he dropped into his seat, forgetting about the dark truth of the world he hated yet protected valiantly.

'Speaking of severe problems, guess who called me?' Brett asked, gratefully lifting his glass. Bermuda shrugged. 'Angela.'

Bermuda suddenly felt his mood change. A sadness infiltrated his mind, taking control of him and shaking a cold flutter down his spine. He felt his heart jolt, a hard twinge of pain at the mention of his ex-wife.

Angela Bennett had been the love of his life. The moment he had looked into her dark, green eyes he had lost himself. Her dark hair, cut into a short bob with a tinge of purple dye, framed a beautiful face that left him breathless. They were young, only twenty-two years old, yet she was the first person to ever make him forget about The Otherside. The only person to make him think completely about this world and the possibilities it held.

They married at the age of twenty-four, a quiet service at a wonderful country estate that provided the backdrop for the majority of his most precious memories.

Chloe arrived four years later.

Bermuda slowly lifted his hand, dabbing a small tear away from his eye. His friend looked at him with a heartfelt sympathy, knowing the struggle he had inflicted upon himself. Finally, Bermuda spoke, his voice fractured with small echoes of heartbreak.

'What did she say?'

Brett waited, watching as his best friend reached for a cigarette with a shaking hand, the pain of the conversation turning the simple task difficult.

'She asked how you were. The usual.' He nervously looked at his friend, contemplating his words. 'She wants to meet you.'

Bermuda shook his head, pushing the smoke out before stumping it out on the glass tray. Another one lit, he shook his head again.

'She said it's important.'

'No. I can't see her. I won't see her. It's not safe'

'It's about Chloe.'

Bermuda looked him straight in the eye. Brett hated these conversations, knowing that mentioning her name was almost forbidden. Bermuda took a few moments of composure before lifting his glass and finishing the rest of his drink.

'Please call her and tell her I'll see her tomorrow. Tell her to come alone and not to mention it to anyone.'

Bermuda reached out and patted his best friend on the shoulder before pushing himself to his feet. Brett looked up at him with a concerned gaze, knowing the burden he had placed upon himself.

'You going to be okay, BJ?'

Bermuda steadied himself, slightly angered that three pints had begun to make the edges of his world fuzzy, replaced with a drunken incomprehension that usually visited a few more pints down the line.

'No. But when am I ever?'

Downtrodden, Bermuda turned and exited the benched forecourt of the Royal Oak, wandering aimlessly towards the large green that lead towards the main road.

Brett sat back in his chair, his fist clenching in frustration for the suffering he had just brought to his best friend, cursing the fact he could do nothing to help him. He finished his beer, watching Bermuda disappear into the shadows that he constantly spoke of as being alive.

6

Bermuda felt the warmth of the sun as it fell on him, soaking up the rays like a blooming plant. Euston Station was one of the heartbeats of London, the hustle and bustle of everyday life marching past him with impatient steps. Young men and women danced through crowds of people, eager to get to work on time. Businessmen nonchalantly meandered through streams of tourists, tutting at the obstacle caused by those with a genuine interest in their surroundings. Students woozily went by, dragging their feet as if they were attached to a hangover and clinging on for dear life.

The normal, everyday routine of the human existence.

How he envied them.

With a jealous shake of the head, he lit a cigarette, the smoke delicately wafting upwards towards the blue sky before latching on to the larger cloud that hung above the smoking section. Commuters surrounded him, all nervously eyeing the timetable screen, many contemplating a final smoke before embarking on their journeys.

With eyes that yearned for more sleep, Bermuda looked around the forecourt of the station, the eateries bursting with the London inhabitants, shops almost busting at the seams with people demanding an early morning caffeine fix. He smirked, lifting his cup and sipping the adequate coffee he had bought, surprised that it was still warm. In the shadows cast by the nearest shop he noticed an Other, latched against the wall with its head turned 180°. Its skin, a faded brown, wrapped over its sharp skull, the ice white eyes glaring at the people walking by.

Bermuda held his stare, burning it through the Other's subconscious till it turned around to face him. He could sense its instant fear, knowing full well the reputation he had among their kind. As if its entire body was made of liquid, it slowly began to slither around the side of the building, away from him and the horror stories that preceded him. Bermuda felt a duty to follow it, question its reasons for being here, but he couldn't muster the energy.

This was the place.

With perfect timing, his mind was brought back to reality when he heard her voice, her words creeping up behind him and slithering over his shoulders.

'Franklyn.'

He felt a shudder, as if a tiny ant raced down his spine. Leaning with his back against the bench table, he refused to turn, feeling the seat shake slightly as Angela Bennett settled onto it. His heart beat faster. He could hear her fumbling in her bag, before speaking again.

'Thank you for meeting me.'

'I have told you, it isn't safe for you to be seen with me.'

He heard her sigh, one he had heard for years, a sigh that had become as regular as breathing. He could sense her eyes burrowing through him, making him feel a twinge of sympathy for the Other he had done the same to moments before.

'Well, it is good to see you. Well, the back of your head anyway.' Bermuda chortled slightly, out of politeness.

'What do you want, Ange?' His words were strained, the pain of talking to the love of his life for the first time in months, hung from each one like an unwanted tumour.

'I wanted to see you. Chloe misses you.' She noticed his head twitch with a grimace. 'I miss you.'

'Well it was your decision to leave me, so sadly, you don't get the right to miss me.' Bermuda took a few breathes, refusing to lose his temper and blow their cover.

'I left Franklyn, because you were losing control. You were so transfixed with this other world that was stalking you. It was terrifying Chloe. I didn't want to leave.'

'But you did, didn't you?' His words were accompanied with a soft cloud of second hand smoke, which Angela fanned away with annoyance.

'Because you pushed us away.'

'I was trying to protect you.'

'From what?'

He couldn't answer. They were re-treading ground that had long since perished. He knew it sounded crazy. Not even the woman he had pledged to love and protect could believe him. The government, although since abolished by the BTCO, filed paperwork that certified him as insane. The easiest thing would be for the Otherside to stop hiding, to blow away the smoke and smash the mirrors and reveal itself to the world. The chance for him to tell the world a big, fat 'I told you so'.

But he would never want those he cared about to see what he had to. To witness just how dark the real world is. For that, for the sake of keeping them safe, he refused to answer.

Angela, spoke to him through sharp intakes of breath.

'Your daughter sits at home, asking me 'why Daddy doesn't visit anymore'. 'Where has Daddy gone?' 'Why does Daddy always seem sad?' What am I supposed to tell her?'

Bermuda shook his head, leaning forward and taking in more toxic smoke.

'Look. I tried to be the doting dad, but I can't be. Okay, I can't be. Not because I don't want to. There is nobody in this or any other world that I love more than you and Chloe, but I can't be that dad. The world won't let me.'

Angela reached out nervously, a manicured hand slowly lowering itself onto his rounded shoulder. He shook slightly, feeling her touch for the first time in over three years.

'This world isn't trying to hurt you, Franklyn.'

'No, you're right. *This* world isn't.'

She slowly removed her hand, weeping softly as she retracted her love from a man she had wanted since the moment she had met. He had been hers, but she knew that somewhere along the way he had lost himself.

The likelihood of him returning had left town a long time ago.

'Franklyn.' Her words stammered out, each one doing their best to disappear before reaching him. 'Look at me.'

As he shook his head, she cast her eyes to his arms. The avalanche of tattoo's. The hideous, random scrawlings of ink. He was gone and she knew it. A new wave of tears crashed through her skull, pouring from her eyes like two waterfalls. Her voice, broken and shaking, rose in volume.

'LOOK AT ME!'

A few commuters turned with interest, seeing what looked like either a domestic in public or a callous break up. Either way, all the sympathy would sit with Angela and Bermuda knew that. Taking a deep breath, he swung his leg over the seat, turning so he faced her across the table. His heart stopped for that moment.

He hadn't laid eyes on her in over a year. His Angela, who he had loved unconditionally from the very moment he knew she existed. She looked so beautiful, despite her face painted with the pain he had caused.

He knew she would never be his again.

The edges of his vision, the frame around the striking woman before him, began to blur, his own tears creeping into his periphery. He tried to speak, but words were impossible. Trapped in his own sadness, he watched as she slowly dabbed at her eyes, shaking her head in disappointment. Finally she spoke, zipping up her handbag and standing up. The sun bathed around her, casting her shadow across his handsome face.

'You were the one who chose to stay away.' She stepped to the side, a blast of brightness hitting Bermuda, sparkling off of the tear that ran down his cheek. 'This is all your doing.'

She turned and stormed through the adjacent crowd, barging past surprised tourists before disappearing into the station to head home. Bermuda watched her leave, wiping away the evidence of his broken heart. He sat in the sun for a while, an ever-increasing pile of cigarette butts scattered around his feet.

'None of this is my doing,' he angrily said to himself, cursing the world for the 'gift' it had bestowed upon him and hating himself for losing all that he cared about.

Heading towards the nearest entrance to the station, he wanted to jump on the first train that would take him to anywhere that his life didn't exist.

■ ■ |

He stared at them all in disgust. There was something ugly about the human race that infuriated him greatly. An heir of entitlement, a true arrogance. Man thinks man is dominant.

He smiled, crooked, sharp teeth that hung from his grey lips. They were so wrong and it would only be a matter of time before he could show them. Show them all, one by one, what real power and dominance is. He had already demonstrated it to his own kind.

He looked around the ship; the thick, wooden slabs symmetrically tacked together, only a few thin cuts of light breaking through in random gaps. The humans passed him by, unaware of who or what he was.

He was their reckoning.

The wooden vessel was somewhat of a museum, a bewildering tribute to a bygone era that he had never witnessed but had outlived by centuries. These people, of different colours and languages, wandered round, taking empty photos of things they didn't care about. Nothing but a herd, a race that needs to follow.

His arm, covered by the sleeve of his tatty blazer, rested on a nearby stand. His top hat sat proudly on his shaggy, white hair. In his other hand he held the twelve-sided artefact, his fingers coiled around it like an attacking python.

It was almost time. There was no selection process. No criteria one of these useless creatures had to meet. He would just know.

With his jet black eyes scanning the inside of the Cutty Sark, they finally rested on a portly gentleman, wobbling through a small group of people with a camera in his hand and beads of sweat dripping down a flustered face. He spoke with a thick twang, unlike the usual accent he had heard from the regulars.

This man was a long way from home and was about to travel even further.

A high pitch scratch echoed through his skull as he dragged his nails across the wooden stand before pushing himself up right. Like a lion stalking its prey, he slowly circled, walking between a few tourists who shuddered as he passed. The portly man leant in close to a glass cabinet, squinting his eyes to read the small plaque.

The man with the top hat leant in, his nose a mere few centimetres from the oblivious tourist. He took a deep sniff, inhaling the foul stench of a perspiring human. His cavernous eyes emanated hate and he bared his razor teeth.

'You are my one,' he whispered, knowing he couldn't be heard.

With his hands clasped around the strange device, he followed the gentleman as he walked towards the corner of the ship, his interest piqued by another display unit.

It would only take 10 minutes for the rest of his tour group to report him missing.

7

The Cutty Sark sits in the heart of Greenwich, London. Once belonging to the Jock Willis Shipping line, the magnificent wooden structure lays along the concrete in the busy town, now nothing more than nearly a thousand tonnes of British history. Its vast, white sails slowly danced on the breeze, the mast they swung from reaching up towards the sky.

Originally built in the 1800's, the ship had undergone two renovations, both due to fires. Although repaired and components replaced, the ship drew many an interested traveller, all of them walking the narrow interiors or experiencing the warmth upon the deck of the magnificent ship. Middle-aged tourists snapping photos, young couples posing for selfie's.

The beautiful ship brought a touch of elegance and class to an already smart area of London. The surrounding streets, busy with foot traffic, were dissected by alleyways, all leading towards hidden market stalls.

On a day as hot as this there were plenty of people about. So many potential witnesses.

Yet as he sat in the forecourt of The Gypsy Moth, a large pub that overlooked the tremendous ship and the neighbouring Thames, Bermuda knew that no one had seen anything. Not one person had a clue as to how Josh Cooper went missing.

Argyle had found Bermuda as he sat on a train, the heartbreak of meeting his ex-wife earlier that morning had lead him to embark on a journey to anywhere. He was fairly sure he was halfway to Cambridge when his partner sat down next to him. Off at the next stop, Bermuda boarded a train back towards London with a keen interest.

This was similar.

Cooper had been with a tour group, eight in total, and all of them were inside the narrow hall of the Cutty Sark. Portly and standing over six foot, the large American was hard to misplace, especially inside the historic ship.

'What is our plan of action?'

Argyle stood beside Bermuda, his muscular arms folded across his armour. His sword glistening in the sun as it lay strapped to his meaty back. Bermuda, with the white smoke of his cigarette ghosting upwards, reached for the half drunk pint of Doombar before him.

'It's the same. I can feel it.'

'We don't even know what the first one was.'

'I told you. That symbol was not of this world. I could feel it when I touched it. It latched onto me.'

'Latched on?'

'Never mind.' Bermuda lifted his glass quickly, swigging his drink and trying to end the conversation. He didn't want anyone to know about the ever increasing pull The Otherside had. Especially not Argyle.

'We need to inspect the ship.'

'Absolutely.' Bermuda pulled out his notepad, his heavily tattooed arms looking brighter in the glare of the summer sunshine. 'And I guarantee we will find this.'

Slapping the pad in front of Argyle, he tapped the page. Argyle scanned his grey eyes over the scrawled symbol, the rough lines that Bermuda sketched forming a twelve-sided shape unlike any he had seen before.

Before he could speak, a young waitress, who had previously flirted with Bermuda, walked up to the table to collect his now empty glass. With a coy smile, she dropped a card in front of him, her phone number scrawled across it. He smiled at her, imagining what the inevitable sex would be like between them.

Without her knowledge, she walked directly at Argyle, who quickly moved out of the way. Humans pass through Other's continuously, the outcome being a cold chill running down their spine. Always passed off as a sudden chill or 'someone walking over their grave', Bermuda knew the truth. But with Argyle's Latch Stone, she would have collided with something she wouldn't be able to see.

Argyle saved her the confusion. His noble compassion drawing a smile from Bermuda as he stood up.

'Let's go check it out, Big Man.'

He slid the chair back and stood, squinting his eyes through the glare of the sun. Hundreds of tourists were huddled near the entrance to the boat, all of them nattering in annoyance at the police presence denying their entrance. Having been called to the scene by the hysterical wife of the recently missing, they had evacuated the ship and were awaiting a forensics team to search the vessel. Standard procedure that Bermuda knew would be a pain in the arse.

He stepped from the beer garden of the pub onto the street, throwing a glance at a disappointed waitress, berating himself for leaving her card on the table. Argyle, having witnessed his behaviour with women before, raised an eyebrow which Bermuda shrugged off.

'We don't have time for me to be Prince Charming.'

His excuse seemed to work, Argyle refusing to ask any more questions. The last thing Bermuda wanted to admit was that he, for a ridiculous reason, felt like he would be being disloyal to Sophie. He had only met her once.

As they walked across the large, concrete square which accommodated the Cutty Sark, Bermuda noticed another small group of people, gathering round a small outburst of ringing bells and the clacking of colliding wood. He stopped to get a better look, the large thwacks of wood alerting Argyle who protectively drew an arm across his partner.

'Easy, Argyle,' he chuckled, gently pushing away the arm. 'It's just Morris Dancing.'

Argyle, scanning the scene, slowly retreated before stepping towards the group. Bermuda, walking towards the boat, noticed his partner's detour and quickly jogged towards the watching crowd. Having carefully maneuverer between the humans, Argyle stood at the front of the onlookers, his grey eyes wide with enchantment at the synchronised British tradition before him. After excusing his way to the front of the group, Bermuda stood next to his other worldly friend.

'What are you doing? We have to go and inspect the ship.'

'The movements are intoxicating. Such precision.'

Bermuda, aware that a few people were looking at him, smiled. 'You like it?'

'The uniforms, whilst obviously strange, are rich with nobility. Their chanting is a proud voice.'

'Why don't you go and join in?' Bermuda joked, rattling a few mints from their box whilst a concerned tourist stepped away from him.

'I have not been invited,' Argyle responded sternly.

'So what? Go and bust some shapes with them.'

Argyle turned, his frown almost pulling his short, dark hair over his face.

'That would be an intrusion of their display.'

'Ok, Big Man. Tell you what, I'm going to go and investigate a missing person. You know, the reason we are here. You can stand and watch the funny dancers and I'll come and find you.'

'You speak like I am neglecting my duties,' Argyle said, his voice revealing a hint of disappointment.

'Not at all. If I need you, I'll give you a shout, ok?' Bermuda looked back to the dancers, their chanting trying its best to drown out the shrill of the bell. He looked back to his friend, smiling at the surprising delight the performance held for him.

'I'll be back in five.'

Argyle nodded, his face almost relenting and producing a smile. Bermuda waited, but when it never surfaced he meandered through the random people before him, breaking out into the space before he approached the other crowd. A female police officer stood by entrance, behind her two strips of police tape stretched across the glass entrance to the ship.

Officer Karen Riley looked at the angry tourist with her brown eyes, her face displaying the necessary sympathy as the man berated her for ruining his visit. Her blonde hair, tied in a ponytail, bobbed under her hat. She stopped suddenly as Bermuda tried to walk towards the door, bypassing the crowd who looked on with intrigue.

'Excuse me, sir,' she said with a thick Northern Irish accent. 'This location is closed until further notice.'

'I know. I am here to inspect the disappearance of Josh Cooper.'

'Sir, that is a police matter.'

He smiled his warmest smile, slightly upset that his usual charm had no apparent effect on the woman. With a heavily inked arm, he whipped his badge from his pocket, flipping it in front of her scanning eyes.

'I'm sorry, sir. But my orders are that nobody goes in. Please step aside.'

'I literally need five minutes,' Bermuda begged, his patience at the Police rejecting him beginning to reach a boiling point.

'Sir, please step aside.' She hardened her tone, her hand reaching up to her radio. With the potential of being arrested looming, Bermuda held his hands up in surrender. Over her shoulder, he noticed a hulking officer staring in their direction, a keenness etched on his face like a shark coming across a school of fish.

'Sorry to bother you, Officer,' Bermuda said, stepping away and pushing a cigarette between his lips. He blew a cloud out into the warm air, watching it dance against the pale blue background. Circling the mighty, wooden structure, he clenched his fists in a small suppression of anger. Someone had gone missing. Another person, snatched from a world that had no idea how. It annoyed him more that he didn't know either.

Without the chance to inspect the inside of the ship, Bermuda couldn't prove his theory. That crude, twelve-sided symbol is part of it.

He knew it. The engraved marking reached for him, the touch of the Otherside ebbing at his fingertips. If that symbol was inside the boat, then he knew he had something to run with.

As his eyes searched the wooden panels of the ship's hull, a piercing scream of terror tore through the air.

■ ∎ ∣

As Bermuda had exited the crowd, Argyle turned his attention back to the dancing group before him. Fascinated with the elegance of their moves and the regimented formations of their stick striking, he found himself immersed in the show. It reminded him of his life before the BTCO. Before Bermuda.

An existence that was so far away and one which could never be revisited.

Shaking free from his wretched memories of life on the Otherside, he watched as the more seasoned humans before him skipped in unison, their bells ringing like a flock of birds chirping overhead.

Suddenly, he felt something gently collide with his leg. Jolted from his trance, he looked down, noticing an infant human sitting on the ground, confusion spread across its face having collided with an invisible wall. He had seen many of the smaller humans, all of them lacking the intelligence of their elder parents. Whilst they struggled to speak and walk, he did appreciate their innocence and he stared down at this young child. A female he noted. Its face was crumpled with pain, the anguish of hitting the floor etched through its features. Suddenly, it began to cry.

With a growing concern, Argyle reached down with a mighty hand, grabbing the back of the child's t-shirt and scrunching it. As he hoisted her into the air, the surrounding people gasped, moving quickly away at the phenomenon before them.

As Argyle held the child to his eye line, inspecting her injuries, the rest of the world witnessed the infant rising slowly into the air and levitating on the spot.

A piercing scream of terror cut through the air as a young woman raced over, her eyes streaming tears and her panicked words of calm spluttering through short breaths. As the woman approached, she extended her arms towards what he assumed was her infant. Argyle gladly offered the child to the bemused mother, who snatched the child from what looked like thin air, her red eyes bulging with fear as she hurriedly calmed down the wailing child.

Bermuda raced through the crowd and began hastily ushering Argyle in any direction away from the crowd. The gentle warrior looked back in dismay.

'What the hell are you doing?' Bermuda sternly said, trying his best to keep his voice down.

'That young human was injured and I was the cause.' He again looked back in the direction, the mother soothingly tapping the young child's back as it clung to her. 'I was ensuring there was no damage.'

'Dude, you can't do that,' Bermuda said, sympathising with his partner. 'You just put the shits up a lot of people.'

'That young child needed assistance.'

'Yeah, and now her mother is probably going to need counselling.' Bermuda slapped Argyle on the arm in comradery. 'Remember, they can't see you like I can.'

Argyle nodded his understanding, failing to keep his sadness hidden. Bermuda didn't know much about Argyle's past, but knew that he was anything other than a monster. He offered him a smile before turning his attention back to the Cutty Sark, the doorway still guarded by the plucky Police officer.

'Why did she scream?' Argyle asked quietly.

'Huh?' Bermuda responded without looking.

'The mother. She screamed with such terror. She was wild with movements that I could not comprehend.'

Bermuda turned and warmly smiled at Argyle.

'She was just scared, Big Guy. That's what us humans do. We get scared and we act out of character. We think everything is coming to an end and we don't really know how to handle it.' He looked over at the mother, who was now sitting on a small wall, playfully bobbing the now happy child on her lap. 'But when we calm down, it's not so bad. Usually the solution is right there and it just takes a little perspective.'

Argyle nodded, reaffirming to himself more than anyone. Bermuda reached for his pocket, but winced in frustration as the box of mints was empty.

'What did you find on the ship?' Argyle asked, his mind returning to the case.

'The what? Oh, couldn't get on. It's fine, we can come back later when they realise there is nothing more they can do.'

'I see.' Argyle nodded. 'What's the plan?'

'The plan? I need to find a shop.' Bermuda waved his empty box of mints at a seemingly unimpressed Argyle before turning on his heels and venturing away from the Cutty Sark back towards the high street. Argyle sighed.

'You humans are confusing.'

Argyle set off, following his partner a few steps behind in the glorious London sunshine.

■ ▮ ▍

The feeling was immense. The raw surge of humanity that coursed through his body almost made him shudder. The man's identity was not important to him, nor would it ever be. All that mattered was he now belonged to him.

He had become another one of his 'stolen'.

As he adjusted his tatty blazer, the creature looked around the rest of the wooden vessel with the same disdain as he had before.

People were now in a state of fear, all of them buzzing around frantically within the narrow confines, as if someone had kicked a hornets nest.

They were all so...pathetic.

He snarled at them through gritted, jagged teeth, his deep black eyes scanning the disgusting race before him. They would all soon belong to him. Each and every one of them. Whilst he witnessed a female crying, urging the others to find her 'missing' husband, he imagined what they would be like if they had walked through the doorway with him.

If they got a glimpse at the world beyond.

The world that forged him.

That held him captive.

The inspiration behind his great pilgrimage.

His turned his head, the white hair fraying underneath the black, top hat. His door was still open, crudely cut into the wooden walls that contained them. Beyond it, nothing but black, the faint hint of a grey smoke wafting near but never crossing the threshold.

The man had passed through as easily as the rest. Another one that was his.

Soon they would be here. Snooping around and trying to find him. He knew of the organisation that existed on this wasted planet, the humans without the blindfold. They would be looking for him, along with their treacherous Neither's and they would be here soon enough. The human they had assigned to it was of great interest indeed. The man who could walk both worlds. Such power. A power he would duplicate.

As he gently tapped his sharp, crooked nails on the wall next to the portal to his world, a sinister smile crept across his decaying face. The three scars that horribly mangled one side of it creased.

With a silent word, he sent the invitation, beckoning the

creature through the doorway with minimal fuss. The respect and obedience were driven by fear. Even a beast as feral as this one knew who he was and what he stood for.

The creature loomed over him, its eyes the colour of recently spilt blood. Its crooked jaw bone, protruding from its long, black face, presented a sharp, jagged set of teeth that had ripped more flesh than he cared to imagine. All it took was a stare from him and the creature slowly faded into the shadows that hid in the corners of the massive, wooden vessel that housed them.

Whilst the humans erupted into blind panic at one of their own going missing, he slowly made his way to the exit, leaving behind the enormous creature as a welcoming gift for the man who could walk both worlds.

The man who scared The Otherside as much as he did.

Bermuda.

8

The sun made its retreat a little after eight o'clock, slowly fading and leaving the streets of Greenwich with a grey tinge. As the moon took charge of the sky, street lamps burst into life, ready for their night shift. The locals meandered through the streets, groups of young adults already merry, chasing their latest alcoholic drink at whatever bar they stumbled upon.

As the moon shone proudly from the darkness above, the Cutty Sark was awash with a white glow. The street lights that surrounded the ship illuminated its grandeur, the large beams shooting out towards the stars like mighty, wooden fingers.

The afternoon had passed fairly quickly for Bermuda, who decided to waste his day away within the surrounding hotspots as opposed to venturing all the way across London towards Hertfordshire. After being denied entrance to the ship, he had wandered down the high street until he found a small, Spanish restaurant. Ordering four separate Tapas dishes for lunch, he ate quietly, allowing Argyle to collect himself after the incident with the small child earlier. After enjoying his multi-layered meal with a cold beer, he paid and walked further from the boat, heading towards Greenwich park.

The vast, green fields were swarming with tourists and locals and he slowly walked through as dogs sprinted around excitedly. Young women sunbathed whilst their other halves threw a Frisbee with random accuracy. The world was a happy place and he scowled, knowing that beyond the brightness of this day, their lay something worse in the shadows.

It was a painful reminder of the life he existed in.

As the afternoon slowly descended into evening, he found himself thumbing through his phone, annoyed that he didn't have Sophie's number and also annoyed that he was letting himself get distracted. He couldn't let people in. It was too dangerous.

Bermuda returned to the Cutty Sark as the sun began to descend, only to find a SOCO tent set up, officers in white jump suits swarming all over the large vessel like brightly coloured ants. Sighing deeply, he turned and walked back into the town, heading towards the Maritime Museum that sat just on the outskirts. As the day faded to dusk, he strode through the immaculate grounds of the famous buildings, the large, white structures standing powerfully. Argyle, who had barely spoken since his introduction to a terrified parent, seemed blown away by their beauty. Bermuda watched him take in their stature, deciding to allow him to enjoy the moment in silence.

It wasn't until the groundkeeper ushered him towards the gate that he realised he had sat for over an hour, ignoring the conclusion of day. Shadows formed in every corner, and he could feel the eyes of so many Others on him.

Now, having walked through the endless sea of people enjoying their 'normal' lives, he approached the Cutty Sark, ready for work.

'Fuck!' Bermuda exclaimed as they reached the opening. The

mighty boat sat in the centre of the concrete ocean, street lights showering it with a flattering glow. Beyond, the River Thames quietly wafted by, cutting through the capital city like a giant vein. On the horizon line, London was lit up with a million lights. The sight of the night-time London landscape always impressed Bermuda, the buildings illuminated and lights twinkling like a swarm of fireflies had ascended upon the city.

But the view was spoilt, not by the boat in front of them, the ship even more striking in the moonlight. Standing in front of the glass entry doors, was a Police Officer.

A large, chubby man with a thick beard, the officer was visually the opposite of the plucky lady who had confronted Bermuda earlier. From the look on his stern, hair covered face, Bermuda could tell that he would probably be just as obstructive. To the side of the ship, another Officer had been temporarily distracted by a couple of tourists. The young PC was pointing at their map and then across the street, his face a picture of frustration.

Bermuda felt his pain.

'Why are we not approaching?' Argyle spoke, his first words since Bermuda had berated him earlier that afternoon.

'What's the point?' Bermuda said, snapping his zippo shut and blowing a cloud of smoke into the conversation. 'I literally can't recall a time that my badge has gotten us onto a crime scene.'

'Two years, five months and six days ago.' Argyle stated to Bermuda's amazement. 'You were granted access to the Montogomery household in Liverpool.'

'Thanks. That was useful.'

'You are most welcome,' Argyle replied, once again failing to grasp the concept of sarcasm.

Bermuda stood in a smoky silence, his eyes flicking over everything. He noticed a couple of Others beyond the ship against the far wall. The edges of their bodies looked smudged, as if they were on a TV screen that couldn't quite get the right signal. The tourists had finally started to head in the direction that the now visibly relieved Officer had been pointing. He slowly returned to his partner, who was chuckling.

'I thought for sure they would have been gone by now,' Bermuda moaned, stomping his cigarette out in frustration.

'So?'

'What do you mean, so?' Bermuda said, turning to his friend, the light shimmering off his dark skin.

'When has that ever stopped you before?'

'That's a good point.'

'Our job is to inspect this crime scene and see if there is an Otherworldly influence on this man's disappearance.'

'Which there is.'

'We need proof.'

'Proof is in there, Big Man.' Bermuda pointed.

'Then let's go.'

'Well, we need those cops to piss off.'

Argyle's grey eyes lit up. 'You leave that to me.'

■ ∎ |

PC Connolly watched as the two tourists slowly shuffled away from him, his relief escaping his body with a loud sigh. It had taken over ten minutes to direct them towards Greenwich train station, yet he was sure the two minute walk would take them a life time. Standing by the door to the ship was his partner, PC Stokes, a large chuckle emanating from his thick, brown beard.

The evening had been dull.

When he was told of another disappearance, he was excited to be allocated the task until he realised he was effectively babysitting a massive, immobile, wooden child. He was counting down the minutes to the end of his shift.

'Hurry up. I need to take a leak,' Stokes's voice boomed across, shaking him from his boredom.

'I'm coming.'

Connolly trotted towards the door of the ship to relieve his partner, when suddenly, he stopped still. Panic set in quickly as no matter how hard he tried, he couldn't move his head. Nor his neck. The rest of his body worked fine, his legs tried their best to move forward, his arms waved wildly but his head stayed still. As a human, he couldn't see Argyle standing behind him, his mighty hands holding his head and neck in place.

'Fuck! My neck!' Connolly shrieked, his partner racing over as a few civilians turned with interest.

'What the hell are you doing? I'm going to piss myself...'

'There is something wrong. My neck. My head. I can't move them.'

'What?' Stokes, nervously moving, approached his fear stricken partner. Argyle slowly manoeuvring so as not to collide with him.

'Call medical. I don't know...maybe it's a trapped nerve. Something is seriously wrong!' Connolly's voice shook, his eyes searching wildly for an explanation.

Argyle, with his firm grasp in place, looked beyond the oblivious police officers at the glass door to the Cutty Sark. A few moments later, his grey eyes sparkled with delight as Bermuda skilfully snuck around the corner of the ship, quietly opened the door and slipped inside.

He released his hold.

The straining young officer suddenly lurched forward, his feet slapping against the concrete as he collided into his partner. A passer-by chuckled at the two officers stumbling around in the street light.

'What the hell are you playing it?' Stokes asked, angrily shoving his younger colleague away.

'It's gone. My neck, it works.'

'Well your fucking head doesn't.' Stokes quickly began jogging towards the Gypsy Moth pub opposite, hell-bent on relieving his bladder. 'I'm going to piss myself!'

Those were the last words Argyle heard, as he quietly slipped through the glass doors, to catch up with his partner.

■ ▌ ▎

The wooden walls and ceilings of the ship loomed around Bermuda, creating a shadowy tunnel of rich history. His footsteps echoed, each one reverberating off the thick planks and cascading amongst the information stands. Bermuda pulled out his mobile phone, flicking through the menu until the front casing burst into light. The torch app was always handy.

Slowly navigating down the hallway, he passed many glass cabinets, the sudden burst of light launching shadows up the walls until he wasn't sure if they were moving or not. Walking slowly towards the supposed corner were the man had last been seen, he brushed the light over the walls, scrutinizing every surface. Looking for the link. Looking for that symbol.

'Something is wrong.'

Argyle's voice shattered the silence, causing Bermuda to slightly jolt with surprise.

'Jesus. Word of advice Argyle. Don't sneak up on people in the dark, okay? Especially not someone with a supposed history of mental health issues.'

'There is something here.' Argyle's voice relayed his worry, turning his head to scan the surroundings.

'Yup. And we are going to find it.'

'Not the symbol.'

'What are you talking about?' Bermuda turned, his phone spraying Argyle with brightness, his armour shimmering angelically in the glow. Without answering, Argyle turned, his head cocked as he searched, before walking through a side door that lead to a small, presentation room. Bermuda exhaled in bewilderment, turning his light and attention back to the wooden strips that surrounded him. As he ventured nearer the corner, his face drew back into a grand smile.

The symbol.

The crudely, uneven, twelve-sided shape was unmistakable. The lines cut into the wood, as if someone had branded it with a crooked cattle prod. As he reached out, he could feel the tips of his fingers shake. The lure of the Otherside began to pull, he could feel its ghastly reach beckoning him closer.

He clenched his fist, refusing even the slightest to touch.

'Hey, Argyle,' he called out without turning. 'I found it.'

As he reached for his notebook to compare it to his previous scribble, he slowly heard shuffling behind him. Although a big man, Argyle was usually very light on his feet but the footsteps began to grow in volume.

Having been staring solely at the wall for the last few minutes, Bermuda had failed to notice the large Other that had slowly slunk across the Cutty Sark, its huge, sharply clawed feet causing the ship to gently shake with each step. As he slowly turned, his body stiffened with fear at the behemoth before him.

Standing over ten feet tall, the feral Other loomed over him. The skin, a musky brown colour, drew tight over an imposing frame, with thick, elongated arms that hung from its spike-covered shoulders. Its legs, crookedly bent, slowly straightened, pushing the giant beast further towards the ceiling. Its jet-black eyes burrowed through Bermuda, resting in a large skull with two small horns on top of its head. Its long snout reached a few feet from its face and it roared at Bermuda, revealing razor sharp teeth. The volume shook the ship, the pictures on the wall swung terrified from their hooks. As its ear piercing roar ricocheted through Bermuda's body, the beast's bottom jaw split down the middle and swung out in two separate directions.

It lurched forward, snapping at Bermuda who ducked and threw himself to the hard, wooden floor. Scrambling between the unwelcome guest's legs, he turned onto his back, his eyes widened in fear.

As if disconnected from its spine, the Other's shoulders and pelvis twisted, turning the beast on the spot. Its neck cracked, allowing it to turn its monstrous skull around to face him.

'Fuck!' Bermuda exclaimed, before scrambling backwards across the floor as a mighty, razor clawed hand slammed down where his legs were. Bermuda clambered backwards down the wooden ship, the wild, gargantuan Other gave chase, its vicious claws slamming holes into the floor as each hand missed his feet by a matter of inches.

Aiming for the door, Bermuda collided with a marble plinth, the glass dome atop it housing a small piece of paper that recollected a moment of the ship's history. He was sure that fighting a wild, giant beast from another dimension wasn't on it. Blocked in, the hulking monster stood before him. Its jaw flew open and it let out another roar as it hunched onto its back legs, before driving both hands down onto its cornered prey.

Bermuda closed his eyes, expecting his death to be quick.

'GO!'

Argyle's voice bounced off the wooden panels as Bermuda opened his eyes in surprise. Standing before him, with his mighty arms holding up the beast, Argyle shook with power. The beast snapped its jaws, snarling at the soldier who was holding him at bay. Argyle held onto the wrists of the wild monster, the veins in his arms protruding, the muscles shaking.

'GO NOW!'

Bermuda needed no second invitation, quickly clambering to his feet before racing back down the ship, away from the evidence of the Otherside's most recent attempt at extinguishing him.

Argyle had been inspecting the smaller, more intimate rooms of the ship, his instincts alarming him to a presence of his world amongst them. This happened regularly, and a quick inspection usually revealed a legal Other just finding solace in a shadowy dwelling. This time, however, he had been right. Once he heard the roar, he raced back to the main chamber, just in time to see this magnificent behemoth haunch up on its hind legs before aiming to kill his friend.

He had grabbed its arms just in time and now, as rows of razor sharp teeth snapped at him, he shifted his weight, letting out a yell of fury as he began to push the creature back. As he took one step, the creature suddenly twisted, its shoulders turning at such a speed that Argyle was whipped from his feet and the momentum sent him shooting towards the wall. The sheer power sent him clean through the wooden panels, and he erupted into the side streets in a downpour of shards and splinters. Crashing face first against the concrete, he lay motionless, faintly hearing the two terrified policemen frantically radio in for an Armed Response Unit.

Inside the ship, the crazed beast immediately gave chase to Bermuda, dashing past the recently created hole in the wall, its powerful legs bounding as it used its claws to scale the wall, the entire ship rocking as if it were in the eye of a storm.

Bermuda ran as fast as he could, his eyes fixed on the brightness of the moonlight that reflected off the glass doors.

Ten more steps.

The beast dropped down in front of him, its eyes and teeth glistening. Bermuda tried to slow down, but his momentum carried him forward and the sharp claws slashed his chest. The beast swung its thick, tree-trunk-esque arm, its claws striking Bermuda straight in the chest.

The impact was unlike anything Bermuda had experienced, the strength of the Otherside colliding with him at full power. He left the ground at speed, his back clattering into the roof of the ship, his body smashing through the wooden planks. He shot another ten feet into the cool, summer air before landing with a sickening thud on the deck.

Another frantic call was put through on the police radio.

Another hole had been blown through the ship.

Bermuda cracked the side of his head on the hard wood, the impact shaking his skull like a maraca. He could already feel the blood trickling down the side of his face as the darkness of the night began to mould itself to his vision.

He knew he had to run.

The world around him spun and his last vision was of the arm of the monster reaching through the hole, its jaws snapping with anticipation as it clambered through.

It would finish what it had started.

Bermuda wanted to get up. Fight or run.

The blood trickled down and joined the small puddle that was pooling from the three jagged gashes across his chest.

He lost consciousness.

■ ■ I

Through a sea of broken wooden splinters, Argyle placed both hands flat on the concrete and slowly pushed himself to his knees. He had hit the concrete a few feet back, his face scraping against the unforgiving stone as he skidded. His skin was screaming in agony, the rawness telling him he had lost the top layer of his cheek.

It would heal.

As the two police officers stood back, looking warily around the hole in the ship, he heard a crescendo of sirens ripping through the night. Backup was on the way but not for him.

He was the backup.

He pushed himself to his feet with a grunt of annoyance, dusting himself down as he turned back to the face the ship. Bermuda was still trapped within its confines, being hunted by something worse than death itself. He took a few steps towards the ship as a white van hurtled around the corner, its blue lights casting a glow across the entire battlefield. At that moment, another loud crash exploded from the ship, as the body of Bermuda soared into the sky followed by a downpour of wooden rain drops.

He didn't have much time.

Twelve heavily armed men leapt from the back of the van, their faces hidden by black visors, their arms carrying heavily loaded rifles.

He heard the roar from the deck above, the cracking of more wood as the beast was breaking through, ready to finish his partner. The man he had sworn to protect.

As the police went over their tactics quickly, Argyle broke into a sprint, barging past a few of the officers who yelled in bemusement. His armoured boots hammered the pavement as he rounded the front of the ship, looking up towards the decking. Raising his right arm, he aimed his 'Retriever' at the large, wooden mast above. He released the spike, the chain cutting through the air before impaling the wood with a large crack. Picking up speed, he took a few more steps before he began the retrieval. The chain began to retract, lifting him into the air and zipping up into the night sky. He shot upwards, beyond the deck where he saw the beast finally emerge from the hole, violently thrashing into the crisp, night air.

Bermuda wasn't moving.

As Argyle continued his climb above them both, he pulled the hook from the wooden pillar. It ripped through, the chain retracting rapidly to the gauntlet around his arm. With twenty feet of air between himself and the boat, Argyle hurtled back towards the deck.

The beast leant forward, its jaws opening as it readied itself to rip the motionless Bermuda apart.

Argyle reached a powerful arm over his shoulder, his hand gripping the handle of his sword. As he plummeted towards them, he swung it out from its clasp, spinning the blade around. The moonlight bounced off the pristine metal with a mesmerising beauty.

Swinging it into position, he steered the blade straight into the back of the beast's neck.

The sword burst through, before exploding out of the other side of the creature's throat before impaling itself in the wood. Argyle dropped down next to it, landing on a bent knee to steady his massive frame.

The life left the Other instantly, its huge body slumping forward. The weight of its head caused it to slowly slide down the sharp, blood stained blade until it hit the deck. Argyle slowly returned to his feet, sliding the sword from the lifeless body before spinning the blade up and resting it up against the back of his armour. There would be no banishment, not for this Other. The BTCO would be here soon, they would remove the body. Word would spread of how he had slayed another of his kind.

It didn't matter. Bermuda had almost been killed.

He turned towards his motionless partner, concerned for the blood that was pooling around him. Suddenly, the doors to the roof of the ship burst open, a flurry of flashlights and footsteps breaking through. The Armed Response Unit slowly circled Bermuda, their guns focused on him, itchy fingers ready to squeeze triggers.

'I will see you at headquarters,' Argyle muttered, before trotting to the edge of the ship and leaping off into the darkness of the light.

Loud voices and shouted commands rang through Bermuda's ears as he slowly returned, his eyes blurry and his head feeling like an overstuffed balloon. He could feel the stickiness of blood against his forehead, his hair trapped in it. He slowly murmured, instantly drawing the aim and attention of all the armed officers around him.

'Don't move!'

'He's awake!'

'Hold your fire!'

His vision solidified, his return to consciousness welcomed by the muzzles of a dozen guns. Beyond them, masked men faced him, their bulletproof bodies surrounding him completely. He recalled the mighty beast, being chased....

'Fuck!' Bermuda murmured, before resting back on the deck. Moments later, he was roughly lifted to his feet, his t-shirt ripped and blood-stained from wounds the officers would never understand. Beyond them, the motionless body of his attacker was slumped, its wounds fresh and fatal. He knew Argyle had saved him.

Again.

With the weapons trained on him and with slow, measured steps, he was taken back through the Cutty Sark, the formerly dark ship now glowing from the torches around him. He woozily reached for a cigarette, only for the officer behind him to roughly tighten his grip of his arm.

They pushed him through the glass doors, the coolness of the air registering with him, allowing him to take a few deep breathes to return to something resembling normality.

He had been brutally attacked by one of the most terrifying Others he had faced. It wasn't luck that the creature was there. He knew that much.

He was now being arrested for apparently blowing two large holes in a London landmark.

Argyle? Before panic set in, he knew his partner would be safe. An officer said something about his rights which he barely heard, the throbbing pain in his head had returned. The feeling of someone hosting a rave inside his skull drowned out the world. The door to the police car opened and he was roughly shoved into the backseat. As inconvenient as it was, he was glad to be safe. Soon he would be taken to a police station and away from this place. He had found the mark. Twelve sides. The two disappearances were linked.

As the night sky around the ship interchanged with darkness and bright, blue lights, Bermuda planned his next move. He needed to go to the BTCO HQ. There, he could use the archives to find the symbol and solve this case. Two officers, both armed, enter the front of the car and the engine kicked into gear. Almost smiling to himself, Bermuda laid his head back to rest, taking one final look at the ship.

A man with a top hat stared back.

Bermuda shot up, his face pressed against the window as the figure stood on the edge of the boat, looking down at him. His black eyes, like two pieces of coal embedded in a grey stone, burnt through him. The wind whipped his wild, white hair in sporadic directions, all kept in place under his tatty black hat.

The stare was relentless.

As the car pulled away, Bermuda tried to turn in his seat, his handcuffs and seat belt restraining him. He eventually struggled through, and peered out the back window.

The man was gone.

'Hey!' A rough voice yelled from the front of the car. 'Sit still.'

Bermuda slowly turned back, his mind, still bursting with pain, trying its hardest to make sense of it all. Those black eyes. They bore through him with sheer disgust. It took him a few moments to realise that the hairs on the back of his neck were standing to attention.

A voice broke his thought pattern.

'I don't know what the hell you were doing tonight. But man, I can't wait until the Sarge gets a few minutes with you.'

The officers in the front sniggered to each other and Bermuda just rolled his eyes. Suddenly, the stress and pain of the evening washed over him like a tidal wave. He rested his head back and closed his eyes.

'Just give me my phone call.'

As soon as they had arrived at Greenwich Police Station, a nurse lead Bermuda into a guarded room. She strapped a bandage across his chest; the gashes crudely interrupting the tattoos that crawled across his skin. She threaded eight stitches to close the cut on his head, assuring him the pain would subside.

He needed a drink.

Instead, with an ice pack firmly pressed against his battered cranium, he was lead into an interrogation room, where a Detective Bright was waiting for him. Sarcastically asking how his head was, Bermuda would have retorted if it didn't feel like someone was chipping away at his skull with a chisel.

As the Detective began, Bermuda asked him if he could have his phone call, knowing full well he would be out soon enough. Under the impression he was merely humouring his suspect, the Detective handed him his phone.

He called a number that not even a blow to the head would cause him to forget.

It rang four times.

'Hello. Please state the destination of your flight?'

'I tried, but the damn light is still green.'

Bermuda forced a smile as he hung up the phone, sliding it back across to the sceptical Detective. Bermuda pressed the ice against his beating brain, slowly counting down in his head.

Three...

Two...

One...

Knock! Knock!

The door opened, a young officer beckoning the detective out. Flashing Bermuda a suspicious gaze, he pushed his chair back and exited the room, the door slamming firmly, sending an extra jolt of pain rattling through Bermuda's skull. He winced, pressing the cold ice against his head. He knew he would be free within a few minutes, the BTCO held considerable influence that baffled even him.

As he sat quietly, he slowly turned his head to the left, catching his reflection in the two-way mirror. His face was starting to bruise, a faint purple spreading around the stitches. They had provided him with a new t-shirt, but a little blood was seeping through his bandages that strapped his chest.

Goddamn, he needed a drink. He sat back, exhaling and closed his eyes. All he saw was the two black eyes staring at him. The pure hatred in them. Who was the man in the black top hat?

Suddenly, the door swung open and Detective Bright marched in. The frown on his face brought a smile to Bermuda's. Without making eye contact, the Detective began to mutter.

'You are free to go.'

Bermuda nodded, slowly lifting himself from the uncomfortable chair. His body ached and he slowly walked towards the door, the ice pack held firmly in place. As he was about to cross the threshold, Detective Bright reached out with a powerful arm, his fingers wrapping around Bermuda's bicep. He leant in close.

'Just for the record. I don't like you.' His words were full of menace.

'Don't worry about it,' Bermuda said with a smile. 'Not many people do.'

The Detective roughly let go and Bermuda entered the corridor, feeling the eyes of the entire Metropolitan Police follow him as he made his way to the front door.

Yet the only eyes he could see were those black eyes.

They had almost been daring him to come looking.

Those black eyes.

■ ▮ ▮

It was almost two thirty a.m. when the cab pulled up outside London Bridge Station. The moon was still illuminating the sky with its magnificent glory, casting an eerie glow over the capital. Cutting through the sky was The Shard, its windows twinkling with the reflection moonlight.

Bermuda paid the cab driver, handing him the notes in his wallet and leaving before the discussion of change arose. As he exited the car, the cool, midnight breeze of London swirled around him.

'I'm glad you are ok.'

Argyle stood before him, his arms folded across his broad chest. His grey eyes reached out for Bermuda with relief.

'Let's face it. I've been in worse states at two in the morning.' Bermuda smiled then immediately scowled as his head thumped the joy from him. 'I guess their pissed?'

'They are not impressed.'

'Excellent. As if I didn't already have a bad enough headache.'

Bermuda lit a cigarette, the smoke cascading into the air, reaching towards the mighty structure before them.

'I informed them of your injuries and they have requested you rest before debriefing.'

'How generous.' Bermuda slowly began to walk towards the entrance of the shard, his slow steps minimizing the agony that pulsating from his chest. Argyle calmly walked beside him, scouting the area to ensure his safety. They noticed an Other sitting on a bench. With one magnificent solitary red eye browsing the neighbourhood, it quietly turned away as it noticed them. It sat idly as they shuffled by, Argyle reaching a hand to Bermuda to steady him as he finished his cigarette.

'I'm fine, Big Man.' He smiled at his partner who nodded. The large glass doors to The Shard were closed, guarded by a burly security guard who was used to some of the regulars talking to themselves. As Bermuda fished in his pocket for his badge, he glanced up to his partner.

'I know I blacked out back there, but I have a pretty strong feeling that I'm only alive because of you.'

'It is my duty to protect you,' Argyle replied uncomfortably, the scarring on his face beginning to heal. Bermuda smiled and flicked his cigarette.

'Even so, thank you for saving my life.'

Argyle nodded and Bermuda turned and presented his badge to the guard, who eyed him warily.

'Rough night?' The man asked, his eyes scanning the badge.

'I've had rougher.'

With a smile, the guard pulled open the large glass doors and Bermuda entered, Argyle following him with powerful strides.

The ground floor of The Shard served as the concierge for the many businesses that were homed within. Large and profitable trading companies had clambered over each other to get their name on the list when the building was completed in mid-2012. The building, a masterpiece of eighty-nine glass floors became the second tallest building in the UK and shot to the top of the list for many tourists. With the grand observation deck raking in the money, the building became a hub of activity, shooting up towards the sky with a glittering beauty and hefty profit margin.

With a separate entrance for the public, lined with history and tourist- friendly photos, the only foot traffic Bermuda met in the reception area were those who worked in the building.

And at two thirty in the morning, that consisted of nobody.

His footsteps echoed loudly through the hallowed foyer, the pristine hall containing an eerie silence. His head throbbed as if it had its very own heartbeat and the slashes cutting through his chest were begin to overwhelm him. As they approached the lift, Bermuda stumbled. Argyle shot out a steadying arm, averting an unwanted collision with the marble.

'Thanks.'

Argyle nodded, his face a stern mask.

The elevator door opened and the two of them entered, the large metal container awash with the glow of the halogen light above.

Bermuda approached the control panel, the circular buttons aligned symmetrically in rows of five. Each one would send the lift racing towards its destination at over thirteen miles per hour. Below the buttons was a small, dark glass panel which Bermuda pressed his ID badge against. Waiting a few moments, a little light flashed green and the doors to the lift slowly shut and it began to descend.

As the metal box plummeted slowly towards the earth's core, Bermuda caught a glimpse of himself in the large, wall-covering mirror. His scruffy hair flopped over his tired, bruised face. The stitches ran across his eyebrow, framing his dark, sleep hungry eyes. His police issue t-shirt now bore large, red patches.

Compared to the regimented and regal Argyle who stood purposefully next to him, he looked like he'd been dragged through a hedge backwards. More than once.

In a few moments, he would be there and they would let him sleep in one of the agent's chambers. His eyelids suddenly gave into gravity and closed.

He saw those piercing black eyes again.

With a shudder, he awoke, the burning pain from his skull sending him stumbling forward. He rested his hand on the metal doors as he hunched over, trying his best to stay conscious.

'Are you alright?' Argyle's concerned voice ricocheted around the container, vibrating wildly through the pain that had consumed Bermuda's skull.

Just stay conscious, he told himself.

The bell dinged as they reached their destination below The Shard. The doors slowly opened.

And an unconscious Bermuda slumped into the corridor.

10

'HELP ME!'

Bermuda shot up in a panic, his face damp and laced with sweat. The dream had been the same.

The same voice.

The same cry for help.

The same feeling of failure.

He took a few moments, his heart beating like a pneumatic drill in his rib cage. His eyes, blurry with tears, blinked rapidly as he scanned the room. The walls were too white, the lights above beating down on him with an overbearing brightness. The buzz of them was too strong. The walls began to spin.

Here we go, he told himself.

Hunching over the side of the single bed, he puked onto the floor. The burning sensation added to the tears as he wretched, a repulsive concoction of bile, alcohol and ready meals. The diet of a singleton.

'You missed the bin.'

Bermuda took slow, deep breaths as he sat back, wiping the

edges of his mouth with the thin, white duvet. He slowly opened his eyes, letting them return to normal. On the opposite side of the room, sat comfortably on a fold out, plastic chair, was Vincent.

The most senior Neither working for the BTCO and the personal Neither of the BTCO Director, Lord Felix Ottoway III.

With a calm smile, Vincent was the polar opposite to Argyle. His skin was a deathly pale, which he attributed to having been alive for over six hundred years. His hair, although now wafer thin, was a jet black colour, matching the irises of his eyes. His small frame was wrapped in its usual black robe; his delicate hands clasped together in his lap.

'Sorry about that. My aim is a little off,' Bermuda said dryly, his throat gasping for water. Instinctively, Vincent rose from his chair, his movement so light that Bermuda often wondered if he floated through the air. He handed him a cup of water, which Bermuda gratefully gulped down. Vincent glided to the side table, picking up a clipboard and glancing over the paper.

'You still have the same dreams?' He asked, not looking up from the sheet.

'Dream,' Bermuda corrected. 'And yes.'

'Hmmm.' Vincent mused over the sheets before returning the clipboard. 'You humans like to place a lot on the meaning of such events. Perhaps a psychological assessment could sniff out the cause?'

'Don't know if you recall but the last time I had a shrink speak to me, they locked me in a padded room.' Bermuda sat up, shaking away the cobwebs and the lurching memories of his past.

'Quite. Your wounds will heal.'

Bermuda grunted, turning slowly and draping his legs over the white sheets of the bed. A patch of blood smeared them, creating a ghastly Rorschach test on the mattress. He shook as he tried to lift himself.

'Perhaps you should rest some more?' Vincent said concerned, walking back to his chair.

'I need a cigarette.' Bermuda's legs trembled with each step, his sense of direction slowly returning as he stumbled towards his belongings.

'This is a no smoking facility'.

Click.

Smoke filled the air.

Vincent sighed.

'I take it Felix is pissed?' Bermuda asked, his words pushing a thin, dark cloud into the room.

'Lord Ottoway is less than impressed, if that's what you mean?'

Bermuda shrugged.

'What do you recall?'

'I remember...the ship. I remember something big.' Bermuda frowned, his skull ready to rip through his skin at any moment. 'I remember almost shitting myself.'

'Do you recall blasting two large holes in a London landmark?'

'Not really. I was too busy being beaten unconscious.' Bermuda stubbed the cigarette out on the side table, drawing a tut from his guest.

'You were attacked by a Gorgoma. An ancient, feral breed of behemoth. How it got into the Cutty Sark, we do not know. They are prohibited from this world for the safety of your people.'

'Well, then how the hell did it get where I was sent?' Bermuda's voice rising a little in anger. 'And how the fuck did it get its hands or whatever it has, on a latch stone?'

'Our investigation is ongoing on that matter.'

Investigation.

The symbol.

The man with the top hat.

Those piercing black eyes.

'He brought it!' Bermuda exclaimed loudly, bounding back towards the desk that housed his belongings. He instantly began flicking through his notebook. Vincent approached slowly.

'Who?'

'The man.' Bermuda flicked through the pages eagerly, the grogginess diminishing with every page turn.

'What man?'

'There was a man. Well, an Other. His eyes. The way he stared...'

Bermuda trailed off much to Vincent's frustration. For a few moments, the only noise was the swish of paper and the low hum of the halogen bulb. Bermuda finally turned to the Neither, his eyes twinkling with excitement.

'Have you ever seen this symbol before?'

Vincent reached out his long, spindly fingers as Bermuda handed him the notebook. Sketched on the paper was a crude drawing, a twelve-sided shape that was obviously scribbled in a hurry. Having been involved in the peace talks between Earth and The Otherside, Vincent was a fount of knowledge. Educated in the complete history of the truce, he was a walking archive. Bermuda had lost count of how many times Vincent had pointed him in the right direction.

'Hmmm.' Vincent mused, his fingers rubbing his sharp, bony chin. 'Where did you find this?'

'I found that symbol on the wall where that Lambert girl went missing. I found the same symbol in the boat, right before Captain Fingers found me.'

Studying the paper, Vincent flashed a concerned glance towards Bermuda. 'Follow me.'

They exited the room, making their way into the brightly lit corridor. A long, endless tunnel that was lined with large, concrete doors. A few of them to the left housed more agent chambers. Down the far side were the Neither quarters, a place for Argyle and the other 'defected' to find solace amongst the two worlds that had turned their backs on them. Beyond those rooms was the combat arena, where Agents and new recruits were trained. Vincent took a sharp right, heading down an identical corridor, the doors bolted tightly shut, locking in the recently banished who would soon be deported back to the Otherside for further imprisonment. The truce between the two worlds hinged on the law that captured Others were sent back to their own world for trial - and usually a fatal punishment. Bermuda knew that Argyle despised the banishment, knowing that he was effectively sentencing those they had apprehended to death.

As the corridor broke into a T-Junction, Vincent stopped at a set of grand doors, the metal slabs decorated in an intricate, carved pattern. Reaching out his delicate fingers, he spoke quietly.

'Wait here.'

The door opened slowly, the brightness of the room violently trying to escape through the crack in the door as he used all his strength to open it.

The Archive.

The effective heartbeat of the BTCO, access to the room was strictly prohibited without Level One clearance, an honour bestowed upon only a few. Bermuda was not on the list. Before entering the room, Vincent slowly turned his head, his movements slow and jerky, like someone had removed a few frames from his full turn.

'This may take a while. Ottoway wishes to speak to you.'

'Where is he?' Bermuda asked, shuffling uncomfortably.

'Where do you think?'

Vincent offered a smile, and Bermuda nodded, watching as he ghosted through the opening and the doors closed with a loud thud. He exhaled, rattling the box of mints in his pocket before popping a few into his mouth. Just as he was about the leave, a thick French accent broke the silence.

'Monsieur Jones.'

Bermuda cursed under his breath and turned to face Hugo LePone. With his slick, black hair combed back over a head that housed sharp cheek bones and a perfect jaw, Bermuda wanted to punch him for being so strikingly handsome.

That, and for his obnoxious attitude.

'Hey,' Bermuda half-heartedly offered.

'What brings you here?' Hugo placed his hands on his hips, his biceps bulging through his black, turtle neck jumper. 'Oh wait, could it be that you decided to reckless once again?'

'Reckless? Awesome? Depends on how you look at it.'

'What good can it do for agents who are being discreet, when people like you do not give a shit?'

Bermuda clenched his fists, turning on his heels and coming nose to nose with the clean-shaven smirk of his fellow agent. He could smell the expensive coffee lingering on Hugo's breath.

'It's called being a damn good agent. Maybe if you got out there and actually did something once in a while...'

'The two Others we have in the cells are thanks to me and Marco,' Hugo retorted. Marco, his Neither, stood a few feet behind. Small and thin and his movements almost reptilian, he was fundamentally different to Argyle. His skin a darker brown than Argyle's, but with eyes just as grey, he was incredibly agile and an effective interceptor when needed. Hugo continued. 'However, we didn't leave large, hole shaped traces when we were done.'

Bermuda held back from responding. Hugo had a history of jealousy that had led to confrontations before. Although he had 'The Knack', the same as all the other agents, he envied the strength of Bermuda's curse. The ability to walk in and interact with both worlds. The curse that ruined Bermuda's life.

Bermuda shook his head in disbelief.

'I'll tell you what Hugo; I'm going to go speak with Ottoway now. Would you like me to ask him if he can give you a gold star?'

Hugo reached out with a muscular arm and forcefully shoved Bermuda in the shoulder, sending him back a few steps. Gritting his teeth and willing himself not to react, Bermuda regained his balance. He felt the stinging pain from his chest wounds rising up through his body, manifesting in an explosive rage.

'I wouldn't do that.'

'Why's that?' Hugo asked, confident in his training.

Before Bermuda could react, the large bolt of the Archive door unlocked, echoing down the long corridors. It slowly opened and Vincent leant through the gap, a frown across a face that had seen centuries pass.

'Jones, please enter. And whatever petty squabbles you two have, bury them.'

Hugo sneered, his eyes flicking from Bermuda to the senior Neither. With a grunt, he stormed passed Bermuda, purposely bumping his shoulder and trying to knock him off balance. Bermuda stood firm, absorbing the impact without reacting. Marco slithered by, following his partner like a slippery shadow.

'Come with me.'

Slightly seething, Bermuda stepped over the threshold, into one of the most secluded rooms in the entire building. The vast chamber, lined with hundreds of book shelves, was a chronological history of the entire Otherside. Ever since the existence of another world was discovered, the BTCO had documented everything. Every case, every incident, every conversation. The entire passage of unity between the two worlds lined the walls, all wrapped in large, leather covers. Although he had entered the Archive once before, the sheer volume of it was breathtaking.

'This way.' Vincent glided gracefully across the marble floor - his footsteps, if he took them, made no sound as they travelled. They passed rows of benches, used for the more senior analysts as desks, all of them empty. Beyond them, a small maze of filing cabinets, each one containing individual case files. Bermuda often wondered if his disciplinary files were somewhere inside and how much space they would inevitably take up.

He fumbled for his box of mints, the rattle echoing in the silence, drawing a scowl from Vincent. They stepped beyond the cabinets and Bermuda slowed down, his gaze drawn to the extraordinary sight before him.

In four separate reclining chairs, lay the Oracles. Completely nude and pale blue, they were the four most precious Neithers belonging to the BTCO. Each one was attached to a series of wires, linking them to the large computer screens that surrounded them. They never spoke, nor did they hardly move.

They informed.

Their ability to be linked to the Otherside, not by their birth but by the Others themselves, allowed them to pinpoint events within our world that humans could not comprehend. They were the ones to notice the peculiar nature of Jessica Lambert's disappearance, and every case could be traced back to them. When a pattern or an occurrence is relayed into the system, it is passed on to a Neither, who will then relay it to the agent. Whenever Argyle showed up with a new case, Bermuda knew it would have found its way from here, the very heartbeat of the BTCO.

'Over here.'

Vincent broke Bermuda's stare, having walked beyond the sight he saw every day to a large book, laid open on a wooden alter. Each sheet was A3, the paper thick as if written on pig skin. The writing that criss-crossed the page was indecipherable to the human eye and Bermuda nodded at the page, before looking blankly at Vincent.

'Shall I explain?' His voice was calm.

'Please do.'

Vincent smiled warmly before turning to face the pages before him.

'When peace was sort between our two worlds, your elders agreed to designated doorways between the two realms. These would be manned on both sides of the divide, by humans here on earth and by Others on the Otherside. All who cross the threshold would need certification. Permission, if you will.

'To ensure that the peace would last, all artefacts pertaining to cross-world travel were deemed illegal and stored away by the Elders; locked away in a vault somewhere within the higher reaches of The Otherside.'

'So basically, no border hopping?' Bermuda suggested, popping a mint into his mouth.

'To put it crudely, yes. As you well know, the travel is one way. From my world to yours. Beyond yourself, no human has survived a trip through the gateway. We here at the BTCO act as a deterrent to those who do not abide by the truce. To those who see this world as merely an extension of their own.'

'So what you're saying is...' Bermuda let his question hang, raising his eyebrows at the ghostly entity before him.

'The symbol you have found is that of an Arko Feld.' Bermuda's vacant expression urged Vincent to continue. 'A Gate Maker.'

'A Gate Maker?' Bermuda pulled out his notepad and scribbled onto a free page.

'Yes. Whoever is creating these doorways is doing so of his own volition.'

'I know who it is,' Bermuda said, the pencil flicking around the page with wild scratches.

'You do?' Vincent responded, closing the book with a loud thud that echoed through the vicinity. Bermuda etched a few more lines before turning his crude sketch to his audience.

'This guy.'

The rushed lines formed a jagged face, one with no discernible features apart from the large, black eyes that sat in the middle. Sitting on the uneven head, Bermuda had sketched a top hat. Vincent stared at it intently, Bermuda wondering if he would be able to hear the cogs in his brain turning.

'Who is this?' Vincent asked.

'He was there. At the Cutty Sark. He was watching.'

Vincent smirked dismissively.

'They always watch you, Bermuda. Remember, you are the one that genetically broke the rules.'

'I'm telling you, this guy here, he knows what is going on.'

Vincent took a deep breath, calmly looking over the page one last time. Bermuda shuffled on the spot, eager to get going. He respected Vincent for his catalogue of knowledge and constant flow of answers, but something wasn't sitting right. It was as if something was being held back.

Eventually, Vincent turned, a warm smile across his ancient face. He handed Bermuda the notebook, his long, bony fingers retracting quickly.

'Well you better find him then.'

Bermuda nodded, turning towards the door as Vincent gazed

at the Oracles, their company screens flashing with numerous patterns and images.

'I will consult the Oracles; see if they can provide any more information. In the meantime, Ottoway has asked that you see him before you leave.'

Bermuda stopped in his tracks; a summoning from the head of the organisation wasn't a usual occurrence, nor one to take lightly.

'Where is he?' Bermuda asked, his hands fidgeting in his pockets.

Vincent smiled warmly.

'Where he usually is.'

Bermuda took a deep breath and walked back across the archive as Vincent glided towards the prone Others, hoping for answers.

11

The sun had burst through the clouds, shrouding the city of London in a wondrous glow. The streets were awash with people, all zig-zagging impatiently around each other, scuttling to a destination of relevant importance. The roads were gridlocked. Buses, black cabs and cars, all honking their horns and jostling for a few extra inches as the traffic lights did their best to filter them. The buildings shot up to the sky like a row of jagged teeth, all of them filled with employees, unrealistic targets and minimal profit margins. The hustle and bustle of everyday life. The human condition, evolved to the modern society in which we live.

The rat race of life.

Lord Felix Ottoway III looked over it all and smiled. At eighty-one years old, he had watched the world rebuild itself into the technological labyrinth it was today and he couldn't have felt prouder. To be part of a species that could not only create such wonders but be driven to further develop. A species that could construct the capability to walk on the moon. One thing that he knew, having been part of the BTCO for over sixty years, and the UK Director for over thirty, was one thing; humans are survivors.

Ironically, it was at that moment that the cancer tightened its grip on his lungs, causing him to splutter violently into his handkerchief. Pulling the cloth away, he saw the blood and sighed.

It wouldn't be too long now.

He tucked the handkerchief into the pocket of his navy blazer and straightened up. Dressed in an immaculate three-piece suit, he straightened the cuffs of his shirt protruding from his sleeves. His waistcoat, neatly buttoned, held in the considerable gut that retirement from being a field agent was always going to bring.

He missed it.

He and Vincent had been partnered for over sixty years, since he first became an agent. His 'Knack' was never the strongest, but his gift for puzzle solving had been lifesaving on numerous occasions. He afforded himself a smirk when realising it was now used on the daily Sudoku at the back of his newspaper.

The city of London.

Knowing the work he had undertaken to preserve the peace between the two worlds (unbeknownst to the inhabitants of the fine city) made him swell with pride. And standing on the sixty ninth floor of The Shard, before the viewing gallery was open to the public, he felt like he was gazing protectively over all of them.

'Sir?'

Ottoway turned slowly, offering a warm, world-weary smile as Bermuda slowly walked through the high staircase, his footsteps echoing slightly on the wooden floor.

'Ah, Jones. I'm glad you stopped by. Come, join me.'

Bermuda slowly meandered next to his superior, following his gaze out of the large, ceiling high pane of glass before them. Below them the SS Belfast lay dormant on the Thames, the glass creation known as City Hall nearby on the bank of the river.

'Look at the city, Jones. Everyone going about their lives with the mental clarity that they are safe. That their world is as black and white as they believe it to be. It's a truly mesmerising view, don't you agree.'

'It's high,' Bermuda mused, cautiously looking downwards and battling vertigo.

'Indeed. From here, we can see it all. The heart of this city beating.'

Bermuda nodded, allowing his boss this speech. The wind whipped through the gaps in the corner of the viewing platform, ricocheting off the panels.

'You caused quite a commotion last night.' Ottoway's voice was rich with authority.

'In my defence sir, I was under attack.'

'Quite. You will be happy to know that our extraction officers removed the body during the aftermath. Although slain by Argyle, it has been sent back to The Otherside for burial.'

'Let me know if they cremate it so I can piss on its ashes.' Bermuda gently placed a hand over his chest, the pain emanating from his stitches.

'Now now. Let us show respect for the dead, this side and the other.' Ottoway rested a reassuring arm on Bermuda's back. 'Our gift is designed to bring peace and order between our two worlds. Not to scorn each other nor to bring bloodshed.'

'Hey, I am all for better worlds. But that thing attacked me. What's more, I don't think it was a wrong place, wrong time kind of thing.'

'No?' Ottoway spoke as he walked, his slow steps leading him towards the west side of the gallery. Beyond the glass, the sun exploded against the Houses of Parliament, the shadow of Big Ben drenching the streets below it.

'There is no way something that big would live in a place that small. I think it was invited.'

'Invited? By who? And for what purpose?'

'By the guy with the top hat. He was there, watching as they put me in the back of the car. His eyes, they were so black.'

Suddenly, Ottoway looked slightly uncomfortable. He slid a hand through hair that was so grey and fluffy; it was as if he had his own personal rain cloud.

'Are you sure?'

'Yeah. Why? Who is he?

Ottoway shook his head, dismissing the idea.

'What is it, sir?'

'For an Other that size to pass through, we would have registered it. It was too feral to be allowed in our world.'

'I found this too.'

Bermuda handed Ottoway his sketch of the Gate Maker. Ottoway squinted, his beady eyes magnified by his spectacles.

'A Gate Maker? It can't be.'

'It was at the scene of Jessica Lambert's disappearance too. And I believe this guy has it.'

Bermuda flicked the page to the sketch of the man with the top hat. Ottoway mumbled under his breath, Bermuda was sure he murmured 'It can't be'. Ottoway snapped the pad shut.

'Your number one priority is to find this Gate Maker. We cannot have unsanctioned travel between the two worlds.'

'I'm gonna find this guy and I'm gonna kick his arse.'

'No!' Ottoway's voice rose, bouncing off the glass walls surrounding them. 'Leave the personal attack aside and concentrate on the case. That Gate Maker needs to be destroyed.'

Bermuda looked agitated but nodded. Throughout his life, be it school or on the rare occasion he held down a job, he hated authority. Teachers and managers had encountered his attitude yet he had nothing but respect for Ottoway.

'Say I find this Gate Maker. How do I destroy it?'

'You will need a lock. One that can fuse with this shape. Combine them both and when put through the doorway it creates, it will close it for good and render it useless.'

'I don't see why we don't just close the fucking door altogether. Then maybe I could have my life back.'

Ottoway shot Bermuda a scornful glance.

'The door stays open for the continued development of our very existence. Do you even understand the leaps we have made thanks to The Otherside? Do you truly believe that our species would have evolved so far without their help? Who do you think cured The Plague all those years ago?

The advances in science we have procured thanks to our truce with their world is why we fight tooth and nail to maintain the peace. What you call a curse is seen as a gift by all. Especially a gift as strong as yours.'

Ottoway nodded in triumph and Bermuda scolded himself for letting his woes embarrass him. All he longed for was a normal life. Where he could hold his daughter without the fear that those waiting in the shadows for him would target her. A lonely existence described as a gift. Crestfallen, he slowly turned and walked back towards the door, the flight of stairs led to the lift that shot through the building at an ear popping speed.

'Jones,' Ottoway called after him. 'You will find the lock at Other's Town.'

'Oh no. Not Other's Town. I'm about as welcome there as a shit in a swimming pool.'

'Look for an Other named Jared. He should still have a shop there. And in regards to your comment, yes, you will probably be met with hostility. Be careful.'

'Yeah, yeah.' Bermuda waved it off, again turning to leave.

'I want you to visit Denham before you go. He will provide you with some protection. Stay safe out there and try not to break any more of London.'

Bermuda grunted as he approached the door. A trip to see Denham was usually as painful as the striking sensation in his chest. Ottoway called out one final time before turning back to his view.

'Remember Jones. Two worlds, one peace.'

Bermuda descended the stairs, with the BTCO slogan echoing behind him. He waited for the lift, behind him the line of unisex toilets that allowed someone to relieve themselves to an incredible view. The doors pinged open and Bermuda entered, hurtling his way through the building with a scowl that would scare Satan himself.

■ ▌ ▏

Ottoway watched the world below him, the silence of his surroundings only penetrated by the doors of the lift closing as Bermuda left. He sighed, knowing how troubled his agent was.

From the shadows, soft footsteps approached him.

'You did well to protect him,' Ottoway said, not turning. Argyle stopped next to his boss, his grey eyes scouring the world below. The world he had sworn the protect but still was yet to fully understand. His mighty sword lay strapped to his back. His mighty arms crossed across his armour covered chest.

'It is my duty to protect him.'

'That is why you were selected, Argyle. You and I both know how important he is.' Argyle nodded forlornly. Ottoway continued. 'The truce is creaking Argyle. I know you had no other option, but the more dead bodies we send back through the doorway, the more that come through with a bloodlust.'

'I only draw my blade when it is the last resort.'

'I know, dear friend. I know.' Ottoway reassuringly patted Argyles shoulder. 'I fear, however, that those moments are only to become more regular.'

Ottoway shook his head and slowly stepped across the rooftop, taking in the views that South London now offered him. The Battersea Power Station loomed over the surrounding streets.

'Sir, you are afraid?' Argyle asked, joining him.

'Bermuda spoke of a man, Argyle. A man with jet black eyes.'

He turned to face the loyal Neither, whose expression revealed his confusion.

'Never mind. Just keep Jones safe. I have concerns that they are stepping up their efforts.'

'They fear him. They hate him more than they hate me.'

Argyle stood firmly, his jaw straight and powerful, covered in a thin, black beard. His dark skin shimmered in the sunshine.

'You will always be a soldier, Argyle. No matter if you are on this side or theirs. You are a soldier who has never failed to follow his orders.'

Argyle shuffled slightly, his eyes glowing with pride.

'I am ordering you to keep him alive.'

Argyle nodded. Ottoway's smile was fake, his own concerns betraying him. They both knew what would be expected of Argyle should the situation ever arise.

'By any means necessary.'

Bermuda made his way back through the corridors that twisted underneath The Shard like tree roots. A few analysts walked past, nodding at Bermuda who returned in kind. He strode past the cells where Hugo had stashed two illegals, his brow furrowing at the thought of his antagonistic peer. Striding with purpose, he made his way to the training facility and slammed a fist against the steel door.

'It's open!' A gruff voice echoed from the other side of the metal.

Bermuda pushed forward, the heavy slab creaking on its hinges. The training facility was a series of long rooms, all designed to take a new recruit from shit scared to field ready in minimal time. His mind leapt back to his first ventures in this facility, the sheer terror of the scenario rooms, the expectant Neithers monitoring with their computers and clipboards.

Then there was Denham.

The owner of the rough voice that greeted his knock, Denham was a semi-retired field Neither who Ottoway had placed in charge of new recruits, due to his unmeasurable ability to be an arsehole who meant well. As tall as Argyle but stockier, with a shiny bald held wrapped in caramel coloured skin. An eye patch lay jagged across his ageing face; his one good eye shimmered a wonderful shade of grey.

'Mr. Jones. Come and take a look at this.'

Bermuda nodded, joining Denham who stood opposite a large, tinted pane of glass. On the other side, a portly gentleman with short, ginger hair and beard was slowly meandering through a scenario, cautiously checking corners in what looked like a mock library. Denham, with an arm the width of Bermuda's body, reached out to the control panel, his mouth, framed by a goatee beard, angled upwards with a smile.

'Watch this.'

A pull of the lever and suddenly, demonic hands shot through the book cases, ripping at the young recruit who screamed and fell to the floor, panic jolting through his terrified body. Bermuda shook his head in pity, remembering his experience with what Denham called 'The Angry Librarian'.

Denham was chuckling unsympathetically.

'Gets them every time.' He slapped Bermuda on the shoulder, sending a small, shockwave of pain through his chest.

'You are a cruel bastard; you know that?' Bermuda retorted.

'Yes I do.' He turned from the glass panel and looked at Bermuda. 'Jesus, what happened to your face? That eye looks terrible.'

'You can talk.'

The two men smirked, a mutual respect existing ever since Bermuda's first six months with the BTCO when Denham put him through his paces. Although strict and thorough, Denham was a Neither of principal, appreciative of hard work and a strong spirit. Bermuda begrudgingly had both.

'What can I do for you?'

'Ottoway sent me. Told me you could hook me up with a chest plate.'

Denham turned and marched to one of the large, metal cabinets that adorned the walls of the control centre. As he rifled through its contents, the door to the scenario chamber opened and the dishevelled recruit entered.

'Everyone falls down the first time.' Bermuda smiled, offering a handshake which was duly taken.

'Thanks. I'm Thorpe. Bobby Thorpe.'

'Jones. They call me Bermuda.' He responded, slight embarrassment at the goofiness of his nickname.

'Wait? Thee Bermuda Jones?' Bobby looked ecstatic. 'Man, you are a legend. This is such an honour.'

'Trust me. It really isn't.'

Bermuda retracted his hand, an uncomfortable smile on his face. He hated the legend that seemed to precede him with the other agents, it made people like Hugo jealous and the higher ups like Ottoway interested.

He just wanted to be left alone.

To have a normal life.

Oh, for a normal life....

'This should fit you.' Denham broke Bermuda's depressing trail of thought and tossed a black vest at him. He caught it with both hands, surprised by the lightness of the material. He knew the texture; it was called Argiln, a rare material from the Otherside. Removing his t-shirt slowly, Thorpe and Denham cast their eyes over his tattooed body. Although the scriptures curved with every defined line of his chiselled body, it was the three large scars that dominated his chest that drew their attention.

'Jesus. I thought Argyle was supposed to protect you,' Denham said, a hint of sarcasm hanging to his words.

'He saved my life.'

'Yeah, looks like it.'

Bermuda didn't respond. Denham had a long history of not liking Argyle, a trait that many of the other Neithers, as well as all of the Otherside, seemed to share. Bermuda didn't know why, nor did he want to ask Argyle.

'Whatever. Thanks for the vest,' Bermuda said, tapping it under his shirt.

'Just stay safe. Otherwise we will have to rely on Bobby here and he is only good for shitting in his pants!'

Bermuda flashed a sympathetic look to Bobby Thorpe, who was sheepishly looking at the ground. Denham gave him a playful slap, the muscles on his arms rippling beneath his black t-shirt. The man possessed so much power; Bermuda constantly wondered what he would be like in battle.

He said his goodbyes and quietly left Denham to torture the new recruit and as he approached the lift to take him back to the surface, Vincent appeared causing him to jump.

'Jesus!' Bermuda exclaimed, perplexed by the Neither's silence.

'Apologies. The Oracles have been able to source this information from the police. It isn't much but it's something.'

Vincent handed him a few sheets of paper and a photograph, a lone paperclip holding the sparse evidence together. Bermuda raised his eyebrows unimpressed.

'Thanks, I guess.'

'It's names of people taken recently. They detected a pattern of two days between each one and mystery surrounding their disappearances. Witnesses have claimed they saw nothing except a split second between their existence and their vanishing.'

'Existence? You think they are dead?' Bermuda asked, the swelling on his eye impeding his vision as he scanned the sheets.

'It is likely. It depends on the gate. I suggest you see Jared at...'

'At Other's Town, yeah. Ottoway has already told me.'

'Then best of luck, Jones.' Vincent reached out with his ghostly fingers, patting Bermuda on his arm. 'Find these people.'

The lift pinged open and Bermuda entered, grateful to see the imposing figure of Argyle, arms folded and ready for action. He pressed the button for the ground floor, eager to leave the building and to be back above ground. As the lift ascended, Argyle broke the silence.

'I do not wish to go to Other's Town.'

Bermuda didn't look up from his sheets of evidence.

'Me neither, Big Guy. Me neither.'

12

The sudden burst of sunlight was blinding.

As Bermuda stepped out onto the concrete, he shielded his eyes with a grazed hand. The air was clean; he could feel the stuffiness of the underground offices leaving him, the cool air swirling around him in the breeze.

It was nice to be outside again.

The BTCO Headquarters always got to him. Not a claustrophobic, yet he hated being confined to the space where every move and rule was scrutinized. As he recounted his disdain for the authority, he clasped a cigarette between his lips and quickly lit it.

'Your injuries will heel,' Argyle said, assuredly.

'Yours already have,' Bermuda noticed, smiling at his partner. Argyle's genetic makeup had always stunned Bermuda, his ability to heal; had already begun to graft the skin back to his feet. 'What would it take to kill you?'

'A better swordsman.'

'Unlikely.' Bermuda patted his friend on the arm as he trudged towards London Bridge station. He was eager to get back to

Bushey, to lay in his own bed and go over the case. He needed a coffee. As he scanned the station for the inevitable coffee stand, he switched his phone on. After a few screens of swirling colours, his phone kicked into life. A few messages from Brett, followed by a couple of emails pertaining to bills and memberships he had long since ignored. Then something caught his eye:

You have 1 New Voicemail.

Stubbing his cigarette out on the wall and dropping it into a man-made flower bed, Bermuda lifted the phone to his ear, ignoring the aching pain that shot from his chest and brightness of the sun that hammered his vision. The message brought a smile to his face.

'Errr....hi. Bermuda....Mr.Jones...It's Sophie. Sophie Summers. We met the other day and you gave me your card. I...ummm...I just wanted to know if you had any news about Jess. The police have been round but they have nothing. I guess if they don't...ignore me...I'm just worried.'

Bermuda nodded; a small concern at how much he wanted to see her was instantly batted from his mind.

'Anyway....If you hear anything or have any information, please call me back on this number. Thank you.'

A slight ruffle and the message ended. Argyle noticed the grin.

'Was it a message of happiness?' He asked, drawing a shake of the head from his human friend.

'I have to go.'

'Go? We have this information to look into.' Argyle held up the files that Vincent had provided. Bermuda straightened his t-shirt and parted his hair in the ghostly reflection of the train station window.

'I will meet you back here.'

'Where are you going?'

Bermuda grinned sheepishly.

'I just got a lead.'

The train from London Bridge to Peckham Rye took less than fifteen minutes, and before he knew it, Bermuda was strolling through the multi-cultural streets that surrounded the station. Even before midday, the streets were an explosion of music and languages, all fighting for supremacy as potential customers sauntered through. With less excitement around, he found the streets nearer to Sophie's block of flats quieter, the hipster scene busy with their jobs before their inevitable takeover once the pubs were open.

He was nervous and it angered him.

Bermuda knew he was a handsome man. His chiselled, stubble covered face was topped with thick, light brown hair and piercing green eyes. He trained regularly, usually with Argyle, and maintained a muscular, toned physique that drew even more attention due to the vast amount of ink scrawled across his muscles.

The tattoos were always a talking point, gallons of ink infused with his body, scrawlings of incantations and bizarre symbols, all of which seemed to have a defensive effect against the creatures from the shadows that constantly tried to remove him from his own world. How would he explain them to Sophie?

'One step at a time!' He told himself. It had been a while since he felt the touch of a woman. Even longer since he had cared for one. The last thing he needed now was for a distraction. As he approached the cafe where he had agreed to meet Sophie after he called her back, he wondered if telling her he couldn't start a relationship due to a paranormal thief would go down well.

The bell dinged above the door as he entered, a barrage of grease, over cooked bacon and lukewarm coffee assaulted his sense of smell. The dingy eatery was lively, a large number of construction workers boisterously tucking into their fry ups, high vis jackets slung over chairs and the discussions about last night's football turning the air blue. Inexplicably, a fruit machine stood in the corner, an unwashed, elderly gentleman pushing coppers through for another shot at the measly jackpot.

Behind the counter, a large man with a stained t-shirt and greasy hair hurled orders to the women working by the cookers, his accent thick with an eastern European twang, his gestures anything but friendly.

His eyes landed on Sophie.

Sat in the corner, wearing a faux leather jacket and a white blouse, she looked a picture of controlled beauty. Her striking, brown eyes were gently topped off with eye shadow, her lips a shimmering scarlet. Her delicate hands wrapped themselves around a steaming cup of coffee. She saw Bermuda, their eyes met, and the smile that spread across her perfect face caused his heart to jump. He approached the table and her expression changed from relief to horror.

'Oh my god. What the hell happened to your face?'

Her concern was genuine, leaping from her words as she scanned the stitches above his eye that sat amongst the darkening bruising.

'Oh this.' Bermuda looked across to the proprietor, motioning for a coffee. He turned back to the gorgeous woman before him.

'Sailing accident.'

'Sailing?' She responded, sceptically.

'Well, near enough.' A coffee was placed in front of him and Bermuda hoisted it to his lips, allowing the caffeine full control of his veins. 'So? You called?'

She retreated into herself a little, her shoulders sagging and Bermuda could see the terrified girl he had met when her friend went missing.

'It's been a few days and the police have nothing. They say they are still looking but I haven't seen an officer since. I don't know. I guess I'm...'

'Scared?' Bermuda offered, nodding her his acceptance of her circumstance. She smiled gratefully.

'She is my best friend. She really is the only person I know here in London.' Tears began to form, a few cracks in her voice. 'I'm just so worried that something bad has happened.'

She broke. Tears began to cascade down her chiselled cheek bones, shimmering under the halogen lights above. Bermuda offered a napkin. After a few moments of self-contained sniffling, Bermuda calmly spoke.

'Can I be honest with you, Sophie?' She nodded. 'I can't tell you that nothing has happened to Jess, because I don't know that. But I am onto something. Tell me, did Jess ever see things?'

'What do you mean?' Sophie asked, dabbing at her eyes with the napkin.

'Like, did she ever suffer from what you might have thought were hallucinations?'

'She thought the guy in the flat opposite us was spying on her. He is a bit of a creep though.'

Bermuda smiled politely, trying to hide frustration.

'I see. She never mentioned that she saw...how can I say this...

monsters?'

Sophie stared at him, unimpressed. 'Monsters?'

'Please hear me out.'

'Seriously? You know how upset and worried I am and you ask me if she sees fucking monsters?'

In a small explosion of anger, Sophie pushed her chair back, the wood screeching across the greasy tiles, drawing a few looks from the grizzly builders. Bermuda calmly leant forward.

'I was not trying to offend you, Sophie.'

'Miss Summers!'

Bermuda's heart sunk. She wanted nothing to do with him. The pain in his chest wasn't from the three gashes that ripped across it.

'Miss Summers. I believe your friend was taken and I have a lead on what may have caused it. I just wanted to eliminate something from my enquiry.'

'What? That monsters did it?' She shook her head, her hands planted on her hips. 'This is a waste of time. What do you even do anyway? You are not even police.'

Bermuda looked at the last mouthful of coffee that sloshed the bottom of the mug in his hand.

'You wouldn't believe me if I told you.' He finished it with a swig. 'And you wouldn't stay if you did.'

With an apologetic smile, he dropped a tenner on the table for the two beverages and then rose from his seat. He sent a nod in Sophie's direction, her face a mural of confusion and sorrow. She watched as the peculiar man left the cafe, stopping outside briefly to light a cigarette. She knew nothing about him. Only that he spoke of monsters and theories of a possible horrible demise for her best friend. He seemed eager to help, but almost a little too cautious in how he spoke to her. He was attractive, she could tell he had muscular arms and had seen the edges of extensive tattoos.

The man was a complete mystery.

And right then and there, as she watched him disappear into a cloud of cigarette smoke, she knew she hadn't felt safer than when she was with him.

■ ▮ ▏

When Bermuda returned to Argyle at London Bridge station, he said nothing. The look of defeat told Argyle not to press, that his partner wasn't happy nor in the mood to explain why. With their joint disdain for Other's Town leading to procrastination, Argyle had suggested checking out Regent's Park, where a ten year old Alfie Evans mysteriously went missing eight days ago whilst playing hide and seek with his friend.

Bermuda had merely shrugged his shoulders at the suggestion, pre-occupied with cursing himself for upsetting Sophie.

Argyle reconnected with Bermuda the moment he stepped through the gates of Regent's Park, the tranquillity of the place was over powering. The sun was beaming down, almost dishonestly due to the cold whip that surfed the breeze. Ducks aimlessly paddled along the river that divided the park, a few joggers marched past with impressive stamina.

Bermuda lit a cigarette.

This was it. Another missing person and due to the strangeness and lack of police evidence, the Oracles had concluded it matched significant traits of the other recently stolen. Bermuda sighed, his mind still repeating his exchange with Sophie, the look of pain and frustration at the first baby steps he took of introducing her to his world.

How could he have been so naive? People don't believe in monsters or ghosts. People don't believe the words of a crazy person.

'This way.'

Argyle's booming voice shook Bermuda back to reality, the image of Sophie's sadness melting into the greenness of his surroundings. He followed his partner who walked with authority, careful not to collide with the passers-by. Groups of young work colleagues scattered the park, sharing laughs and gossip over open Tupperware boxes and unbuttoned shirts.

The normal life of a London worker. Bermuda had tried, yet found he could never envy the working life a of a normal person. The nine to five life of logging in and grinding out. People gladly repeat their days in jobs they don't like for organisations they don't care about for money that they spend on houses they don't own. Yet he was considered crazy?

They followed the footpath, the sun slowly blocked out as they turned onto a path that cut through the trees. Lined by large, thick tree trunks and draping, leaf covered vines, Bermuda could feel the presence of the Otherside. He turned, looking back over his shoulder to witness a dead Other, its head resting against the base of the tree. What disturbed him most of all was the Other that was clambering down the trunk, its razor sharp teeth reared and ready to sink into the skull of its fellow species. He shook it off and turned to continue walking only to collide with the stationary Argyle.

'Jesus!' Bermuda exclaimed as he stumbled back. Argyle didn't even budge.

'Apologies.' Argyle scanned his eyes from the photo to the trees ahead of them. 'I believe this is the spot.'

He handed Bermuda the photo, who accepted after popping two mints into his mouth. He glanced at the photo and then at the trees ahead of him. They looked similar and as he peered more, he could see further beyond the trees. A broken log lay to the left of the tree, a few feet away from the edge of the mud. Beyond that, the river flowed by with a peaceful calm.

Yes, it looked similar. Bermuda was adamant he would find the symbol should he venture closer. That was the spot that Alfie Evans was last seen, his head pressed against his arms, counting loudly as his friends raced for hiding places.

He looked at the area ahead of him, then back to the photo. It was the exact spot. He had to investigate.

He looked up again.

The black eyes stared back at him.

The photos fell from his hand, carried down the concrete path by the passing wind.

Bermuda stared ahead, through the dangling vines of the surrounding willow trees. There, goading him in broad daylight was the man in the top hat. The hat itself sat angled to one side, the white, broken hair shifting messily in the wind. The marble-like skin shimmered, although from this distance, Bermuda couldn't make out the marking that ran down the side of its face.

Jagged teeth formed a cruel smile.

The black eyes burnt through him.

He was right. They were connected.

This Other was responsible.

He was the gatekeeper.

Bermuda's footsteps echoed in his mind, each step blocking out the clichéd sound of dogs barking and people enjoying each other's company. He slowly walked, his eyes not breaking the fierce look that rested upon him.

The black eyes burning into Bermuda.

A hundred feet away now.

The air felt cold and heavy.

Bermuda could feel his eyes watering, his peripheral lost to an ever growing tear. He hadn't blinked; his refusal to break the exchange an act of defiance against what he could already feel was evil.

Three scars became visible, crudely etched down the side of the face that bore the look of an entity with a purpose.

Bermuda knew the look all too well. It was the same one that had greeted him in the mirror after a night of heavy drinking.

Disgust.

Fifty feet now.

Twigs crunched under his feet as he slid between the trees, the river growing larger as he neared its edge.

The Other had not moved. Nor had it blinked.

Bermuda took a few more careful steps, when suddenly a large hand grasped his shoulder, spinning him around.

He yelled in anger.

'Where are you going?'

Argyle's words were laced in concern. Bermuda's heart raced wildly, slamming against his rib cage in a flurry of panic. He turned back quickly.

'Argyle, he's right....'

His voice trailed off.

The Other had gone.

No top hat. No jet black stare.

Just the wind sliding across the river, small ripples bursting out as far as they could.

'What did you see?'

Bermuda didn't answer, walking forward slowly towards the base of the tree that The Other had stood beside. The tree trunk that Alfie Evans used to begin his hide-and-seek countdown.

The twelve-sided symbol displayed proudly in the bark.

Bermuda sighed deeply, patting his pockets until a cigarette leapt into his mouth. He exhaled the smoke, willing his adrenaline to leave and his heart rate to drop.

'What did you see?' Argyle repeated, his bulging forearms crossed against his chest.

Bermuda searched for words but all that left his mouth was second hand smoke. After a few more drags, he sent the butt to a watery grave before marching back towards his partner.

'We need to go to Other's Town. Now.' He looked back, still shaken by the presence he had seen. 'This place is giving me the fucking creeps.'

Within a few moments, Bermuda was back on the path, marching to the exit. Argyle hurried behind him, neither of them realising they were followed every step by a set of jet black eyes that sat above a crooked smile of razor teeth. The man in the top hat.

The time was soon approaching.

13

The bus indicated and joined the main road, Aldgate East station disappearing into the distance. London, even during the middle of the day, was busy with traffic, a number of buses, cabs and angered civilians battling it out for road supremacy. Cyclists dodged in and out of traffic, daring drivers to take their lives.

All Bermuda saw were the two eyes.

The blackness of them.

The hatred he had felt.

As the bus slowly meandered towards the Docklands, he tried to refocus. He was about to enter Other's Town, the only place he was less welcome than his ex-wife's house. To the normal human, the Tobacco Docks were just a London landmark. A vast, historical structure that had since taken importance as a place on London's storied tapestry. It was more than just a measly storage facility and in recent times, had been the location of a few raves and film nights. Annual conventions were held inside its dusty brick walls, a tattoo convention that Bermuda owed for the inscription that ran across his right shoulder blade.

As he stepped off the bus and rounded the corner, he saw the large iron pillars with the word 'Tobacco Dock' punched out. The entrance arched ahead, encasing the surrounding concrete in shadows, which moved erratically. A long queue of Others lined the wall, each one as unique as a finger print.

This was their town. Their market place.

Bermuda clicked his lighter, ignoring the hundreds of eyes which landed on him, the entire queue now focused in their fear. Through the smoke that he stepped through, he knew he looked like a demon to them.

He enjoyed it.

'We need a plan'. Argyle stepped ahead, blocking Bermuda from his tried and tested 'hit now, ask later' technique.

'I have a plan,' Bermuda said, smoke surrounding his raised voice. 'I'm going to go in there. I'm going to ask who the fuck is stealing my people and where I can find him.'

'That is not why we are here.'

'It isn't?' Bermuda stomped his cigarette into a gravelly grave.

'We are here to locate Jared. He will be able to create our lock and maybe shed some light.' A few hisses and murmurs emanated from the crowd, all eyes, whatever the colour, focusing in with extra venom. Bermuda scowled back at them, considering the bizarreness of his life before sighing.

'Fine. Let's go.'

Argyle nodded and the two of them entered the Tobacco Dock, their ID badges enough to not only gain them access but also spread fear among the inhabitants. The entire structure, recently refurbished with glass fencing around the corridors, may have seemed abandoned to the human eye. Bermuda, however, saw something complete different.

Rows upon rows of stalls, all of them displaying goods that

Bermuda could never comprehend. Other's didn't exchange in currency, their lack of financial dependency replaced with a noble notion of providing what one can with everyone. It didn't promote a healthy economy but it brought those who walked across the divide a kinship with each other that humans would never amount to.

Capitalism is a very human trait.

Bermuda walked a few paces behind Argyle, every step that echoed through the dock drew more attention, the Other's silent in their movements. Hundreds of eyes latched on him, many willing him to be ripped limb from limb.

They hated him. Because they feared him.

Bermuda stopped at a stall, its offerings bizarre - a long, black material cut into thin strips. He had seen an Other wearing something similar before, a fashion statement he would never understand.

Suddenly, a commotion ahead of him drew his attention.

'TRAITOR!'

The large Other reached out and slapped Argyle across the face, an army of its smaller minions circling like baby sharks. Argyle stood calmly, his face a picture of sternness. A few more others joined the group, one of them hurling a strange, orange stone that clattered against Argyle's eyebrow.

'HUMAN LOVER!'

'KILL HIM!'

'YOU'RE A DISGRACE!'

Bermuda felt the rage boiling as the large Other, a brute with an unseemly lock jaw, the bottom teeth sticking up over his top lip, approached Argyle with menace. Argyle gallantly stood his ground, refusing to engage in any form of altercation.

He was the living embodiment of the BTCO's creed.

Two Worlds. One Peace.

The large Other drew back and then spat a large batch of saliva straight into Argyle's face. Bermuda saw red.

Fuck the creed.

Bermuda pushed past Argyle, his hoody zipped up to cover the body armour that encased his frame. The Other took a small step back, its ragged teeth upturned in a snarl. The gathering spectators fell silent, a number of them cursing the very human before them. Staring straight at the large Other, Bermuda clenched his fists.

'I think you all need to back off, right now!'

'Bermuda.' Argyle reached out, trying to draw him away. He was shrugged off.

'You're in our town now, little man,' The Other provoked, prodding Bermuda in the shoulder.

'You're in my world.'

The Other grinned.

'Well, let me show you what I think of your world.' Its yellow eyes glistened as it suddenly reared back, hawking up another dollop of phlegm. As it lurched forward to spit in Bermuda's face, a human fist collided fully with its nose. Blood and bone exploded forward as Bermuda landed a perfect punch, sending the Other reeling and the entire audience into a frenzy. Shaking with fear, the Other swung a lazy fist at Bermuda who ducked, expertly locking the arm and wrenching it backwards, slamming the Other face first into the random items that scattered the table.

The entire 'Town' had come to a standstill.

'Listen and listen good!' Bermuda yelled, wrenching the arm slightly. 'We are here on a case. Someone or something from your world should not be here. We have been sent here to find the one you called Jared.'

Bermuda looked around, his gaze returned by a hundred

worried faces. He wrenched the arm, the tendons twisting as the Other howled in pain.

'WHERE IS HE?' Bermuda addressed the room, his words reverberating off the hollow walls.

A few Others sheepishly pointed towards the far exit, leading to some of the more illustrious stalls. Wrenched the arm again. Another shriek of pain filled the air.

'As for you. If you so much as look at me or Argyle again, I will snap this clean off. Understand?' Bermuda twisted the arm again. 'UNDERSTAND?'

The Other nodded, before mumbling in pain. Bermuda released his grip before storming off, barging past a few of the terrified onlookers. All eyes rested on Argyle again, who slowly followed his partner, striving to maintain his indifference. The large Other sat on the ground, its back against the wall, arm hanging loosely from its socket.

Bermuda walked to a clearing near the corner, sparking up a cigarette and slowly quashing his rage.

'I do not need you to fight my battles.' Argyle calmly approached.

'I know.'

'I made peace with their hatred a long time ago.' Argyle looked at Bermuda's fist, the balled hand shaking slightly. 'Hatred and rage will only lead to downfall.'

'Look, I know you can handle yourself. And I know we need to maintain the peace and blah blah. But I'll be damned if they are going to spit in your face and get away with it.'

Argyle reassuringly reached out, placing a fingerless gloved hand on Bermuda's shoulder.

'Your gesture is duly noted and appreciated.'

The two of them nodded, appreciative of the other's presence. Ghoulish monsters of another world slithered around, all of them with nothing but pure hatred for the two of them. They needed each other.

'I'm going to locate Jared.' Argyle began to walk. 'Are you coming?'

'I'll be there in a minute.' Bermuda motioned with his cigarette.

'Well, don't do anything rash.'

'As if I would?' Bermuda smirked. Argyle, stern faced as always, shook his head and took his leave. Others parted, letting the solider through with fear and hatred circling him in equal measures. As soon as Argyle exited through the doorway to the other section of the dock, Bermuda quickly whipped his notebook from his back pocket, the pages flicking until they landed on the crude sketch.

The top hat was clumsily drawn. The face was misshapen.

But the eyes. The dark, black eyes. He could feel them. Just as he could when he was put in the back of the police car last night and just as he did earlier that day in Regent's Park. He shook the horrible stare from his mind and turned to a sheepish, rat like Other that scuttled past.

'Excuse me. Have you seen this guy?' Bermuda flashed him the drawing. The vile looking creature muttered in a tongue Bermuda didn't recognise before slinking off.

With a sigh, Bermuda strolled back into the group of Others, flashing the picture and asking the same question.

Had anyone seen the gentleman in the top hat?

A few Others recoiled at the image, a fear that Bermuda thought he witnessed in Vincent back at the HQ. A few of them shrugged. The majority however, retorted with venomous threats and lurid insults.

After ten minutes of non-stop and utterly fruitless questioning, Bermuda found himself standing to the side, eyes closed, slowly massaging his temples.

'OUT OF MY WAY, HUMAN!'

A large Other pushed past, knocking Bermuda into the wall. His already bruised cheek slammed against the stone, his body armour absorbing the impact in the chest. Bermuda muttered under his breath. The Other turned, egged on by a few more creatures scuttling across the walls.

'Didn't see you there. I don't pay attention to garbage.'

He chuckled, a large jaw displaying three crooked teeth. Its eyes sat back in its skull.

Bermuda again muttered, his fists clenching.

The Other leaned right into Bermuda's personal space, its ear a mere inch from Bermuda's mouth.

'What did you say? Speak up.'

'I said,' Bermuda's whisper rose in volume, 'how are you going to eat shit with only one tooth?'

The Other frowned in confusion, then stumbled backwards as Bermuda swung a vicious elbow straight into its mouth. The crack shook the room as blood spurted up the wall, two of the large teeth ricocheting off the brickwork and clattering to the floor.

The Other scurried around on all fours, weeping and trying to secure its teeth as Bermuda slowly walked through the crowd, annoyed at losing his temper once more. Word would get back to Ottoway and Vincent. Complaints would be made of excessive force and once again, Bermuda would face the Committee and his 'punishment'. Only it wasn't punishment to be suspended. It was punishment to be at goddamn Other's Town.

Downhearted, Bermuda squeezed through a group of Others, making his way up the corridor towards Jared's shop. A few Others ran from him, climbing the walls and making their getaways on the walkways above.

He opened the door to the outlet, striding towards the counter that Argyle was patiently waiting by. Behind it, an Other with an angular head embraced him with his eyes. The Other had no mouth.

'Jared,' Bermuda offered, nodding his hello. It was reciprocated.

'Jared has agreed to construct our lock,' said Argyle.

'Goody gum drops,' Bermuda said, uninterested. He slowly scanned the bizarre shop. Jars and trinkets lined the shelves, all of them containing substances this world could never comprehend. Jared scratched the counter in a systematic fashion, before gesticulating with his free hand. Bermuda raised an eyebrow.

'What is he saying?'

'He says that it will take an hour of earth's time to create the mechanism.'

'Earth time?' Bermuda asked. Blank looks. 'Never mind.'

Argyle turned back to the shop keeper. 'We will wait. Thank you.'

Jared motioned again, before scuttling sideways from the counter like an anxious crab. Argyle slowly retreated to the seats that lined the wall of the empty shop, slowly lowering himself down.

'You should rest,' Argyle offered, his partner looking agitated.

'I might step outside. Ask some questions.'

Before Argyle could answer, Bermuda stormed to the door, hoisting it open and stepping outside. Thousands of eyes landed on him, the entire section filled with Others looking straight in his direction. He could feel the anger and hatred swirling around him like a furious tornado.

He placed the cigarette in his lips and leant forward, cupping his hand protectively around the flame.

He didn't light the cigarette.

He could feel them.

The black eyes.

Slowly, he raised his head, above the swathes of other worldly creatures before him.

They were burning into him.

His vision continued to climb.

The walkway above Other's Town cast a large shadow over the hustle and bustle of the world below it.

The grey hands clasped the rail tightly.

Bermuda latched onto the stare and could feel it goading him, daring him to come and play.

The man with the top hat stared back at him.

He had found him.

14

The time was always going to come.

Locked away in his cell for over a hundred years, he knew the moment would arrive when he first heard the rumours. The muted whispers of a human who could survive in their world. A human who crossed over and didn't perish.

And that moment, when he himself would rest his jet black eyes on such a specimen, was upon him. While the embarrassment of his people hid in the dark corners of the world, he stood in plain sight, wishing and waiting for this human to look up at him.

He had locked eyes at the ship, the ghastly welcoming gift dying slowly on the deck as the human was led to safety by his own authorities.

By the river, where the young boy had become his. Just like the other ten.

They all belonged to him.

This world would be next. Be his.

All that stood in his way was this moment. Standing above the insult of a town led by his own kind, his bony, grey fingers tightened their grip on the railing. His top hat slanted across his hard skull, the shadow hiding the three brutal scars that dominated his face.

His black eyes fixed on him.

The man looked up.

The invite was offered in silence and the man's sudden dart towards the stairs told him it had been accepted. The final phase of the plan. The only possible obstacle that would stop him remodelling the world. The chosen human, a man whose ability was not befitting the despicable race he belonged to.

With slow, measured steps, he strode into the back room, the windows boarded up and the brick work old and decaying. The shadows adorned the wall like curtains.

They would be alone. There would be no audience for this.

The meeting would be completely private.

His mouth twisted into a crooked smile, two rows of razor sharp teeth zig-zagging across one another like a broken bottle.

Time to meet the one they call 'Bermuda'.

■ ▮ ▎

Bermuda took a deep breath as he reached the top of the staircase. Bounding up the steps two at a time, combined with years of smoking usually equalled discomfort. He took a few moments, straightening the hoodie that rested over his body armour before slowly walking along the narrow walkway.

The wooden platforms, held up by pillars were lined by glass railings. Below him, Other's Town was scuttling about, a dark mass of shadows all crashing over each other like a furious ocean.

Each step echoed, the hustle and bustle below fading out so all that Bermuda could hear was his own footsteps and beating of his heart.

Another step forward.

The Man in the Top Hat was gone.

Deflated, Bermuda took a few more steps, drawn to the place where he stood merely seconds ago. Nothing but empty space and another dead end.

'Almost.'

The voice cut through him like nails down a chalk board, the 's' playing out like the hiss of a wild python. Bermuda spun suddenly, following the booming resonance of the voice through an archway and stopping dead.

Standing on the other side of the room, with his back to the entrance, was the Man in the Top Hat. From behind, Bermuda was surprised by how tall he was, his wiry frame deceptively hiding the slight bulk of a strong back. The white hair flared out from under the hat like a scarecrow.

Bermuda slowly entered the room, standing directly behind his adversary with a distance of another ten metres between them. The shadows on the wall stopped dancing.

The noise of Other's Town fell to below a whisper.

It was just the two of them.

'So, who the hell...'

Bermuda was cut off by a raised finger. The Other let it hang in the air, refusing to turn. His voice, deep and booming, ricocheted off the walls with a fury.

'Do you know what power is?' Rhetorical. 'Power is what controls the outcomes of so many insignificant moments. Having the power to walk, one foot in front of the other, can change the outcome of whether or not you make it work. The power to do the mundane, such as turn on a light bulb, effects whether or not you see the intruder in the house. These tiny outcomes are taken for granted by you humans, these powers are considered nothing more than everyday tasks. You and I know that real power, the power to change worlds, THAT is the power of true consequence.'

Bermuda shifted uncomfortably on the spot. The Other before him hadn't turned, although he had shot a few sideways glances, permitting Bermuda a brief glimpse of those harrowing eyes.

'You humans know nothing of consequence. Even a man such as yourself, bestowed with this unique gift, has reacted with such ignorance and disdain of his circumstance. But that will change. Oh, it will change.'

The Man in the Top Hat chuckled, the sinister laugh spreading through Bermuda's body and chilling him to the bone.

'Who are you?' Bermuda asked, his voice shaking.

'I am the consequence.'

'Turn around and let me see your face,' Bermuda ordered, trying his hardest to reinforce his authority. 'I am an agent of the BTCO and I am ordering you to turn around.'

'I do not bow to such meaningless authorities.'

'Tell me your goddamn name!'

'I am your reckoning. Humanity's chance at a new beginning.'

He slowly turned, the black eyes trembling with fury. The mouth, twisted at the side in a snarl that disturbed the three, thick scars. Bermuda took a moment to compose himself. The Other before him oozed nothing but pure danger.

'But you my friend. You can call me Barnaby.'

Bermuda held the gaze for a moment, every second passed with a feeling of foreboding.

'You had me attacked and almost killed. You are no friend of mine.'

'Ah yes,' Barnaby smirked. 'How is the face?'

'Better than yours.'

Barnaby nodded, the three scars that ruptured his skin a testament to a darker time.

'Do you know why they gave me these scars? What they stand for?'

Bermuda curiously looked around the room before responding.

'Can't say I care too much.'

'This is the mark of a traitor. They branded me for having the gall to try and save my race. I watched my people, day after day, surrender to your race and I grew to loathe you both with equal measure. They branded me a traitor. Ironic really, considering this is a mark they should bestow upon your precious Argyle.'

Bermuda turned sharply, angered by the insult of his partner before an increasing awareness of loneliness spread through him.

'Argyle isn't a traitor.'

Barnaby scoffed, his sharp laughter roaring through the air like a freed demon.

'Tell me, Bermuda, what would you call a man who judges, arrests, banishes and slaughters his own kind?'

'He is just keeping the peace...'

'PEACE!' Barnaby's black eyes flashed with fury. 'There is no more peace than there is an understanding of one's place in the food chain. Tell me, on what level of peace sees my people, resigned to the shadows and afraid to walk amongst humans? In what way does peace constitute a constant stream of analysis of their behaviour and swarms of agents keeping them in line?'

Bermuda could sense the emotions within Barnaby heightening, regretting not equipping his tomahawk when he left the house over a day ago.

'Well, this is our world. Rules are different here.'

'Under whose authority? The humans?'

'Well, yes. As the dominant species of this planet, we have

authority. So when I ask you what you have been doing and where the hell Jessica and the rest of those people are, I expect you to tell me.'

Barnaby looked to the ground, his jaw flexing into a cruel smile.

'And why is that? What makes you humans so special? Humanity? Answer me this, in what world is it 'human' to slaughter and kill other creatures, who have just as much write to inhabit the world, for food and sport?'

Bermuda stepped back, steadying himself as Barnaby continued.

'What is so glorious about a race of people who will slaughter one another in the name of an unproven god, yet claim there is more than one? Or a world where the majority are dying of illness and famine, yet the rich and powerful withhold the necessary treatments to increase their pathetic reliance on wealth?'

Barnaby shook his head in frustration.

'Don't you dare tell me your world is any better than mine. Open your eyes, Bermuda. You will see a whole lot more if you choose to.'

'I've seen more than enough in my time.'

'Your time? Your measly thirty-four years walking this planet is no more than a blip on the map of time. Try watching your world fall apart for centuries, confined to a darkness that not even you could comprehend. What pain could you possibly know?'

Bermuda's mind quickly flashed to an image on Angela and Chloe, the three of them walking through a park with nothing but love and laughter for company.

'I've given my fair share to this world.'

'Ah yes. The BTCO. Keeping the peace and maintaining the balance.' Barnaby clicked his tongue around his mouth. 'What is the creed again? Two worlds. One peace?'

Bermuda didn't answer, his eyes scanning for any other routes of escape. Barnaby continued, his eyes burning like coal.

'Tell me, Bermuda. Why save a world that doesn't believe it needs to be saved?'

'Just because others don't have my curse, doesn't mean they don't deserve a normal life.'

'And what is a normal life? Being blind and naive to what truly goes on and what is resigned to the shadows of your pathetic existence? Or is a normal life one where you see behind the curtain, as your organisation so poetically calls it?'

Barnaby shook his head, the top hat swaying atop his skull. Beneath the floorboards below, a congregation of his people slithered amongst themselves, trying to survive in a world that refused to acknowledge them.

'Where are you taking those people?'

'They are mine now.'

'What have you done with them?' Bermuda demanded. Barnaby flashed him a look of sinister glee.

'I took what they have taken for granted. A free passage and existence in this world. Each and every one of them, they have all passed through and they belong to me now. I can feel them; their connection to this world is coursing through my veins like an unstoppable cancer. And soon....soon I shall be the same.'

'Nothing is unstoppable.'

'Naivety is a cruel trait that you humans are blessed with. Soon I shall be as at one with this world as you are. The clock is ticking for your race, Bermuda. And I am the judgement when those seconds run out. What do you do, Bermuda, when something finally loses its power?'

'You replace it?'

Barnaby sneered, dissatisfied.

'You remove it entirely.'

Bermuda shuffled uncomfortably on the spot, Barnaby turned,

admiring the brink work of the wall before him.

'Tell me again, Bermuda. Why are you humans in control of this world?'

'Because we are the dominant species.'

Barnaby turned to face him again, his jagged teeth contorted in a ferocious snarl. His words shot out like whispered bullets.

'Not anymore.'

Before Bermuda could even move, Barnaby shot across the room, his movements faster and sharper than anything seen by human eyes. Through the blackness of the blur, a bony hand shot forward, the palm striking Bermuda in the centre of the chest. The body armour that protectively encased his torso shook, the power of the blow rupturing the layers and shaking Bermuda's rib cage like a rattle. The pain was monumental.

Bermuda felt his internal organs scatter, his feet swept off the ground as he hurtled towards the concrete wall behind him. The brick and cement shattered like glass as he exploded through, the sheer force of the strike reducing the wall to confetti around him. The impact hammered the back of his skull and shoulders, the world suddenly going fuzzy as his consciousness swirled.

Launched from the room, he hit the floor, sliding down the walkways supported above Other's Town. Brick rained down on the Other's below, confusion breaking out and spreading through the town like a virus.

Bermuda rolled onto his front, gasping for the breath that had been driven out of him. His hands shuffled for balance, gripping shattered pieces of brick and stone with broken fingers.

Barnaby stepped through the Bermuda shaped hole in the wall, his footsteps slow and measured as he stalked his prey. A sinister grin appeared across his scarred face. As Bermuda pushed himself onto all fours, Barnaby launched a thunderous kick to his ribs, the impact breaking a couple of bones. The strength of the vengeful Other's strike launched Bermuda up into the air, and shattering through the glass banister that surrounded the platform. Hurtling fifteen feet, he slammed through a table, the other worldly goods it displayed exploding over the panicked consumers like a snowstorm.

Bermuda's world went black.

As the Others gathered around in confusion and concern, they began to part as Argyle raced through, his shoulder shoving those still obstructing. He slowed down, quickly checking on Bermuda who lay amongst the wreckage before racing to the stairs, bounding up them three at a time. His footsteps echoed across the platform above, hundreds of eyes peering up at him as he searched methodically, one hand drawn to the handle of his sword that adorned his back.

Each platform was empty. Every room was clean.

Barnaby had gone.

15

Bermuda's eyes slowly opened, revealing the white tiled ceiling that greeted him earlier that day. For the second time in the space of twenty-four hours, he was waking up in a room hundreds of feet beneath The Shard. He rubbed his bruised eye and slowly sat up, groaning with anguish at the crunching in his chest.

'You have three broken ribs.' Vincent's calm voice filtered through the air and Bermuda reached for a glass of water. 'Ottoway is waiting outside. He would like to see you.'

'Whatever,' Bermuda grumpily replied, shuffling through his personal affects which lay on the bedside table. He slid a cigarette out of its box as Vincent opened the door. The authoritative figure of Ottoway strode in as Bermuda flicked his lighter to life.

'This is a no smoking facility,' Ottoway stated, his voice borderline angry. It worsened when the response was a cloud of smoke. 'What did I tell you in regards to protecting public property?'

Bermuda winced; fresh bandages circled his increasingly beaten body. He took another puff, letting the nicotine sooth his throat.

'Something about not breaking it.'

'Exactly.' Hands on hips, Ottoway was not impressed. 'So tell me, how the hell you managed to smash another hole through a wall?'

Bermuda sat silently, not wanting another facetious comment to get him in more trouble.

'I understand you were attacked, Jones. But you need to ensure we keep a low profile. Leaving a trail of damage to public property raises questions and our existence already causes too many people too many worries.'

'Forgive me if I don't feel their pain,' Bermuda said, shaking his head as he stubbed out the cigarette.

'Well I do. The Committee are discussing disciplinary sanctions as we speak. I have been kept out of it on account of bias.'

'Bias?' Bermuda scoffed. 'I'm a pain in the arse.'

'Quite. But you are also a damn good agent.'

Bermuda nodded his thanks, swinging his legs over the edge of the bed. He ached, longing for a pint of Doombar and his own bed.

'Can I have a shirt, please?'

Vincent glided across the room, his elegance cutting through the tension as he obliged Bermuda. He uncomfortably slid it over his head, his hair messy and unkempt.

'Where is Argyle?'

'Argyle is in the Archive, reviewing his report. We have concerns that he left you unattended.'

Bermuda laughed.

'Concerns? You should be concerned that if Argyle hadn't been there I would most likely have been dead. Twice in the last day I have been attacked by that world. Argyle isn't a concern, he's a goddamn saving grace!'

'Well, we shall review his actions later. The Governance have also questioned your actions over the last twenty four hours and have requested a meeting.'

'The Governance? What the hell has it got to do with them?' Bermuda moaned, knowing full well why. The Governance were the council that managed the truce between our world and The Otherside. A clan of eight elderly Others, all of whom despised Bermuda for his ability to walk through their world. His intrusion, so to speak.

'The Governance have just as much as authority as our committee.' Ottoway spoke with a calm assurance. 'Let's face it; your actions haven't exactly been subtle.'

Bermuda rolled his eyes as he plonked his feet onto the cold, tiled floor. His face ached, the searing pain in his cranium bouncing around like a ping pong ball. He caught a glimpse of himself in the mirror. The bruising around the cut that framed his eye was a dark purple. A few splatters of blood were beginning to decorate his t-shirt. His chest wounds would take a while to heal properly. Time he didn't have right now. Not with Barnaby still out there.

'Who the hell is Barnaby?'

Bermuda's question filled the room with tension, Ottoway and Vincent exchanged awkward glances. Angrily slamming two mints into his mouth, Bermuda shuffled back to the bed, resting on the edge of it with his tattooed arms crossed.

'Well?' Bermuda asked, his eyes shooting back and forth between the two most senior members of the BTCO.

Vincent sighed.

'Hundreds of years ago, the connection between your world and ours was discovered. The first to go through and return were amazed at the sheer colour and vibrancy of your world. The potential. You have seen my world, Franklyn; you know how dark it is. We saw earth as a second chance. 'For the first hundred or so years, my people lived quietly within the confines of your world. The odd discrepancy yet your race is so young and undeveloped it went unnoticed. It was only when humanity became educated that we slowly began to be discovered.'

Vincent slowly walked across the room, forcing himself from making eye contact. Bermuda looked at him, a look of boredom on his face.

'Barnaby was one of the first to oppose the truce that was struck between these two worlds. He felt that it would weaken their position, would make them remove their power. He believed that the strongest lay claim to the world and tried to rally an invasion.'

'Sounds like an arsehole,' Bermuda said, stretching his back and feeling his broken ribs click.

'Well you had the pleasure of meeting him today,' Ottoway chimed in. 'How did that go?'

'Point taken.'

'Eventually, the decision was made to imprison him,' Vincent continued, as if talking about the past was painful. 'He tried to overthrow the general of the Legion, but was captured. They burnt him with the mark of the traitor. Three permanent scars that run deep through his face. Then they threw him in the darkest hole and threw away their strongest key.'

'Hate to break it to you, Vincent, but that didn't fucking work.' Bermuda pushed himself off the bed and walked past the senior figures in his room, pouring a glass of water and draining it in one swig. 'He isn't locked away anymore.'

'Yes. Well we suspected he may have been involved but we didn't want to concern you needlessly. Especially with your temper.'

'My temper? He almost fucking killed me! A heads up would

have been nice.' Bermuda shook his head, frustration taking control.

Ottoway stepped forward.

'We were curious as to a few dead bodies found on the Otherside recently. They didn't appear connected but it now seems likely it lead to Barnaby's escape. Wherever he found or forged that Gate Maker, we don't know. We just know he needs to be stopped. We can't let him open a doorway and not know what he is bringing in.'

'Or sending out.', Bermuda mused.

'Excuse me?'

'He isn't killing these people. Jessica, that American from the ship. That list you gave me, they were all two days apart. Every two days, he seems to opening a doorway but he isn't killing them.'

'What could he possibly want with humans?' Ottoway asked, his chubby face writhe with confusion.

'I don't know. He said they belong to him now. That they were coursing through him like a cancer.'

Vincent suddenly turned around, facing them both. His sharp face was awash with worry.

'Vincent?' Ottoway asked, concern for his friend obvious.

'It can't be.'

'What?' Bermuda asked, slowly feeding his arms into his hoody.

'What else did he say?' Vincent demanded, his voice rising with the tension.

'That they were passing through. That soon he will be as connected to this world as I am or some shit like that.'

'A convergence?' Ottoway asked. Bermuda's eyes shot between the two of them as Vincent slowly nodded. Ottoway shook his head in disbelief, his thought process playing out through the sternness of his face.

'I must inform The Committee. This is a serious matter.'

Ottoway turned on his heel and marched out as Vincent watched him leave. Bermuda watched the Neither, admiring the calmness of his movements despite the increasing levels of fear.

'So what the hell is a convergence?'

Vincent extended and placed a comforting hand on Bermuda's shoulder. 'A convergence is a joining of two worlds at an unplanned section.'

'Meaning?'

'Barnaby is trying to fuse himself with this world. Genetics is what binds humans to this world just as genetics denies them the ability to interact with Other's. There are anomalies in the code. Hence your abilities.'

'My curse.'

'Your gift,' Vincent corrected. 'However you are the anomaly amongst the anomalies aren't you? The only one to have gone to the Otherside and returned. You are what Barnaby craves. The corridor between the two realms. The doorway to a different future.'

'He wants to merge himself with our world?' Bermuda asked, not wanting to discuss his issue.

'Yes. He takes their life essence, stealing the genetic coding that merges him with your world. Just like you are still doing with mine.'

Bermuda looked up shocked to a comforting smile.

'I don't know what you are talking about.'

'Please. Franklyn. It is just us in the room so do me the decency of not thinking me a fool.'

Bermuda shuffled uncomfortably on the spot, looking towards the door which Ottoway had slammed shut behind him. They were completely alone.

'How long have you known?'

'I had my suspicions early on. It doesn't make sense for someone to travel through such a shift in atmosphere and there not be some symptoms.'

Bermuda sighed; a part of him that he wanted to keep to himself was slowly slipping away. Just like every other part of his life; taken out of his control.

'So? What are they?'

'They're not symptoms as such. It's more of an effect.'

'An effect?'

Vincent glided next to Bermuda, a concerned hand reached out. 'Tell me.'

'I can't tell you what it is. It just feels like the Otherside is trying to pull me back. Every time I touch anything to do with. Be it the markings of the Gate Maker or even when I punched that thing in the face earlier. Every time I touch it, I can feel it physically pulling me across.'

A moment of silence sat between them as Vincent pondered. Bermuda pulled out a cigarette, nervous fingers fumbling at the lighter. Vincent went to warn him of the rules, but thought better of it as a waft of smoke danced around the room.

'I will need to do some research however it would appear something from my world is fusing to your genetic coding and hasn't finished. Whatever it is, it seems to have connected with your gift.'

'Gift?' Bermuda questioned, flicking ash to the floor as he headed to the door.

'It is. You may not see it, but this is a truly wondrous gift.'

Bermuda stopped at the door, flicking the cigarette to the ground and turning back. His soul crushed.

'Gifts aren't supposed to ruin your life.' He forced a smile, in hope of a solution. 'See you around, Vincent.'

With that, Bermuda closed the door, leaving the senior Neither to ponder their chat and to prepare for the inevitable inquest from The Governance.

■ ■ |

Bermuda trudged down the corridor, the bright halogen bulbs above only adding to the throbbing pain that shook inside his skull. Each step was careful and considered, the impact of putting his weight down scraped his ribs together. The gashes across his chest were half opening. His eye had almost swollen shut. He had been through hell in twenty-four hours.

Just as he rounded the corner, Bermuda swore to himself that his day couldn't get any worse. He proved himself wrong as he collided with none other than Hugo LaPone.

As they crashed into each other, a pain shot through Bermuda like a bolt of lightning. French curse words spring from Hugo's mouth, his perfectly chiselled face was even handsome whilst snarling.

'Are you blind?' Hugo remarked, before looking at the state of Bermuda's face. 'Well half at least.'

'Brilliant. If you wouldn't mind, I'd like to go home.'

Bermuda slowly stepped to the side only for Hugo to block his route.

'I heard you destroyed another wall. The docks. Yes?' Bermuda nodded. 'You are, how you say, a complete fuck up?'

Bermuda chuckled silently, before looking Hugo straight in the eye.

'Seriously mate, I have had a pretty shit day. Now I'm going to get in that lift, I'm going to get on a train and I'm going to go home. So please. If you don't mind.'

Again Bermuda tried to squeeze past and again Hugo stepped in his way.

'A real agent would not be going home. They would be out, trying to fix the problems they have already caused. But you, Bermuda, with your pathetic nick name, think you are abo...'

CRACK!

Despite a day of anguish and energy sapping disappointment, Bermuda's fist hurtled with pinpoint accuracy onto the bridge of Hugo's nose. As blood burst out, covering the symmetrical face in a crimson mask, Hugo fell backwards, cursing and yelling. His eyes dripped with tears, as blood dripped over the white tiles.

Bermuda didn't hear the insults or threats that were thrown his way in a French tornado of abuse.

He ignored all of the commotion, BTCO office workers and jobsworths gathering round to witness the one bit of excitement they would see all day.

He ignored all of the announcements in the lift and the foot traffic that ran through London Bridge Station as he made his way to Euston.

The train journey from London back to Bushey, in the calm, quiet evening of Hertfordshire didn't register with him.

On autopilot, he cracked open a can of Doombar as he entered his flat, struggling to recall any moment of his journey home.

Undressing, he ignored the agonising pain of the crushed ribs, ruptured skin and a mild concussion cocktail his body had been treated to.

His mind removed the horrible sense of foreboding, of the black eyes that belonged to the biggest threat the world didn't know about.

He ignored his impending doom.

The end of the world.

Bermuda was asleep before his head hit the pillow.

16

Every step left a footprint in the ash.

Flaming embers rained down from the grey clouds ahead, basking the world in an intermittent glow. The buildings beyond the horizon line roared with flames, the orange flicking upwards like eager fingers. There was no sky, just a thick, grey smoke that merged into the cloud.

Each step crunched on the dead world.

The scorched grass crumpled under Bermuda's footsteps, crackling like hey as he moved. He could remember this street, not by name, but by memory. A happier time, when he and Angela stood either side of Chloe, a hand grasped each as they swung her into the air. Her giggles filled the world with joy.

The buildings that lined the street crumpled to the ground, bricks clattering against each other as dust exploded upwards.

Somewhere in the distance, Bermuda could hear the screech of an Other, something large and world ending.

Each step took him closer to oblivion.

As he walked, the nearest lamp post flickered, before evaporating into ash, gently filtering off on the hard winds that scattered the flaming embers around with a chaotic beauty.

There she was.

Angela.

His ex-wife stood meters away, her back to him. Her hair danced in the wind, the strands flicking away the flames. Bermuda opened his mouth to speak, yet his words failed him.

Another step closer to her. He reached out.

Just as his fingers grazed her shoulder, it began to crumble, ash filtering down to the ground in slow motion as his wife faded from him.

'Goodbye,' he finally managed to mutter.

Slumping his head forward and trying to hold back tears, he turned, only to see Brett. He smiled, relieved to have found his best friend during the end of the world. A glimmer of hope.

As he walked through the violent wind towards his friend, the street came crashing down, more buildings tumbling under the weight of extinction.

More dust and smoke filled the sky. The world was ready for death.

Brett turned to face him but before he could say anything, the wind blew him to ash. Scattered across the dead street, Bermuda watched the essence of his best friend disappear. Lost forever.

'Daddy'.

Bermuda stopped dead. The voice, the one thing that could stop his beating heart, danced through the wild air, blocking out the devastation that had set itself upon his world. He swallowed deeply, composing himself before he turned.

Chloe.

His eyes filled with tears, the drops descending down his cheeks towards a mouth that cracked a smile. She was so beautiful. Her bright, blue eyes stared at the father who had removed himself from her life. They welled with tears, the death and destruction around her only multiplying her beauty.

She began to run towards him.

Behind her, every building exploded, brick and stone reigning down around them as he raced towards her. The street seemed to stretch, placing more meters between him and the most precious thing in his life. If the world was to end, he would meet it with his arms around his daughter. Fire fell from the sky, surrounding him and his daughter as they raced towards each other. Suddenly, the street was lined with people he knew.

Sophie.

Argyle.

Ottoway.

All of them crumpled to the ground, an ashy cloud all that remained.

Bermuda dropped to his knees as Chloe launched herself towards him. She stopped in mid-air. Her eyes wide with terror.

Tiny black hands extended from the shadows, wrapping themselves around her.

Bermuda begged, scrambling to his knees.

The world exploded around them.

The shadows tightened their grip.

Chloe looked at her Father, his outstretched hand just too far away.

'Help me!'

And with that, the hands pulled in different directions, ripping his daughter into several pieces. He screamed as the world burnt to the ground.

Bermuda woke up, his whole body covered in sweat.

The water coolly splashed against his face, washing away the few hours of distressing sleep. Bermuda stood upright, staring at the dishevelled reflection in the mirror. The bags under the eyes, the ever-growing stubble. It was a face that screamed for a good night's sleep.

Slowly he raised his arms up, the agony of shattered ribs and a slashed torso reminding him of just what he had been through. Never in a million years had taking off a t-shirt been so painful. As he grasped the scruff of the collar, he slide the shirt over his head, the material stuck to his skin through sweat. With a painful grunt, he finally removed it, dropping it to the floor with a slight slap.

The mirror now told him a lot more.

His body, chiselled from years of regular exercise and Argyle's survival training, was usually one of his better features. The artistry that adorned it, many hours spent under a flaming hot needle, the ultimate adornment.

Now it was a monstrosity.

Unravelling the bandages that wrapped around his torso, he gritted his teeth in pain. The right side of his ribs had turned a sickening shade of purple. A deep bruise, the internal bleeding wrapping around the shattered bones that rattled inside him. He pressed two fingers against his ribs, instantly withdrawing them with a gasp of agony.

He composed himself, remembering the severe power with which he had been struck.

Barnaby.

He instantly shook the image of the dark eyes from his mind, refocusing on his chest. The three large gashes that crossed his pecs were starting to heal. Worryingly, a little too fast. Bermuda scanned his chest, trying his best to witness the fibres of his skin threading themselves back together. Although he saw nothing, he was sure he was recovering rapidly, terrified that the Otherside may be having more of an effect on him than he would have ever acknowledged.

How could Vincent have known?

He held his own gaze in the mirror, his brow fraught with worry. What if he had brought back more than just the ability to interact with The Otherside? He could feel it calling to him; he could feel himself physically being pulled across every time he touched something that belonged there.

Did he belong to The Otherside?

He shook his head, catching his reflection once more to inspect the gash across his eyebrow. The bruising was slowly fading, the swelling of his eye lids slowly starting to part.

He looked like shit. Which was ten times better than he felt.

With a deep sigh, he entered the shower, allowing the warmth of the water to splash over him, the water turning orange with blood before it vanished down the plughole. Stood, naked and alone, with pain emanating from all over his body, Bermuda wished for a different life.

A better path.

After a few minutes of quiet pondering he slowly ended his shower, drying himself off with bleak acceptance. He trudged back into his bedroom, changing his underwear and popping on some jeans and a fresh t-shirt before lowering himself cautiously on the edge of a bed he was sure he would never share again.

Immediately shuffling the image from his mind, he gently slid open his bedside table drawer. Sighing to himself, he removed the envelope that housed the most treasured item he had ever owned.

His photo of Chloe.

A drop of water splashed onto her perfect face as Bermuda failed to wipe the tear in time. He missed her so much. All he wanted to be at that moment, was an attentive dad, tucking his daughter in after a bad dream.

He knew a thing or two about them.

Instead, he was nothing but a myth to his daughter, a rumour of a man who once cared but was now running. A life he had thrust upon him had led to a family he chose to abandon.

The Otherside couldn't know. Chloe would always be a secret.

Wiping the relentless tears from the edges of his eye, Bermuda glanced towards the alarm clock.

It was two thirty a.m.

'For fuck sake!' He muttered, stomping to the kitchen and furiously searching for a coffee sachet. After twenty seconds of fumbling, he decided to crack open a can of Doombar and strolled to his living room. The nicely decorated flat was a testament to how much the BTCO appreciated his struggles but it was all for show. He rarely watched anything on TV barring the football and his Xbox was only good for gathering dust.

Amongst a cloud of smoke, he flicked through the channels, apparently the monumental scale of adverts told him he needed the entire cable package yet he found each channel as mundane as the last. He had finished his drink and turned the TV off before he had finished his cigarette.

He checked his phone in a self-deriding hope that Sophie had sent him a message. He had a missed call and a voice mail. Quickly thumbing through his phone, his excitement faded as the call was from Charlotte Foster, his sister.

Like the rest of his family, Bermuda kept his distance, refusing to allow someone he cared about be taken from him by a world he despised. Unlike everyone else, Charles, as he called her, had stuck by him, believing him and the bizarre worlds that he spoke about. She may have just been humouring him, but he appreciated it. He wished he could spend more time with her, form any sort of relationship with her husband and his nephew.

But he wouldn't risk his happiness if it would risk their safety.

The message clicked in.

'Hey Frank. It's Charles. Just ringing to see how you were. It's been a while. I know you are probably hunting some spooky stuff but I just wanted you to know that everyone is fine. George is getting so big now, he is talking and he is really funny.'

Bermuda choked back a tear; his only memories of his nephew were based on photos.

'Mark got promoted which is great but he works late a lot. George will be starting nursery this year and then I will go back too. Anyways, I just wanted you to know I saw Angela and Chloe the other day. Chloe is so beautiful. I took a few photos. I know you won't want them but my god, Frank, you did well there. Ange told me she saw you the other day, said things were the same. She misses you. I miss you.'

Bermuda sobbed, punching the wall in frustration as Charles's voice cracked.

'Give me a call soon, yeah? I love you.'

The line went dead. The phone was hurled across the room in a frustration born from being denied a family.

Bermuda slid his back down the wall, landing on the floor and sat in silence. Time flowed past. Several cigarettes evaporated to smoke. Eventually, when the final tear had perished on his lap, Bermuda wiped his eyes and pushed himself to his feet.

Grabbing himself a beer and fed up with procrastination, Bermuda clicked the light of his office, the desk and papers awash with their sudden brightness. The reports that Argyle had received from Vincent lay on his desk, his two PC monitors lay inactive, usually flashing with the latest video's on YouTube or his latest game of Football Manager.

On the wall was a large, cork pin board which was fairly empty apart from a few receipts and a scattering of business cards. In the corner, the spare pins had been arranged into a smiley face, an ironic notion not lost upon Bermuda.

He slumped into his chest, arching slightly at the pain that shot through his ribs, the bones rattling around like a box of his mints. A few empty boxes lay on the desk, next to the folders from HQ. Swigging from his can and sparking a new cigarette into life, he began to slowly weave his way through the paperwork, begging for semblance of a pattern or story to emerge. All he had so far was:

Barnaby was real.

The world is fucked.

Page after page revealed very little, allowing Bermuda to mutter his views on the police under his breath. He appreciated the losing battle they fought, yet he couldn't help but feel they were on the same side. The constant obstruction and lack of co-operation he was met with had lead him to almost despise them. Ten people missing yet all they had provided were names and locations. A few of them had photographs as well, along with the odd witness statement. Nothing to make a connection. None of the people were related or linked to each other in anyway.

Bermuda had quickly shut that down, using Facebook and Twitter to find any connections between the people. He found himself distracted when he arrived at Jessica's profile, her links leading to Sophie's.

Scowling at the potential feelings growing for the concerned friend, he decided to print out a map of London, dissected into nine sheets of A4 paper. Carefully, he tacked them to the board, lining up the edges perfectly to bring the city to life in his office.

He stood back for a moment, taking a long, concentrated pull on his cigarette before shifting through the folders once again. Slowly, he tacked a photo of Mark Fenton, a forty two year old bus driver, to a street just outside of Brixton.

The first of the stolen.

Systematically, Bermuda pinned the rest to the board, replacing photos with names where needed. All ten of them, logging where they were taken. The whole thing laid out in front of him, the Stolen. Every photo or name tried its best to call to him, to tell him that they themselves had lives. People who cared that they were missing. A life that was stolen.

Bermuda swivelled in his chair, smoked countless cigarettes and made the sensible decision to switch from ale to coffee. His concentration was broken by a knock at the door, a postman with a package for a neighbour. Bermuda hadn't even realised the sun had come up and the world had begun another rotation of its repetitive cycle.

He stared at the wall.

He had discovered nothing.

■ ■ I

The entire complex was a cavern of darkness, a large, spacious arena, lined with metal shutters and glass protected balconies. Potted plants shot out of man-made structures, trying to give the dour décor a sense of nature.

Barnaby sneered at the feeble attempt.

This entire building, a living heartbeat of the city, was usually awash with masses of faceless humans, all slithering over each other in a thirst for consumption. Parting with their pathetic currency for belongings and possessions they would never need. Humanity was a stain, a race of people who pride themselves on what they have, as long as others haven't got it.

Barnaby shuddered at their very existence.

As he sat on the wooden slats that comprised the bench, he looked around, his sharp, bony face taking in all directions. His jet black eyes steered through the darkened corridors, the emptiness of the grand building a harrowing, yet peaceful experience.

Soon his menu will arrive, a walking selection of disgust, all of them idly wandering past, their heads in the proverbial clouds and none of them aware of who – or what - sat amongst them.

The change that was coming.

He was so close now, he could feel it. His tongue sloshed inside his mouth, the muscle running gently over jagged, razor teeth. This wouldn't be the final one, but he was so close. Soon, the convergence would be complete.

He would walk in both worlds.

Just like Bermuda.

A thin smile crept across his scarred face as Barnaby thought of the agent. The pathetic denial of the inevitable. The faint hope he held that he could somehow stop what was coming.

The fool.

Slowly, he wrapped his long fingers on the wood, the echo only for his ears. A shuffle rose from the shadows, Others hiding in the dark and wanting to stay out of his eyeline.

They feared him.

Soon, humans will fear him as well.

Bermuda did. He saw the fear in the man's eyes when he sent

him hurtling through the brick wall. The pathetic realisation that his puny race was just waiting to be vanquished by a supreme being. Bermuda had the gall to question him. To insult him. To stand against him. Barnaby chuckled slowly to himself, knowing he would make Bermuda suffer more than the rest of his appalling race. He would witness how easily Barnaby could change the world.

He would be the first to realise the true consequence of power.

Slowly, one by one, the large halogen lights exploded into life above him.

The soft hum of a floor buffer echoed not long after.

Within hours, this place would be full of people, all of them different. Each one on a different mission, but so like sheep, merging into one as they followed the signs to their latest bargains. They would all walk past, oblivious to his existence.

His next would be among them.

17

It had taken a number of failed relationships and many fractures to his heart before Kevin Brecker knew he had met the love of his life. Carla Peters was everything he could wish for. She combined model looks with her PhD, a high salary and a sense of humour that had him in stitches on a daily basis.

Love had finally dealt him a winning hand.

Now, stood outside the window of a H.Samuel in Westfield Shopping Centre, he gazed at the rings the jeweller displayed so lavishly. The price tags alone should have sent him running, but this was for Carla; he was doing his best to mentally build a savings plan.

Was he really thinking about proposing so soon?

He knew his mother would be ecstatic, the thought of her only child starting a family with such an incredible woman, would cause her to overflow with emotion.

His dad, strict and retired military, would shake his hand. He knew his career in IT hadn't exactly made his father proud, but he knew that having Carla on his arm had garnered a few nods of acceptance.

Yes, he would propose.

The decision was so huge; he wanted to tell her about it and chuckled at having this little secret. His eyes shot about and eventually landed on the ring. To anyone else, it would have been just another golden hoop in a row of hundreds more. But to him it jumped out. It demanded his attention. Thin and understated, it displayed one jewel, a white diamond that glittered gracefully in the shop lighting. His heart began to flutter as he imagined sliding it onto her perfect finger, completing a hand he would hold for the rest of his life.

'Boo!'

Carla's whisper hit his ears, causing him to jump. She laughed playfully.

'Why are you so jumpy?'

'Sorry. Was in a world of my own,' he replied, smiling and running a nervous hand through his thick, curly brown hair.

'What you looking for?' She asked with interest, peeking over his shoulder at the expensive rows before them.

'Just a new watch.'

He smiled, convincingly enough for a frown to fall on hers, her hopes of jewellery seemingly quashed for now. She sighed, two shopping bags swung from her hand as she linked his arm. She looked at Kevin and smiled, his dopey face causing her to squeeze him tighter.

'Where to next?' Kevin asked, knowing their shopping trip was far from over.

'Well, I wanted to pop into Top Shop to see about those shoes. Then I thought maybe we could stop for some food?'

'Sounds good to me. I'm starving. What do you fancy? Cheeky Nando's?

'Babe, it's not cheeky if you plan it.'

They chuckled, walking through a sea of consumerism, waves of people crashing through shop doors and flooding them with purchases. The faint sound of a trashy pop song could be heard, doing its best to float between the thousands of voices of happy shoppers.

They walked silently, Carla scanning the windows of shops, ranking the fashion choices bestowed upon the mannequins that posed awkwardly. Kevin was trying his hand at quick maths, working out a saving plan for the huge decision he had just made.

The sign above stopped him. TOILET.

'Oh, hang on a sec. I need a pee.'

Carla playfully rolled her eyes as he let her go, shuffling beside an elderly couple as he made his way towards the Gents. She watched him pass the vending machines, as well as the large queue of people, waiting to pay for their parking tickets before they tried their best to tackle the London traffic.

She did not see the large man in the top hat, whose jet black eyes had followed her boyfriend the entire walk. She did not see him follow him through the door, into the rest room. Nobody did.

She did not know that Kevin would never return.

■ ▮ ▎

A loud thud against the front door drew Bermuda from his fiery dream, pushing himself up from the desk he had slumped over. Empty cans of Doombar clattered to the floor as he hoisted himself upwards, paper and files strewn erratically around the desk.

He had no idea what the time was, the only thing resonating with him was his ever growing hangover, his brain on a conquest to escape his skull. The moment he saw Argyle he knew what had happened.

Another stolen.

In a silence that only amplified their failure, Argyle waited whilst Bermuda got ready. After a shower and coffee, the BTCO agent was out of the door, the brisk Spring breeze returning and ensuring his long black coat made a reappearance.

Argyle walked beside his partner, carefully dodging the pedestrians that lined Bushey High Street as Bermuda ventured to the shop before heading to his car. He could sense the pain in his partner, the lack of patience he seemed to have and the bags around the eyes. He understood, the notion of sadness, and could only sympathise with the human race for being brought to such a sad extreme it results in actual tears. Pain so hard, it manifests physically.

Bermuda had spoken no more than a greeting as he roughly ripped the plastic off of his cigarettes, lighting one up and coughing out a cloud of poisonous smoke. He thought of his sister's words, the answering machine message that did it's best to rearrange his heart through a million breaks.

'You seem distracted,' Argyle pointed out, standing a few feet away from and towering over Bermuda.

'I'm fine.'

'Do you wish to speak about your feelings?'

Bermuda spluttered a little, smoke etching its way from his stunted chuckle.

'No offence big guy, but I don't think you would understand.'

'Is it about a personal matter?'

Bermuda gave a warm grin, a sign of appreciation to his warrior friend. He puffed a few more times before obliterating the cigarette against a wall.

'Argyle, I'll tell you what. When we catch Barnaby, send his arse back to the Otherside along with a few broken ribs for good measure, you can get me on the couch for a whole fucking session.'

They stopped walking as Bermuda pulled the door open, his car welcoming him with a musky smell of stale nicotine. He dropped into the seat and slammed the door shut. Reversing out of his space, he opened the window, his eyes meeting Argyle's, the genuine concern they emanated made Bermuda question how alone he was in the world.

'See you there, big man.'

As he raced up Bushey High Street, Bermuda laughed at the hand life had dealt him. He had a child. He had friends. Yet the closest person to him, was from a different world entirely.

He turned off of the high street and hurtled towards London to revel in his own failure.

It took a little over an hour to reach Shepherds Bush, the traffic growing in stature as he inched ever closer to the capital's centre. The concrete jungle that surrounded him was alive with movement; people scuttling everywhere like a human ant farm. Not far from the Westfield's Shopping Centre was Loftus Road, the football ground of Queen's Park Rangers. Luckily for Bermuda, the streets weren't awash with a blue and white striped traffic jam.

Bermuda slowly pulled into the parking lot that accompanied the Westfield's, eventually finding a space after navigating the narrow floors and incompetent drivers. He took in the enormous shopping centre as he entered, recalling a visit with Ange a few years ago when it had first opened. Shopping wasn't exactly a keen past time and the idea of being swept up in the avalanche of needless consumerism wasn't one he held favourably. As he stood with his hands on his hips, watching the world slide in and out of shops, his focus was broken by the bass of Argyle's commanding voice.

'Humanity's obsession with money is incredible.'

Bermuda nodded slowly, popping two mints into his mouth.

'I'm not going to argue on that one.'

They both walked through the crowds, Argyle carefully weaving in and out of random groups of people and swinging shopping bags. Bermuda scouted the area, questioning why any place on earth would need three of the same fashion stores. On the first floor, just beyond the escalator, was where they needed to be.

As they slowly ascended, Bermuda sighed deeply as he reached into his jean pocket for the badge that never worked, prepping himself for the same discussion he always had with the law.

He approached the first Police Officer with a look of residual rejection.

'Hello there. Special Agent Franklyn Jones, I believe you are expecting me.'

'Ah, Agent Jones. We have been waiting for you. I'm Sergeant Matthews. Right this way.'

The senior officer strode quickly towards the toilets, leaving a bemused Bermuda standing, his mouth wide open in shock. It had never worked before.

'Are you coming?' Matthews asked, raising his eyebrows in confusion.

'Yeah. Sorry.' Bermuda followed. 'What's the situation?'

'Kevin Brecker. Twenty-eight. Out shopping with his partner, Carla Peters. Goes to take a leak, doesn't come back.'

The Sergeant stopped as they approached the corridor towards the lavatories, the surrounded area taped off, police chattering with intrigued shoppers. A few SOCO's danced in and out of the doorway to the gents, their white suits and masks adding a thin layer of excitement for the viewing public. On the few benches that lay opposite a GAP store, sat a weeping woman, her eyes overflowing with mascara laden tears, a paramedic in attendance.

'That Carla?' Bermuda asked, knowing the answer.

'Yup.' Matthew leant in, his voice reduced to a mere whisper. 'If you ask me, the guy bolted.'

'What? He ran?'

'Come on. She said they were looking at rings at the jewellers. Probably shit him up and he made a break for it.'

'Did she see him leave the toilet?' Bermuda asked, his eyes drawn to Argyle's hulking presence as he scanned the area, his gargantuan arms simmering, preparing to act at any moment.

'Well, she said she watched him go in and then waited right there watching the door.'

'So she would have seen him,' Bermuda stated, trying to end the lazy trail of thought.

'Perhaps. Unless she was Facebooking or what not.'

The Sergeant chuckled, nudging Bermuda in his broken ribs with a bony elbow that sent an explosion of searing agony through Bermuda and made him immediately wish he had been rejected from the crime scene.

'Bermuda.'

He spun, the unmistakeable voice of Barnaby whispered nearby, coiling itself around his head like a snake before evaporating. With a degree of fear, Bermuda spun a few more times, his eyes frantically searching the crowd of people, looking for the black eyes, the top hat.

For anything.

Nothing.

Suddenly, a hand grasped his elbow and he jumped.

'Jesus,' Matthews retorted, jumping himself. 'Did you want to see the crime scene?'

Ghostly pale, Bermuda nodded. With careful steps and a

watchful eye, he slowly trudged behind the commanding officer, following him towards the toilets. As he walked, Argyle's muscular frame loomed over him.

'Are you ok?'

'Yeah.' He scanned the crowd once more. 'Have a feeling he is here right now. Watching us. Goading us.'

'I do not share your worry. I cannot sense his presence amongst your kind and my own in this facility.'

'Don't you get it, big man?' Bermuda stopped, looking up at his partner with a warm, sympathetic gaze. 'He is something else entirely now.'

The words hung between with menace, a damming realisation of how powerful of an adversary Barnaby was becoming. Bermuda continued down the hallway, passed the vacant ticket and vending machines before entering the facilities. The white, shiny floor was awash with forensic gear, the whole team scouring every inch of the bathroom, a few unluckily scanning the often used urinals in search of a clue. The two cubicles were being dusted down, a hopeful SOCO believing they would find at least one bread crumb.

They wouldn't. Bermuda knew this was Barnaby. He had felt eyes on him since he stepped into the shopping centre. Never out in the open, but the eyes lurking from beyond the shadows. The vicious entity existing in the gaps left between people's movements. The final consequence just waiting whilst he played with his humans like pawns.

Suddenly, a crackle from Matthews' radio brought Bermuda back into the situation, the Sergeant excusing himself before making a swift exit, almost colliding with Argyle as they passed.

'He was here,' Bermuda said, not even turning to his partner.

'I agree.' The grey eyes covered the walls, searching for a sign. 'But where?'

Bermuda slowly stepped forward. Carefully treading around the SOCO's as they worked, he approached the first bathroom cubicle. He sighed. Sure enough on the inside of the divider, the same jagged symbol he had found before.

An Arko Feld.

A Gate Maker.

Bermuda shook his head, fighting back the anger of being too late again. There was no way of knowing. No set pattern that Barnaby was using, no selection process for those that he stole.

He had no answer.

Slowly, he felt his arm reaching forward, his fingertips waggling slightly as they yearned for the indent. With every fibre of his being he retracted his arm, unable to stop the contact his fingertips made with the burnt symbol. Instantly he could feel The Otherside, the darkness of its world trying their best to lasso him, wrap him up and drag him through.

'Bermuda.'

Argyle's voice boomed from outside the cubicle, severing the connection. Panicked, Bermuda stumbled backwards out of the cubicle, knowing that Kevin Brecker unsuspectingly walked into that cubicle and was now lost between worlds, his essence now residing in the swirling evil that was Barnaby. As he stumbled backwards, Bermuda almost collided with a SOCO, apologizing with stuttered words.

Argyle's massive frame blocked the other cubicle doorway, his sword shimmering in the light that rained down above them.

'You might want to see this,' Argyle spoke, taking a few steps back to allow Bermuda entrance. He obliged, entering the cubicle before stopping dead.

He saw what no one else had so far. What Argyle had called him to see. Smeared on the wall, in crude, dripping letters, Bermuda had his answer. Barnaby was mocking him. Goading him. He stared at the tiles above the toilet, his fist clenching with rage at what he saw.

'Keep up, Bermuda. Keep up.'

18

'Bermuda, where are you going?'

Argyle's voice boomed through the cordoned area of the shopping centre, the deep bass of his words reaching only Bermuda. Ignoring the question, Bermuda stomped through the cordon, ripping the tape and colliding with the agitated crowd of onlookers.

As a few people gasped or muttered, Bermuda broke free from the group, stomping towards a balcony, his hands grasping the pole and squeezing until his knuckles turned white.

He was failing.

'What is the matter?' Argyle's calm voice followed him. Bermuda shook his head.

'You just don't get it, do you Argyle?'

'What is the it that I need to retrieve?' Argyle stood proudly, his words sincere.

'For fuck's sake. There is no it. We have got people going missing and we can't fucking stop it.'

'It is our duty to...'

'Fuck our duty! Our duty is to stop the Otherside taking over this side and right now, I have as much to go on as anyone else walking in this building.'

Bermuda shook with anger, ignoring the increasing number of eyes that had latched onto him, onlookers stopping to investigate the commotion.

'Then we will find him.'

'Don't you see, Argyle? He has found us.' With an erratic rage, Bermuda pointed to the nearby crowd. 'He is here, watching us. Fucking laughing at us.'

A group of teenagers sniggered to the side, a few of them filming this one man breakdown before them.

'You are upset.' Argyle tried to reach out towards Bermuda, who batted his arm away in anger.

'I'm not upset, Argyle. I am scared.' Bermuda shook his head, accepting the onlookers and their perceived judgement. 'Scared that this is one step too far for us.'

Solemnly, Bermuda began to walk towards the exit, people quickly stepping aside, their fear of a crazy man apparent. Argyle took a few steps to stand directly behind his partner, before reach out with his booming voice.

'You are just scared. It's what you humans do. You get scared and you act out of character. You think everything is coming to an end and you don't know how to handle it.'

Bermuda slowly turned to face his partner, his eyes watering as he heard his own words repeated back to him. Argyle, his concern evident across his face, continued.

'But when you calm down, it's not so bad. Usually the solution is right there and it just takes a little perspective.'

Nodding in agreement, Bermuda wiped his eye with the back of his sleeve. He took a few deep breaths, which rocked his broken ribs before offering Argyle a forced smile.

'There is no solution. Not this time.'

With the grey, pupiless eyes of Argyle watching him, Bermuda turned and continued to the exit. As he passed the rows of designer shops, he could feel the eyes of hundreds of people, all of them backing away and concerned for his mental strength.

He refused to look up.

He could feel one set, amongst the crowd, daring him to.

They burnt straight through him.

The black eyes of Barnaby.

■ ▌ ▏

The lift doors opened, several feet below The Shard and Argyle slowly walked out. His head down and shoulders hunched, the warrior carried the look of a man defeated. The empty hallways of the BTCO headquarters felt tiny, slowly closing in on him.

Bermuda had given up hope.

It was a rare feeling for Argyle, to feel genuine pain at the thought of another person. However, since being teamed with Bermuda, he had found himself genuinely caring for his partner. The sacrifices the man had made, not just for the good of the world but for the good of his family, were astonishing.

Argyle was honoured to protect him.

The sword swung slowly from its clasp, gliding across his powerful back with each step. The sheer number of his own kind that had met the end of the blade would mean he would never be accepted back.

Never be able to cross that threshold again.

This world was his home now.

Ever since his earlier years on The Otherside, the gruelling training and punishing regimes, he knew he would protect. His rise through The Legion's ranks to one of their top ranking warriors felt as natural as breathing.

Then they found out.

Once they knew, he was never allowed back. They would have slaughtered him and all he had held dear.

Bermuda would never know. The facts would remain between himself, Ottoway and his trusted Neither.

He would die before revealing it.

With large, silent steps, he turned a corner, almost colliding with Saira Hunter, a highly respect agent with a penchant for flirtation. Her black hair was tied back in loose pony tail and her brown eyes complimented her brown skin perfectly.

Argyle found her one of the most beautiful of the species.

'Well hey there, handsome!' She offered, her thick, Texan twang escaping her voluptuous, red lips.

'Miss Hunter.' Argyle nodded with respect.

'What brings you here? Don't tell me your gorgeous partner is in trouble again?'

Argyle shook his head as she searched the corridor for Bermuda. Her attraction to his partner had been evident the few times they had acquainted. Behind Saira was her Neither, a small, childlike being with grey skin and a mess of dirty, brown curls that covered its eyes. Argyle was sure it was a female, yet never said a word to it. She was a true outcast of the species, not even named.

Yet she was one of the most deadly Neither's within the entire organisation, linked only to Saira, and Argyle prayed for mercy on any creature, be it human or otherwise, that ever had the inclination to lay a finger on Saira Hunter.

Around its fragile, bony neck was a metal collar, prepared to administer an almost fatal dose of electricity should it get too feral.

Saira loved it, yet was fully aware of the danger that was encased within its tiny frame.

'Well, tell that fine boy of yours to give me a call when he is free. Been dying to take him to the rodeo, if you know what I mean.'

Saira nudged Argyles chest plate with her elbow, winking playfully. Argyle nodded politely before slowly stepping aside. He watched as Saira's heels clicked against the marble floor, admiring the beauty of her body as she headed towards the lifts. Behind her, the Neither scurried, a mop of curls bouncing. Argyle watched until they disappeared into the lift, the small creature reaching up to grab Saira's hand. Even a creature as dangerous as that needed some measure of comfort.

Argyle made his way to the agent chambers, passing a few doors until he came to his own. It slide open, the mechanism recognising his unique DNA on the pad that rested to the side of the entrance.

Once in, he unclasped his weapon. The mighty blade was rested on its stand, Argyle lighting a few incense sticks before falling to one knee.

As he spoke his silent prayer, he wondered of the validity of it all. Should he still persevere with this training? His spiritual connection to the life of a Legion Warrior, when they were so ready to turn on him?

Was he still linked to The Otherside at all?

Tired, he collapsed onto his bed, not thinking of The Otherside. He thought of his new world. The danger that was coming and the seemingly inevitable battle that would ensue.

His fingers reached under his pillow, wrapping themselves around a small ribbon of fabric that was not of this world, but was rich with memory. It intertwined with his fingers, causing a small sense of calm to drift through his veins as he remembered her embrace.

Even a creature as dangerous as he needed some measure of comfort.

His eyelids collapsed over his pupiless, grey eyes and he slept.

■ ▮ |

'Yeah. Am pretty sure you looked like a crazy person.'

Brett offered a kind smile with his words as he raised his pint glass, the last few drops of Doombar slithering down his throat. Sat in the beer garden of The Lord John Russell in Euston, Bermuda nodded in agreement, sparking a cigarette to life and sighing out a cloud of disappointment.

'I just don't know if I can fix this one.'

'I've heard that before,' Brett responded, twirling a cigarette into existence with his fingers. Bristles of tobacco fell from the end, escaping through the cracks of the bench between them. 'Pretty sure you sorted that one.'

'Not this time, mate. This one is different.'

'Why?' Another cloud of smoke into the air.

'This is unlike anything I've seen. Yeah, I've had the odd nasty bastard from their world come over here, but not like this. This thing, this Barnaby...he is more than just a bad shadow.'

'Really?' Brett asked, his eyebrows fraught with concern.

'He threw me through a wall like it was wet tissue. He moved faster than anything I have ever seen. And with every person he steals he gets stronger and closer.'

'Closer to what?' Brett stubbed his cigarette into the ashtray between them. Bermuda took a final puff before following, looking at his friend with resignation.

'Ending the world.'

Brett slammed his hand down on the table.

'Okay, that's enough.'

'I'm not drunk,' Bermuda proclaimed, sipping the remnants from his glass.

'No, I mean we need more alcohol.' Brett flicked his empty glass with a harsh ping. 'This is getting morbidly depressing.'

Bermuda chuckled, edging his way out from the bench, almost colliding with a couple of foreign students who were stood in the alleyway that ran alongside the old pub.

'It's my round.' Bermuda stood, collecting their two empty glasses. 'Watch my stuff.'

Brett gave a thumbs up, watching with a regrettable sadness at the pressure that hung from his friends neck like a medallion. It seemed like a life-time ago that he was best man at his friend's wedding, struggling to hold back tears as his friend tied the knot.

Comparing those times to now, following the divorce, the commitment to a mental hospital and this ongoing war between worlds that he truly believed he was a part of, Brett knew he didn't get the good moments anymore. All those evenings when he was starting out in his band, the lame pub gigs, crammed in the back of baking rooms, performing for the inebriated for minimal credit and constant heckling. Bermuda was there. When he fell off the wagon all those years back, the constant stream of parties as Frozen Death Cull began to pick up fans, their singles slowly beginning to chart. The time he had to be rushed to the hospital due to one sniff too many. Bermuda was there.

Brett sighed, rolling a cigarette between his fingers as he made a silent promise to never turn his back on his best friend. To always make sure that, despite everything, Bermuda was not alone. All he needed was to just let someone in.

As he tapped the now complete cigarette on the table, he glanced through the large, glass windows that ran down the side of the alleyway. There, inside the cramped pub, Bermuda was by the bar, fumbling for cash as the bar maid passed across two more pints.

On the table before him, Brett found Bermuda's phone, the last call registered to him, begging him to join him for a pint. They compromised on Euston.

However, it was not his own number that had caught his attention and Brett smirked as his thumbs quickly began to scatter over the screen as quickly as possible before his friend could return.

■ ▮ ▎

Empty pint glasses began to pile up.

Slowly, the surrounding buildings began to blur, the concrete merging like one constant shade of grey. Bermuda hiccupped, the alcohol bubbling inside his stomach, sitting heavy over his lack of food. The ashtray was over flowing, cigarette butts slipping over the edge like a melting ice cream.

The world was ending and no one believed him.

Sat, staring at the fine indents that ran the length of the wooden panel he rested his arm on, he envisaged the end. The darkness seeping in over the edges as he tried wildly to wave a torch above his daughter.

Chloe. His Chloe.

'Hey, dipshit. Lighter.'

He snapped out of it, lifting his head and catching the glazed eyes of his heavily drunken best friend. Sat next to Brett was a pretty blonde lady, late twenties with a large grin that flashed pearl-like teeth. Without answering, Bermuda scrambled his fingers over the table before him, somehow gripping the lighter and obliging his friend.

Trying his best to look composed, Brett lit his cigarette before continuing his conversation.

'So, Elena, what do you do?'

'It's Elaine and I'm a nurse.' Her accent was thick and deep.

'You're a Scots person?' Bermuda asked, trying his best not to sound accusing.

'I am Scottish, yes.' She flashed her smile again. 'However, I have to go, so are you giving me your phone or not?'

Brett smiled, handing his phone but then playfully pulling it back. She scowled.

'Babe. It won't work.'

'Oh really? Why's that?' She was playing along, slowly getting to her feet, revealing a lovely black top and skinny jeans which Bermuda followed all the way to her boots.

Brett had pulled.

Successfully as well.

'Well let's face it darlin', I'm a musician. You're Scottish.' Brett offered, as she snatched the phone and typed what he hoped was her real number. Handing it back and giving him a playful slap on the side of the face, Elaine and herfriend, who Bermuda hadn't met, disappeared up the alleyway and into the darkness of the London night.

The darkness.

Those black eyes.

The end of the world that was fast approaching.

'Hey.'

He looked up, shocked at the mesmerising beauty before him.

'Sophie?'

Drunkenly, Bermuda stood up, straightening his t-shirt and trying his best not to fall over. She smiled, appreciating he wasn't completely in control of his movements.

'What are you doing here?' He asked, holding the glass covered table for balance.

'You text me, telling me you had something important to tell me?'

Bermuda scowled in confusion.

'No I didn't.'

'Err, yes you did. You said it was about the case and to come here quickly.'

As the mystery wafted around them like the thick clouds of smoke he had blown into the night sky, he couldn't help but notice how beautiful she was. The flickering bulbs that lit the beer garden cast a small shadow that revealed her strong cheekbones, her dark hair tied back in a bun. Her thin, summer jacket hung over her stunning physique.

'You look amazing.'

Bermuda cursed his drunken honesty, failing to realise the effort she had made and the subsequent blushing his compliment had garnered. She didn't know why, but she wanted him to notice her. To look at her as more than just the shouting and crying friend of the recently missing.

She wasn't a hundred percent sure, but she knew there was something about this man that she found attractive.

'Thank you.' She gushed, looking away.

Awkward silence.

'So did you invite me here to tell me I look amazing?'

Bermuda shrugged, trying hard to stand straight and appear sober.

'I don't know. I didn't message you.'

'Then who did?' Sophie demanded, a small frown creasing her immaculate eyebrows.

'Guilty.'

Both of them turned as Brett stood up, both hands raised as he surrendered. In one hand he held his glass, which he quickly emptied with a satisfying 'ahhh'. Bermuda scowled at his friend as he slid his arms into his jacket and stepped from the bench with wobbling legs.

Sophie stood to the side, a look of disappointment etched across her gorgeous face.

'What the fuck?' Bermuda muttered through gritted teeth, leaning in close for Brett's ears only.

'You're welcome.' Brett patted him firmly on the shoulder before turning to Sophie. 'Seriously you are more beautiful than he said.'

Turning back to Bermuda, he threw him a wink before strutting confidently to the end of the walkway and trudging towards the train station. Out of sight, it was just Bermuda and Sophie, stood in the empty beer garden. The spring night was warm, the lights illuminating their evening together.

'Sorry,' Bermuda eventually offered.

'Never mind, eh?' Sophie said, smiling as she stepped into the bench. 'Mine's a white wine.'

As he happily headed for the bar, Bermuda allowed himself something he hadn't for a while.

A genuine smile.

19

Ash flicked onto the wooden bench, missing the recently changed ash tray by a few centimetres. Within seconds, a light breeze swung by, capturing it and dancing away to the unknown. The alleyway had slowly retreated to silence, patrons had either embarked on the rest of their evenings or ventured into the small pub, steeped in an old fashioned charm.

Sophie watched Bermuda as he stared into the shadows at the end of the alleyway, the metal gate leading to a local business's car park shrouded in darkness. She saw nothing of interest, a few shadows flickering across the iron bars.

Bermuda saw them. The two Others slowly scuttling across the floor, as if a few frames were missing from their movements. Juddering and glitching, they rummaged through the bins - any human would merely mistake the commotion for a rat or the wind.

Bermuda could see.

'So you really believe all this?'

Sophie's delicate voice retrieved him from his self-deprecation and he looked up at her, his eyes gleaming with appreciation. His hand grasped the glass of diet coke he had ordered on a quest for sobriety.

'I don't believe it. I know it.'

'It's a pretty wild idea,' she said sceptically, her pristine nails clutching her wine glass as she took a sip. Bermuda pushed another cloud of smoke into the air, and then politely wafted it away from his companion.

'Forget I said anything.'

'No, I want to know what you think.'

'Look, you don't have to humour me. You think this is the first time I have told someone EXACTLY what is going on and they haven't looked at me like I just told them the world is run by aliens?' She chuckled. 'I don't need you to pity me or anything.'

'I'm not.'

Bermuda shrugged, stabbing out his cigarette and glancing back to the alleyway. The two Others were now locked in a struggle, both ripping at each other with vicious, talon-bearing hands.

'The world declared me crazy a long time ago. Now you can either believe me or not, I don't care. But your friend is missing and right now, I'm the best chance you've got of getting her back.'

Bermuda took a swig of his drink, his eyes fixed on Sophie has she let the words sink in. Small tears began to grow in the corners of her beautiful eyes, one droplet escaping and gliding down her cheek.

'How did it come to this?' She spoke, her words meant for no one. Bermuda extended his arm, a gentle hand holding her shoulder.

'The world is so different to what everyone believes.'

'What happened?' She asked, her eyes reaching for him with hope.

'Somewhere along the course of history, we discovered their world. Or they discovered ours. To keep...'

'No. Not that.' Bermuda looked puzzled. 'What happened to you?'

Bermuda was, for the first time in a long time, speechless. A man who prided himself on having an answer for everything immediately knew that this one escaped him. Where did it all begin to crumble for him? At what point did he finally discover the truth?

He forced a smile before taking a sip.

'How did you and Jess become friends?' He asked, changing the subject.

'Oh we met at the modelling agency.' It worked.

'You're a model?' He asked, sizing her up with an exaggerated glare. 'Yeah, I can see it.'

'Oh shut up.' She blushed.

'But you guys are close?' Bermuda offered, embarrassed as he lit another cigarette.

'She is like a sister. When I came to London, well, my family were not impressed. My dad wasn't exactly thrilled that I finished my degree and decided to become a model.'

'I can imagine,' Bermuda agreed, a twinge of pain rocked his broken and beaten chest. A pain calling for his daughter.

'Anyway, she really helped. I mean, London is a big city and I kind of don't know anyone here.'

'It's easy to get lost amongst a lot of people.'

'Tell me about it.' Sophie finished the last of her wine. 'She was in the same boat I was and we kind of found each other. Clung to each other. I just don't know what I would do if I lost her.'

Bermuda gave Sophie a moment to collect herself.

'The world can be a lonely place when you feel like the only person in it.'

She nodded; wiping away tears as they tried to break loose. He rattled the ice cubes in his glass before finishing his coke. She took a deep breath.

'What about you?' She asked, trying to stay positive.

'What about me?'

'Tell me about yourself.'

'I'm an arsehole.'

Sophie laughed loudly, her cackle surprising the both of them as it echoed through the alleyway. Bermuda shrugged sheepishly.

'Nothing to tell you really. Dad was a drunk and an arsehole. He left when I was about three. Apparently, I was too much of a responsibility.'

'Oh, Franklyn.' She reached out and grabbed his hand. Bermuda again shrugged.

'Ah well, what you gonna do? I heard he died when I was about eleven. Drink and drugs. A real role model, you know? Since then, my mum sits in her little flat drinking the days away and I fight monsters from a world nobody believes in whilst this one points and laughs.'

Bermuda took a breath, his disdain for the hand life hand dealt him quickly rushing to the fore. Sophie sat back, sizing Bermuda up with a pitying eye.

'I don't think I'm laughing anymore,' she finally offered.

'I'm not trying to bullshit you. Know that.'

'I do.'

'This other world, it exists. The things that go on behind the curtain, you would never comprehend. But what I do know is that your friend was taken by something that doesn't have a happy ever after for us.'

'What do you mean?' Sophie retreated a little, her eyes watering with fear.

'I have looked him dead in his eyes and have seen nothing but hatred. For humans. For this world. It's just a matter of time.'

Bermuda slid his last cigarette from the packet, tapping it on the table before popping it between his lips. A click of a lighter later and smoke surrounded the two of them.

In the darkness, one Other stood proudly over the corpse of the other.

Sophie was pale.

'Time for what?' She asked, her voice laced with terror as Bermuda took another long drag.

'Till the end of the world.'

Sophie shuddered, her belief growing with her fear. Bermuda leant forward, a smoky mist surrounding him.

'Everything you think you know, forget. Every time you feel something watching you or whenever you see a shadow skip and wonder if something is there … there is. You won't see it, but trust me, it's there. And right now, I have no idea how to find the piece of shit who has your friend or what he has done to her.'

They sat in silence, allowing the cigarette to slowly complete its journey to ash and smoke. Eventually, Sophie broke the silence.

'Will you bring her back?' Her words cracked with sadness. Bermuda slowly dabbed the cigarette into the ashtray. He looked at her with as much hope as he could muster.

'I'm gonna try.'

■ ▮ ▎

Argyle awoke in his chambers, the lights flickering to lit at the mere stirring of his body. He slowly sat up, his chiselled, muscular body aching from the attack on that glorious ship a few nights back. The bruising had faded, yet his brown skin would have concealed any notion of injury.

He stepped from his bed, only wearing the loose fitting, issued trousers that were provided by the BTCO. Shirtless, he approached the mirror, daring his torso to heal completely.

Like the rest of his kind.

The reflection never lied. Before him stood a warrior, his broad chest slashed with scars that should have healed. Rips in the skin that were now a part of his identity, a permanent tapestry of war.

He scanned his arms, the veins popping against bulging biceps. They too wore scars, criss-crossing his skin like Bermuda's artwork. He drew a finger across one, feeling the coarseness of the tissue, remembering the valiant battle in his home world. The demon that confronted him that fell at the end of his sword.

His grey eyes took in the reflection one more time, allowing him to make peace with what he was. His world had turned their back on him a long time ago.

This world had taken him in.

He would protect it.

He would protect his partner.

He walked across the spacious room, his footsteps silent despite his large frame. Along the cabinet, his sword rested on its display unit, the mighty blade that had saved Bermuda's life so many times. With lightning speed, he clutched the handle, spinning the blade around his torso before lunging it forward.

Whatever was coming.

Whoever Barnaby was.

Argyle would be ready.

As he sliced the air, his mind wandered to his partner. The abject sadness that resided within him, the need to self-destruct. A twinge flickered through his body, his pity for his partner shuddering through him.

Bermuda's world had already turned its back on him.

They were both outcasts.

As the blade cut through the room with deadly precision, Argyle made a solemn vow.

They would stop Barnaby.

He would keep Bermuda safe.

Swirling the blade between his hands with a display of extreme dexterity, Argyle knew that he needed his partner.

They needed each other.

As two beings that could walk in both worlds, go beyond limits that no other creature could, they only had each other.

Argyle drew his blade up, the light gleaming off it and he swung it towards the wall, determined to never lose his partner.

■ ▮ ▏

'Well, this has been fun. Awkward, but fun.' Bermuda smiled as he stood, patting his coat to ensure he had enough nicotine and mints for his journey home.

'Where do you live?'

'Not in London.' Bermuda smiled, almost boasting.

'How come?' She asked as she stood, sliding her coat over her toned figure. Bermuda struggled not to look.

'Well, I am just not trendy enough to wear loafers with no socks, grow a huge beard and sit around drinking strawberry beer out of jam jars!'

Sophie laughed, her rapturous happiness echoing out of the alleyway.

'That is so unfair and inaccurate,' she playfully protested.

'You live in Peckham, so you can fuck off,' Bermuda chuckled, tensing his solid chest for the punch Sophie teasingly threw at him. 'I live in Bushey. It's not too bad. Twenty minutes from Euston.'

They walked in silence for a few moments, circling a small park amongst the towering London buildings before making their way towards Euston Road, the giant concrete line that sliced through London. As they strolled towards Euston Station, Sophie linked Bermuda's arm.

For the first time in a while, Bermuda felt attached to the world.

She retracted it quickly as he lit a cigarette as they stopped at the crossing.

'You do know smoking is bad for you?' Obviously rhetoric.

'I know. But then there are an awful lot of things that are bad for you as well. Eating too much chocolate. Drinking too much alcohol. Listening to ABBA.'

Sophie chuckled as Bermuda politely blew his smoke away from her. The cool evening sprinkled them with a slight breeze as they obliged the green man and crossed the road.

'But smoking is medically proven to be bad for you.'

'Sorry, but the 'Medical Professionals' had me certified as insane and locked in a white room for three months. I would rather take my chances.'

Sophie stopped for a second, letting the information sink in and registering the bitterness in Bermuda's voice. He marched on, past the few shops and eateries that adorned Euston station. He weaved through the wooden benches, his mind and heart wrenching back to a few days earlier, when his ex-wife spoke of their daughter.

His Chloe.

Shaking it away, he glanced up at the screen above the entrance to the station; rows of destinations were listed with their departure times. He had ten minutes before his train.

'Well, I guess this is where I leave you.' He offered her a warm smile.

'Is it really true?'

Her voice was sincere, a look of fear across her beautiful face. Bermuda took a step towards her, the breeze reappearing to blow his hair carelessly across his forehead.

'Is what true?'

'Everything. The other worlds. The reason Jess has gone missing. Everything you said. Is it true?'

'Absolutely.' He had never meant a word more in his life.

Sophie anxiously bit her lip, her eyes scouring from the entrance to the station and then back to Bermuda. He took a final puff on his cigarette, flicking the remainder towards the wall.

'Show me.'

'It doesn't work like that.'

'Then make me believe.'

They stared at each other, time ticking between them as he sized her up, his eyes searching for any shred of doubt.

There was none.

All he saw was the most beautiful woman he had ever laid eyes on and her desperation to be reunited with her friend. He cursed the world, for dragging her into the murky space that existed between the two worlds.

The place where he resided.

'Are you sure?' Bermuda asked, taking a small step towards her. 'Once you see it, there's no going back.'

'I'm sure. I need to find my friend. Besides, if what you have said is true, then next to you is the safest place to be.'

She smiled at him, her eye liner smudged by the few tears that accompany the thought of her missing friend. Turning on the spot, she walking into the station, towards the platform that lead to Bushey.

Bermuda sighed, following her slowly and doubting her last statement.

20

Lightning struck outside the window, a clap of thunder soon following. Rain pelted down at a ferocious rate, each drop a wet missile that collided with the planet. Inside the small flat, a five year old Franklyn Jones sat up in his bed, his covers pulled over his knees, his face buried behind it.

The fear came every night.

In years to come, he would use it to monitor the activity, but the curse was something he was yet to understand.

All it brought was fear.

He yearned for his father to race into the room, to tell him everything was going to be alright. However he knew his father was never there and didn't even know what the man looked like. His mum had said he 'wasn't man enough to be a dad', but Franklyn didn't understand.

Mum was probably in the kitchen, drinking that red drink as she did every night, an empty bottle being added to the collection as she dealt with her loneliness.

She had given up on his nightmares.

She always told him to stop being a baby and to go back to sleep. There was no such thing as monsters.

He slowly pulled the duvet back, sliding his head out of the end to take a quick scan of the room. As he did, he saw the creature, hunched on his chest of drawers. Its eyes shimmered in the bolts of lightning, its clawed hands scratching at the wall. It slowly turned his head, baring its large, sharp teeth.

It shrieked.

A five-year-old Bermuda screamed.

No one believed him.

When he opened his eyes, he was sat at school. Eleven years old and keen to learn, he watched as his teacher, Mr Stevens led the class, his voice a mumble of words pertaining to a book he was holding.

He envied the other kids, the ease in which they formed friendships and the care-free way they played during the break times.

They shunned him.

He was the odd one out.

They had heard his stories. The monsters that lived in the shadows. The beasts that adorned his walls in the middle of the night, gnashing at him with sharp teeth and glaring at him with ferocious eyes.

As he sat, he looked through the window to the outside world. The wind was alive and loud, throwing the crisp, autumn leaves through the air with reckless abandon. The sky was heavy and grey, the clouds prepared to break at any moment and drench the world below them.

He looked across the playground to the wall, where he usually spent his lonely lunch times.

There it was.

Long and jarring, it moved with irregularity. Its limbs, too long for its body, were trimmed with sharp, child-killing claws. The eleven year old Bermuda began to shake.

It slowly turned, almost as if it knew he was watching.

It had no facial features.

Slowly, it began to move forward, as if Bermuda had accidently triggered a magnet. It progressed into a gallop, hurtling at great speed towards the school, Bermuda's window directly in its path.

It leapt.

Bermuda screamed and fell to the floor, his classmates panicked and the sound of scraping chair legs filled the room.

The beast had gone.

No one had seen it.

The class began to laugh as a urine soaked Bermuda rose to his feet and ran from the room crying, a mixture of fear and embarrassment pouring from him.

The odd one out had become even more odd.

As he ran through the door he stepped into his University halls, a group of drunk lads were staggering down the corridor and cheered him as he walked by. He caught a glimpse of himself in the window as he turned towards his room, his twenty year old self shining back in all his handsome glory.

He opened the door to his room, only to find his friend Brett in there, a bong in his hand and a fresh cloud of smoke circling the room.

They conversed. About what, he couldn't decipher.

The bong was passed back and forth a few times, the evening becoming a series of photo's as opposed to memories. Somewhere in the dark corners of the building, creatures walked. He had seen them a few times but had kept it quiet.

Only Brett knew what he could see and had been the only person not to laugh it off.

He finally had a friend, and as a cloud of intoxication began to cocoon around him, he realised that he wasn't completely alone in the world after all.

He sat up, his body naked and streaming with sweat. The bedroom was grand; the bed he laid upon was surrounded by four, large posts. Beyond the room was the balcony which overlooked the Pacific Ocean.

Something moved next to him.

It was Angela.

Asleep and also naked, Bermuda recalled their honeymoon. A time when they were happy. The night had been filled with passionate love making, the feeling that his curse had finally released him to a normal life.

As the waves lapped at the beach, he heard their gentle echo.

He slowly nestled back into bed, his hands gliding through the sheets until he felt the soft skin of his beautiful wife.

He leant forward to kiss her.

His lips gently kissed his daughters head, a lame attempt to stop her from crying. The delicate child was held close to his chest and he looked at himself in the mirror.

Finally a father.

Little Chloe screamed in a mysterious agony that he couldn't decipher, but he rocked her gently as he stood in her nursery. The room was a light pink, framed with small teddy bears that danced around the skirting board. A selection of multi-coloured toys lined the room, all of them bought out of love for the small creature he had created with his wife.

Angela slept in the next room, the change to parenthood hitting her hard as she tried to recharge.

Bermuda held his daughter close, never wanting her to grow

another inch nor for time to tick another second. To spend eternity slowly rocking her to a quiet, comfortable sleep would have been perfect.

That was when he saw it.

Its jet black eyes peering through the cuddly toys that were bundled in one of the corners. No bigger than a cat, but with sharp spikes the ran the length of its spine, it leapt out, hissing violently before bounding out of the nursery on its claws.

Bermuda sank into the small chair, holding his precious daughter close to his tattoo-less chest.

He wept.

They were not gone.

They clutched both of his arms, dragging him against his will as he yelled for help. His screams were in vain, he could only see Angela getting further and further away from him, the corridors of the hospital a pale cream that exuded blandness.

He couldn't recall what he yelled.

Nor could he contain the sheer panic as he knew they would throw away the key once they had locked him inside. The world had certified him as insane; the investigation was at the request of his wife.

Angela.

She had finally given up hope. She had turned her back on him, seeing him as a threat and a danger to their daughter.

All he wanted was to protect her.

For two years, they had been arguing about his needless worry, the crazy idea that he saw these beasts in the shadows and how they were never safe. The constant public humiliations of his behaviour. The endless nights she spent crying herself to sleep at the thought of her beloved husband slowly losing his grip on reality.

The courts had sentenced him to the hospital, where he would not be a threat to himself, others and in particular, his family.

He screamed that he wasn't crazy.

They shoved him into his padded room.

His memory made it seem cramped, as if the white, cushioned walls were slowly creeping up on him.

They locked the door as he slammed his fists against it, trying his best to smash it from its hinges.

He took a few steps back and launched himself at the wall.

He stumbled out onto the wooden floor of the Tobacco Docks. Somewhere below him, Others were busy, rustling about one another as the Other's Town market burst into life.

The walls were thin, broken brick and then suddenly he saw him. Barnaby.

Instantly, the dark eyes took hold, latching onto him and never letting go.

The jet black eyes.

The imminent threat of the world ending became very real. He slowly stepping into the room, the walls disappearing to blackness.

He stood, opposite Barnaby with nothing but emptiness around them. His enemy seemed to grow in stature, the imposing threat that loomed over Bermuda and his world.

Within seconds, he turned to a blur, zipping through the darkness and then appearing face to face with Bermuda, his dark eyes centimetres from his own.

'BERMUDA!'

21

Instantly, Bermuda awoke, his hand shooting up and angrily snatching the wrist that was in front of him. His eyes blinked away sleep, his sense returning as he realised himself back in reality.

Sophie stood above him, her face a mask of concern as he quickly released her hand.

'Bermuda,' she repeated. 'We are nearly at Bushey.'

Slowly, Bermuda looked around, ignoring the glares from the drunken passengers. Slowly, he composed himself, lifting himself off of his seat and following Sophie towards the door of the train.

'Sorry, I must have dozed.'

She smiled at him, pressing the button to open the doors as they stopped at the station. They trudged along the platform, exiting the station and passing a few pubs, littered with drunken regulars. They walked in silence, the breeze dancing around them playfully as Bermuda obliterated a cigarette and topped it off with a couple of mints.

They entered his building.

As they stood in the hallway outside of his flat, he sheepishly turned to Sophie, her perfect eyebrows raised in expectation.

'Right, not gonna lie. The place may be a bit of a tip.'

'Please. I live with a model. Do you think we do cleaning?'

'Well....yes,' Bermuda answered, smirking as she playfully shoved him. He gritted his teeth, trying his best to vanquish the flaming sensation of his broken ribs. He opened the door and even he was appalled at the smoky staleness that clung to the air.

He instantly stormed in, popping open a few windows in the kitchen and stealthily trying to hide unwashed plates in secluded cupboard space. Sophie watched with interest, slowly losing herself in his unintentional charm. After a few moments of cluttering about, he turned and faced her, an awkward smile etched across his stubbled face.

'Drink?'

'Yes, please.'

He quickly fixed her a glass of wine, cracking open a can of Doombar and uncharacteristically poured it into a glass.

'This way.'

He led her through the hall, passed the neat yet minimalistic front room to his office, which exploded into view at a flick of a switch.

Sophie was speechless.

It was like everything she had seen on TV.

A large map of London was hammered to the wall, photos and post-it notes tacked onto it. The desk was covered in folders and sheets of paper, empty beer cans decorated the edges of the room. Cigarette butts had been strewn around like confetti.

Again, Bermuda opened a window, before taking a swig of his drink and addressing his guest.

'This is it.' He walked towards the desk. 'Ground zero.'

'What is this?' She asked, her eyes glued to the board.

'It's a whole wall of 'I don't have a fucking clue', Bermuda said, defeat straining his words.

'Are all these people missing?'

Bermuda nodded. Sophie shook her head, before her eyes fell on the photo of Jess. It was the one she had provided to the police several days ago. Her friend burst from the page, her vibrant smile betraying the danger of the situation. A tear rolled down Sophie's cheek.

'Can you find her?'

Bermuda rested a hand on her shoulder, knowing any sort of comfort would do.

'I'm doing my best,' he reassured her. 'I know who has her. I just need to find him.'

Sophie sniffed, gratefully accepting the tissue that Bermuda handed her from the chaotic desk. The wind infiltrated through the open window, sheets of paper shuffled.

'What are you going to do when you find him?'

She turned to Bermuda, her beautiful face inches from his.

'I'm going to get Jess, then I'm gonna kick his arse.' Bermuda coaxed a smile from her. 'I owe him.'

'Yeah?' Jess sniffed away her final tear. 'You promise?'

Bermuda looked her dead in the eye.

'I promise.'

She stepped forward and wrapped her arms around him, instantly retracting as he groaned in pain. She bounced back, worried.

'What?' She said, panicked.

'Nothing.' Bermuda struggled towards the door. 'Fuck.'

He stumbled forward, his shoulder colliding with wall of his hallway, a memory worth framing swinging and dropping to the floor.

Sophie hurried after him, helping him to a vertical base when she recoiled.

'You're bleeding?' She said, her eyes wide with fear.

'It's nothing,' Bermuda lied, reaching for the bathroom door and stumbling over the threshold. The door slammed against the wall, echoing against the white tiles. Sophie stayed in the doorway, afraid to encroach on his privacy.

Afraid to leave him in pain.

With a few grunts of pain, Bermuda eased himself out of his t-shirt, the white garment heavy with a crimson stain. He dropped it to the floor, staring ahead at the mirror.

He winced with agony.

Sophie took a breath. She had noticed his physique a few times, aware that he obviously took care of himself. But she was impressed with the muscular shape of his back, the muscles sharp and well defined.

The tattoos were incredible. His entire upper body was covered in ink, a tapestry of letters and symbols. Hours of work, pain and countless sittings. His entire body was a work of art.

She couldn't take her eyes from it and was realising she didn't want to.

'You want proof that The Otherside exists?' Bermuda's question pulled her from her thoughts, reminding her of the blood stained t-shirt that carpeted the floor. Slowly, Bermuda turned around, his chiselled body spoilt by the three large gashes that ran across his chest.

Sophie stared, dumbstruck. Blood trickled down his stomach, sliding across the words that were supposed to protect him. The wounds above were a testament to a job failed.

Under his right arm, a foul bruising was beginning to dominate, his cracked ribs shaking around like a box of his beloved mints.

He was a mess. The walking wounded.

Slowly, Sophie stepped into the bathroom, silently running the flannel under the tap before approaching him. With genuine care, the first he had experienced in a while, she dabbed at the slashes that shook her to the core.

'Who did this?' She finally asked.

'You mean what.'

She gently dabbed, the flannel shifting from a light blue to red instantly. Bermuda grimaced, sucking air in through his teeth and clenching his fists. After a few more dabs, Sophie ringed the flannel over the sink, a faded red rain falling down into the porcelain bowl.

'You need to be careful.'

'This is careful.'

She scowled at him, not reciprocating the smile he flashed. He gently lowered himself onto the edge of the bath, gently lifting a cigarette from his pocket. Holding a now ruined towel to his wounds, he blew smoke into the air.

'You really shouldn't smoke,' Sophie warned him, waving the smoke away from her.

'This is my flat,' Bermuda stated. 'Besides, there is another world trying to end ours and I'm in a shit load of pain. I think I'm allowed.'

Sophie snatched it from his fingers, taking a long draw before exhaling the smoke with a cough. He chuckled, retrieving his cigarette.

'Where am I going to sleep?' Sophie asked, her presumption catching Bermuda off guard.

'Erm, you can take my bed.' Bermuda pointed to the room across from the bathroom. 'I'll take the couch.'

She smiled her thanks before slowly walking towards his room. Bermuda struggled to his feet, eager to ensure the room wasn't too messy. His ribs ached, his chest roared with agony. Yet he found himself smiling.

That faded as soon as he entered the bedroom.

'What the hell are you doing?'

His angered words caused Sophie to spin in fear. The drawer by his bed was open. In her hand, was a photo.

'I'm sorry.' She murmured. 'The draw was open...'

Bermuda stormed around the bed and snatched the precious picture from her hand, sliding it back in the envelope and slamming the drawer shut with a furious slam. He slowly calmed, his breathing deep and purposeful. Sophie waited a few moments.

'Who is she?'

'They can't know about her.' Bermuda shook his head, walking slowly towards the window. The street light opposite cut through the curtain, basking his toned body in a golden glow. He glanced the scowl on his face in the reflection.

'Who can't?'

'Have you not been listening to me?' Bermuda turned, his eyes watering. Sophie slowly walked towards him, mortified by his emotional state. 'They are everywhere and they have ripped my world apart and ruined my life for as long as I can remember. I won't let them ruin hers.'

'Who is the girl?'

Bermuda wiped away a tear, which twinkled under the invasive light.

'Chloe. My daughter.'

Sophie slowly reached out a hand, sliding her palm across his rounded shoulder, squeezing gently as a measure of comfort.

'She is beautiful.'

Bermuda nodded, trying to smile but finding himself battling more tears. He craved his daughter, to feel her arms around him as he hugged her.

To hear her refer to him as 'Daddy'.

To just be part of her life.

After a few moments of silence and a small barrage of tears, Bermuda let out a deep sigh, shaking his head. Sophie gently rubbed his shoulder, her heart beating faster for the broken man before her. Finally, the silence that rested between them was pierced.

'I'm sorry.'

'What for?' She whispered, taking a small step closer.

'I exist between two worlds, yet I don't feel I belong to either one of them.' Bermuda shook his head. 'It's a lonely place to be.'

Very gently, Sophie reached out her hand, sliding it against the stubble that framed Bermuda's jaw. She turned his face, tear stains twinkling on his cheeks. She looked into his bloodshot eyes, the connection between the two of them almost complete.

'You are not alone.'

They leant in, their lips locking as they slowly began to kiss. Their tongues wrapped around each other, slithering like snakes as he slowly ran his hand up her spine. She ran her fingers through his hair, before sliding her hands down the contours of his muscular back.

They fell onto the bed, still locked in their passionate embrace as they allowed the world to be enveloped in darkness around them.

Bermuda forgot what world he was a part of.

He didn't care.

As Sophie held onto him, pushing her lips against his harder and harder he felt something beyond attraction.

He felt his loneliness evaporate.

■ ▮ ▏

The world had succumbed to the night sky once again, the streets empty and tranquil. A light breeze sent litter scurrying along the curbs, weaving in and out of the wheels of parked cars.

The entire street slept.

Even if they were wide awake, they wouldn't have seen him. His long, powerful frame. The tatty suit that clung to it. The large top hat that adorned the scraggy, white hair. The jet black eyes.

Barnaby sneered at the buildings as he strode past, his disdain for the human race even begrudging them sleep. He slowly ventured down the street, waiting until he could feel it.

The call of the Otherside.

He glared into the shadows that slid off of the building, the family of Other's taking refuge in the darkness shuddered with fear. He flashed them a jagged, brutal smile that caused them to shield their eyes.

Pathetic.

Just like the humans.

He approached the door to the building, slowly walking through the barrier as if it was a hologram. He was not yet complete with this world. His convergence would soon be at an end.

This world would be his.

Everything would change.

He lightly whistled as he climbed the stairs, his steps measured and slow. After passing through a few more doors, he had arrived, his dark eyes taking in the humble surroundings.

Soon it would all be dust.

He had only one more doorway to create.

One more life to merge.

This one, it had to count. It had to render Bermuda helpless. He wanted to ensure that his adversary, the man who was foolish and arrogant enough to claim that his species was dominant, would suffer.

He would not only fail.

He would break.

As he slowly wandered through the hallway, he stopped as he approached the bed.

The couple that lay across it were asleep; their arms wrapped around each other, ensuring their proximity would be felt throughout their slumber.

They were half clothed, suggesting to Barnaby that they did not make love, yet found themselves lost in the throes of passion still. He watched as Bermuda and Sophie slept soundly, their bodies moving together as they breathed gently. His eyes burned into Sophie, taking in what he saw.

Not a person.

But a reason for Bermuda to care.

22

Bermuda awoke early, his dreams of watching his daughter ripped into pieces by the world that hated him, apparently calmed by the presence of Sophie. She lay peacefully, dark hair cascading carelessly across her face. Her breathing was soft. Peaceful.

He smiled.

Watching her sleep, he was glad that they hadn't had sex the night before. He had lost count of the number of mornings where he ushered a girl out of the house, the memories of the night messy. Their name forgotten.

Not Sophie. She was special.

They had kissed passionately, falling into each other's arms on the bed. The pain that shot through his body vanished at the mere touch of her lips, an antidote in the form of a kiss. Before they undressed each other, they realised what the moment meant.

They had found someone. Brought together by a tragedy.

They had lain together all night, sharing the odd gentle kiss when one said something the other one appreciated. Eventually they were lost to slumber, Bermuda protectively coiling his arms around her tight body.

He slowly slid his arm out from under her, pausing as she murmured before failing to wake. Calmly, she returned to the pillow, comfortably asleep as Bermuda eased himself off of the bed. His ribs ached, the pain unbearable as he necked two pain killers he retrieved from his cabinet. He looked at himself in the bathroom mirror, slowly shaking his head. The swelling around his eye was starting to ease, the bruising fading leaving his skin a feint brown as if it had been dabbed by a tea bag. The large cut was healing well, the stitches holding.

Across his chest, the three scratches looked fresh and radiated in agony. He slowly dabbed at them with a wet flannel, remembering the tender moment he shared with the woman who slept in the next room.

He was a mess.

Cursing the reflection, he crept from the bathroom towards the kitchen, his body craving caffeine and nicotine in equal measure. As the coffee machine slowly drizzled the final droplets into his mug, Bermuda reached for his cigarettes.

'JESUS!'

Argyle stood in the doorway, his colossal frame filling the entire walkway. Bermuda put a hand on his heart, feeling it furiously rattle against his broken rib cage.

'Apologies.' Argyle spoke calmly. 'I did not mean to startle you.'

'I'm gonna put a bell on you,' Bermuda joked, lighting a cigarette.

'That would merely compromise my armour.'

'Yeah, well it will reduce the risk of my impending heart attack.' Bermuda sipped his pipping coffee.

'Coffee?' He jokingly asked an unimpressed Argyle, who entered the kitchen.

'Yes please.' They both turned as Sophie appeared in the

doorway, holding the frame with both hands and gently swaying. She had tried to neaten her hair, but her face was adorably sleepy. Bermuda flashed her a smile, ignoring the sceptical look on Argyle's face. She slowly entered the kitchen, walking past Argyle and completely unaware of his commanding presence. She slid her hands around Bermuda's waist as he prepared another mug, the coffee machine humming back to life. Resting her head against his back, she felt safe.

He smiled to himself.

Argyle coughed loudly, knowing full well she couldn't hear him. Instantly Bermuda slowly broke from the embrace before sheepishly getting the milk.

'Everything ok?' Sophie asked, her words laced with caution.

'Yeah I'm fine.' Bermuda smiled. 'Did you sleep well?'

'For the first time since forever.' She smiled with appreciation as he handed her the coffee. 'Thanks.'

They stood in silence for a moment, Bermuda opening the window to allow the stale fog of smoke to slowly filter. He glanced at Argyle, the shake of the head told him that his partner didn't approve.

'So what's the next move?' Sophie asked, innocently moving to the counter, causing Argyle to carefully slide around her.

'I'm going to find this guy and bring your friend back. Pretty much.'

'Actually, you have a conduct meeting in front of The Committee.' Argyle interjected.

'What?' Bermuda angrily responded.

'What?' Sophie, confused at the random outburst.

'Sorry.' Bermuda frantically thought of an explanation. 'I thought you said something.'

'Are you sure you are ok?'

Bermuda slowly approached her, aware that Argyle was casting an eye over his every move. He didn't care. He could feel himself falling and he didn't want to hit the ground yet.

'I'm great.'

He kissed her gently, her lips curling upwards into a grateful smile.

'See. This world isn't all bad, is it?' She swung gently on her heels, her arms wrapped around his neck.

'It's not this world I'm worried about.'

He gently released her grip, before heading back towards the bathroom. The shower burst to life and Sophie checked her phone whilst finishing her coffee. Sat at the messy kitchen table, completely oblivious to the hulking warrior that stood next to her.

After about fifteen minutes, Bermuda strode back into the kitchen, his tie-less shirt was open at the collar, the grey suit well fitted. His wet hair was combed backwards, neatly parting at the side.

Sophie smiled.

'You look very nice.'

'Thanks. I feel like a muppet.'

She stood, straightening the lapels of his blazer. He winced slightly, his broken torso sending a painful reminder.

'Help yourself to towels, coffee, food if there is any.'

She reached up and kissed him mid-sentence. They stood for a few moments, gently swaying as their lips locked. Argyle rolled his eyes.

'I have to go.' Bermuda smiled.

'Just be careful.'

Bermuda opened the door to his flat, allowing Argyle to squeeze through, his gigantic sword clanging against the wall. He turned back, smiling one more time at the woman before him.

'Careful is my middle name.' He slowly closed the door, but then pushed his head back through. 'Actually, it's Michael.'

'Go!' Sophie playfully pushed his head out of the door, closing it firmly. Bermuda stood on the spot, smiling. After a few moments, he turned only to find an unimpressed Argyle waiting, arms folded and head shaking.

'What?'

Bermuda protested the entire walk to the train station.

■ ■ |

The meeting went as expected. Ottoway, true to his word, was not in attendance. Apparently, his support was not something Bermuda would ever get to witness. The Committee were, as always, tightly wound, like coiled springs ready to burst forward.

The sneering senior chair, Montgomery Black, was his usual, sanctimonious self. His large nose flopping from a dreary face that had been working alongside The Otherside for over half a century.

Mopped with a dusty, grey comb over, he constantly looked at Bermuda over his spectacles, as if disciplining a naughty school child.

The other three members took their turns, sniping at Bermuda with well-placed misconduct charges and cheap shots at his character defects. When Marion Wiggins, a field agent for thirty years before she retired to a life of BTCO Beauracracy, questioned why he felt it appropriate to punch a fellow agent in the face, she wasn't best pleased with Bermuda's response of 'because he's an arsehole'.

Bermuda put his case forward when given the chance. The constant provocation of Hugo for the past three years. The jealousy of his French victim, who himself was a fine agent, was bordering on obsessive and Bermuda felt that Hugo initiated the confrontation, knowing full well Bermuda had recently been attacked.

When the Committee questioned Argyle's performance, Bermuda took a stand, refusing to allow his partner's reputation or commitment to be questioned.

'We wouldn't be the first.' Wiggins retorted, much to Bermuda's agitated confusion.

After all of the deliberation, Bermuda was sent out of the room for the final judgment to be decided. He slowly lowered himself onto the wooden bench opposite the grand, double doors to the Committee's chambers, sighing heavily. His ribs ached and he longed to be back beside Sophie.

'Not exactly the group you would invite to a party, huh?'

Bermuda offered a smile as Ottoway lowered his slightly large frame onto the bench, his three-piece suit immaculate as always.

'I don't know. I'm pretty sure Wiggins fancies me.'

The two men chuckled and then sat for a moment in silence. After what seemed like an eternity, Ottoway spoke.

'Do you want to know why they are coming down so hard on you?

'Because I don't play nice with others?'

'No. Look, you and I both know Hugo can be a pain in the backside. But you can't just punch people because you don't like them.'

Bermuda rattled a few mints around before popping them into his mouth.

'I don't know, seems like a pretty good reason to me.'

He offered the mints to his superior who politely waved them away.

'They come down hard on you so they can come down hard on me.'

Bermuda turned, his eyebrows raised in confusion.

'I don't follow.'

'You have spent the last three years working for the BTCO, Jones. Sometimes, even with distinction. However, do not think we do not realise you hate what your life has become. You see your gifts as the bane of your life.'

'What life?' Bermuda spoke, his voice rising in volume and anger. 'Whatever is wrong with me, whatever part of my DNA decided to fuck up, it has ruined every part of my life. So don't try and dress it up as a gift.'

'You are more than an agent, Jones.'

'I'm a pain in the arse.'

'No, you are the balance.'

Bermuda turned once more. Embarrassed, Ottoway straightened his tie, coughing slightly and trying to break the tension.

'What the hell do you mean?' Bermuda's question was laced with venom. Ottoway slowly rose to his feet.

'Do you think this job is easy? Do you believe the Otherside is happy living in our shadows? Slowly, the truce is snapping under the weight of expectation and realisation. They outnumber us three to one. There are more cases of Others with latch stones in the past two years than there has been in the previous twenty. The Committee wants to bend over, let more of them in, however I have opposed them at every turn. You want to know why?'

Bermuda looked up, shrugging his shoulders and craving a cigarette.

'Because this is OUR world, Jones. We are the thin line that divides our world from theirs and believe me, that line is getting thinner by the day.'

'So wait, they are pissed at me because of you?'

'No. They are pissed at me because I brought you in. You are the one that can walk in both worlds. That is power that has never been seen before and while it sits on our side, the balance is maintained.'

Bermuda nodded slowly, his eyes widening as realisation grabbed him.

'Wait. Walk in both worlds. That's what Barnaby said. It's why he wants to Converge.'

'Eliminate the balance and the scales tip.' Ottoway stared at Bermuda, his eyes pleading for him to understand.

'What do you need?' Bermuda asked, pushing himself from the bench and approaching his boss. A new respect hung between them, threatening their usual repertoire.

'I need you to go in there and say sorry, agree to the punishment, find Argyle and then do what it is that you do best.'

'Drink and look good doing it?' Bermuda broke the seriousness, hoping to lower the tension. Ottoway smiled politely.

'Finding people.' He patted Bermuda on the back firmly before pulling out his pocket watch. He nodded his appreciation to his agent before slowly walking down the corridor. Bermuda took a few moments, allowing the speech from Ottoway to resonate in his mind a little longer. Just before his boss was rounding the corner, he spoke up.

'What if I can't stop him?' Ottoway turned at the question. 'What if I fail?'

Ottoway snapped shut his pocket watch.

'Then the balance shifts to the point that it can't shift back.'

The words echoed through the empty corridor, surrounding Bermuda like an angry swarm. Ottoway disappeared, his backing of Bermuda coming as a welcome shock.

His hatred for his curse had caused him to despise a world that knew no different. The families and relationships that passed him by in the streets, oblivious to the reality of the world and taking themselves for granted.

All the things he longed for and craved that existed in the world hung on him being him.

Being an agent of BTCO.

Being Bermuda Jones.

Suddenly the large lock unlatched with a clang and the massive door slowly opened. The secretary, who had sat in the corner of the Committee chambers scribing, poked her head through the gap.

'Mr Jones, please come back in.'

The door sounded like thunder as it slammed behind him.

23

Hugo LaPone grew up in Paris, France in a life of luxury. His parents, Yohan and Amelia, were both highly acclaimed doctors, working in Paris General Hospital and forging careers as two of the best medical professionals in the country.

Living a charmed life as an only child, Hugo believed for many years that his visions were just imagination, his need for companionship manifesting in all of its childish exuberance. Slowly, throughout his teenage years, he began to understand the severity of his visions.

We were not alone in the world, yet he was alone in seeing it.

As he approached his late twenties, Hugo began to communicate with The Otherside, as an Other took up residence in the alleyway behind his bachelor pad. Ever the ladies' man, Hugo never settled down into married life. His handsomeness only outweighed by his arrogance.

As his friendship began to grow with the Other, so did his interest. The next few years were filled with research and solitude; with Hugo working like a man possessed to prove that he was not crazy. That another world existed.

But eventually, he kicked one bee hive too many and was brutally savaged by an 'Alpha', a large Other with a penchant for violence. Just before he could land the killer blow, the Alpha was tackled by a thin, reptilian Other who would recruit Hugo to the BTCO.

Marco.

Eight years later, they were the stand out agents in their sector. With the BTCO performing with minimal staff and under the radar, their sectors were vast and few. Hugo could be assigned a case anywhere in Europe, having been sent to investigate disturbances in small village in Hungary, to having Marco battle an Other outside The Coliseum in Rome.

Eight years on and he was the one held in the highest regard.

Then Bermuda was recruited.

Never one to admit jealousy, Hugo took an instant dislike to the man. He was quick witted and handsome, an immediate threat to what Hugo had prided himself on. He was confident without being cocky and genuinely seemed to despise his gift. Yet for some reason, he was bestowed with what Hugo had always dreamt of. The ability to walk in both worlds.

When the rumours began to circle, that a man had been to The Otherside and returned, Hugo refused to believe it. When that man, Franklyn Jones was promoted instantly to an Agent, he almost knocked Ottoway's door down in protest.

The man was untrained and more importantly, unprepared for what to expect yet Ottoway kept saying it was being overlooked due to the benefit.

The man was a ticking time bomb and about as subtle as one to boot.

Whilst Bermuda slowly began to forge a reputation as a man who gets results yet completely ignores the rules, Hugo began being ignored, only being handed the cases that either involved hours of travel or mind numbing paper work. Soon, all of the back slaps seemed to head Bermuda's way.

All because he could interact.

Hugo spent hours, praying and wishing for the ability. For it to be stripped of such a reluctant host and given to an agent worthy of such power. All he wanted was to be seen as what he truly was.

Better than Bermuda.

Now that chance had come. Whilst he stood for the returning Committee members, Hugo glanced to his right. Bermuda also stood, scrubbing up surprisingly well in his suit. If only he had made such an effort to be a decent agent, he wouldn't be here.

The Committee had seen the evidence, heard the eye witnesses and were forced to do the right thing. The plasters strapped across Hugo's obliterated nose, held the bones in place. Both of his eyes wore a dark shade of purple.

There were no excuses and no Ottoway to protect him.

As the Committee took their seats and asked the two agents to be seated, Hugo could barely contain his excitement. Bermuda would be gone.

'Mr Jones, please stand.' Montgomery Black spoke, not looking up from his papers. Bermuda begrudgingly obliged. 'The Committee has reached a final decision in regards to your punishment, regarding the breach of conduct. Enlight of your assault on Agent LaPone, you are hereby sentenced to suspension, pending further investigation.'

'But sir...' Bermuda tried to speak.

'DO NOT INTERRUPT ME!' His words were oozing venom. 'This has taken into account your recent, careless defacing of public property and the cost of damages to London landmarks. You are hereby instructed to issue a formal apology to Agent Lapone and then hand over your badge and any weaponry the BTCO has been foolish enough to bestow upon you.'

Hugo smirked, fist pumping privately as he watched his nemesis ostracized by those who knew best. The Committee waited and Bermuda took a few moments. Slowly, he pushed his chair back and looked at them all.

'Ladies and Gentleman, may I say a few words.'

A few quiet murmurs.

'You have the floor.' Wiggins waved him to the space between their elevated desk and the tables that the two agents sat at. Bermuda slowly walked before them, looking them all in the eye.

'Look at me,' Bermuda urged. 'Take a good look.'

The Committee members mumbled in confusion, theirs drawn to the battered state of Bermuda's face. His eye, still slightly swollen was framed by bruising and a thick scar.

'I didn't ask to be an agent. In fact, I never asked for any of this. All I ever wanted was to see the world the way everyone else does. To be able to work a nine to five and go home to a house full of love and happiness. To be able to at least hold my daughter and tell her I love her. But I can't.

'I can't because this world isn't the only world out there. We all know this but we can't share it. We manage it. We keep an eye on it so the people who have the lives we crave get to have them. Their perfect world surrounded by a more dangerous one they don't know exists.'

'Get to the point, Jones,' Black spoke, agitated at the gall of the young man before him.

'You need me.'

Bermuda stared at the members before him, feeling the words of Ottoway resonating within him.

'Excuse me?' Black responded, veins straining against his

temples with rage.

'You need me. It's ok, because I'm starting to realise that I need you too. I need a purpose. This curse, or whatever the hell it is, has ruined my life but I won't let it be for nothing.'

'You're saying it is your destiny?' Wiggins chipped in, Bermuda sensing that she was slightly warming to him.

'No.'

'Then what?' Black demanded, his thick, grey eyebrows scrunched into a frown.

'Right now, Barnaby is out there and he's stealing people. He's bringing this convergence to its end. He's already stronger than me and when his connection with our world is complete then we are screwed. I don't know when or where that will be but right now, I'm the best chance you got.'

An awkward silence sat in the room as Bermuda looked around the room.

'Now I am an arsehole, I know that. But there are still a few things left in this world worth fighting for. So let me for fight them. Let me find Barnaby and try and stop him. If I do, I will walk back in here, give you my badge and take whatever punishment you want.'

'And if you don't stop him?' A cynical Black asked, his arms folded in disappointment at the sense Bermuda's words relayed.

'Then it doesn't really matter does it?' Bermuda shrugged. 'We will all be erased.'

A look of panic was shared by the senior members. Bermuda stepped forward, experience a feeling of acceptance for the first time.

'Let me be the balance.'

The Committee members huddled together, their scattered whispers inaudible to Bermuda or his adversary. Hugo angrily watched on in disbelief.

Black cleared his throat.

'Very well.'

'Thank you. All of you.'

Bermuda turned to leave as Hugo slammed his fists angrily on the table.

'What the hell?' His French accent more prominent with rage. 'This is an outrage.'

'Oh and on the grounds of apologising to my fellow agent, Hugo,' Bermuda interrupted, looking his sneering colleague up and down. 'I'd rather have intimate, first-hand knowledge of Barnaby's ball bag.'

Wiggins sniggered as Black just shook his head.

'Dismissed.'

■ ▌ ▏

Hugo slammed through the doors, marching angrily down the corridor and turning the air a shade of French blue. Before the doors could rock back on their hinges, Bermuda emerged, a look of determination on his face which quickly turned to surprise.

'I assume it didn't go Hugo's way?' Vincent mused, a wry smile across his ancient face.

'He'll be fine.' Bermuda shook a couple of mints into his hand. 'He just needs to be less of a dick.'

'Quite.'

'What can I do for you, Vincent?'

'I've been looking for you.'

'You and everyone else it seems,' Bermuda joked, crunching the mints between his teeth.

'I have been doing some research in regards to your condition.'

Bermuda reached out, grabbing Vincent by the arm and

leading him to a quiet nook just off of the main corridor. Vincent, taken slightly aback by Bermuda's ability to manhandle him, shook him off.

'Let's not broadcast that, eh?'

'Unhand me.'

'Sorry.' Bermuda held his hands up in apology, looking around to ensure they were alone. 'What have you found?'

'Well, it would seem that Barnaby's actions with regards to his convergence had caused an anomaly in the existence with your world and that of my own.'

'Meaning?'

'Meaning his plan to merge with this world is nearly at fruition. Hence why he was able to hurl you through that wall.'

'No, he had a latch stone. I saw it hanging around his neck,' Bermuda responded, shaking his head in disagreement.

'Well it would seem that would soon be rendered useless. With the results of my tests, I would conclude he need only steal one more person for a convergence, before his dream becomes reality.'

'And our reality becomes a nightmare.'

'Exactly.' Vincent's grey skin looked even paler. 'He needs to be stopped.'

Bermuda nodded, patting the senior Neither on the shoulder before turning to head towards the exit and sweet release of a cigarette.

'The convergence will reach out to you too,' Vincent called out, causing Bermuda to stop in his tracks. He turned, eyebrow raised and a flurry of questions racing through his mind. He strode back across the corridor, footsteps echoing.

'What the hell does that mean?' Bermuda asked, trying hard to mask the fear in his voice.

'Like you said, The Otherside is trying to claim you. Pull you back.' Bermuda reluctantly agreed. 'Well with the anomalies disrupting the link between the worlds, that pull could be considerably stronger.'

'So basically, anything Otherside is a no-no?'

'That is correct.'

Bermuda drew a sharp breath through gritted teeth, weighing up the new information.

'I guess I'll just have to take my chances.' He reached out to pat Vincent on the shoulder, before stopping a few inches away and then retracting. He flashed the Neither a grin, before marching towards the elevator to return him above ground and back to the real world.

As the doors opened, Vincent spoke.

'What are you going to do?'

Bermuda looked up at him, for once, truly accepting the size of the task and the responsibility that rested with him.

He thought of kissing Sophie one more time.

He imagined being able to hold his daughter once again.

The doors began to slide shut.

'I'm going to save the world.'

They closed, the elevator whizzing back towards civilization as Vincent stared at the steel doors before him.

'Good luck,' he quietly said to himself, hoping beyond hope, that Bermuda would be as good as his word.

24

When Bermuda stepped out onto the street, he took a deep breath. The air always felt fresher having been in the HQ, as if he were slowly being suffocated below. He looked around at the tourists all lining up to visit The Shard, peering up and wondering if Ottoway was on the viewing platform, casting a watchful eye over the city.

The fresh air soon turned to cancerous smoke, as Bermuda lit a cigarette, slowly strolling across the bright, white concrete that led to London Bridge station. Decked out in his suit and his hair slicked back, he could have passed for a London office worker, rushing through the rat race to be at his desk on time.

But he wasn't.

He was an agent of the BTCO.

He was humanity's best hope of survival.

Part of him wanted the world to turn and thank him, pat him on the back in gratitude for his sacrifice. The thought of being believed was one Bermuda had experienced every single day of his life.

But now he didn't want to be believed.

He wanted the world to continue in its naivety, to continue with its life without knowing it could come crashing to an end in the next few hours.

If the world was going to end tomorrow, would you want know?

Bermuda distracted himself, pulling his phone from his suit jacket and flicking it open. He clicked the keypad a number of times, before sending Sophie the following text.

'Didn't get fired. Shock. :) x'

He could feel his face blushing; the idea of actually having someone to text was strange. Not only that, this person seemed to believe him.

Even stranger, she seemed to like him.

As he took the final puff and checked there were no litter police in the vicinity, his phone rumbled and he was powerless to stop the smile etching itself across his face.

'Nice one. Who do you work for? Ghostbusters? X'

Bermuda chuckled, losing signal as he ventured across the concourse of London Bridge towards the trains. As he boarded, he recalled the sense of purpose he felt in that chamber. Facing the power of the BTCO and finally realising what was expected of him.

The world didn't know it, but they were relying on him now. Everyone he cared about.

If he wanted to see Sophie again.

The idea of holding his Chloe one more time?

He had to find Barnaby and stop him.

He rode the train to Peckham Rye, following the same path

before that led to Bellenden Road, the place where he was first introduced to this case. Walking past the cosy coffee shops and unique shops where London's trendiest flocked, he made his way to the alley where Jess went missing.

He wanted to race through, up the stairs of Garland House and wrap his arms around Sophie again. But what would be the point if the world was to end. Hands on hips, he stood in the shadows of the alleyway, the Spring breeze whipping through, clattering off the walls like a pinball. The symbol was still there, burnt into the wall, for his eyes only. A few crisp packets slithered across the concrete and Bermuda watched for a few moments. There was nothing here.

Nothing to tell him where Barnaby could be or where he would open his next doorway. He lit a cigarette, allowing the nicotine to infiltrate his body as he pondered. He had already headed back to the station before he took his next puff.

■ ▮ ▮

The queue to The Cutty Sark was not as long as he had expected. Overlooking the Thames, Bermuda took his time, even experiencing a little tourism as he read the informative plaques that adorned the displays. The vessel itself was a colossal demonstration of the human imagination and hard graft. Large, thick beams ran through the centre of the ship, keeping the upper deck supported. Bermuda slowly walked up the stairs, chuckling to himself at the cordon around the hole in the deck. A couple of labourers measured up the breakage, not knowing it was he who had caused it.

Somehow, explaining to them that he had been launched like a lawn dart through it didn't seem like the best idea. He slowly made his way back down to the corner where Josh Cooper went missing, seeing the area for the first time in the daylight. Without the terrifying threat of the giant Other snapping at his heels, he took his time to survey the entire area.

Nothing of any use.

Just the twelve-sided burn in the wood, the key that unlocked the path to The Otherside.

Bermuda could only imagine their experience. Being forced through a portal to a world that only he could survive in. A world he ran from as soon as he could.

Where were the bodies?

Thanking the staff who spent their time on the ship, Bermuda exited, making his way back down Greenwich High Street and to the station, the DLR train making its pre-programmed stop just as he reached the platform.

He boarded the driverless train and made his way back towards the centre of London.

After a few changes, Bermuda walked out of the Underground Station of Regent's Park. Following the concrete path that cut through the beautiful surroundings, he eventually found the spot where Alfie Evan's went missing. He approached the tree trunk, this time prepared for a sudden appearance of Barnaby.

Those piercing black eyes.

He didn't show.

Bermuda slowly checked the surrounding area, but there would be no clues. He knew that.

The symbol was indented in the wood, as fresh as it was on his previous visit. It called to him. Begging him to touch it. With a disappointed sigh, Bermuda headed back towards the station, puffing on a cigarette and hoping beyond hope for some inspiration.

It didn't arrive in the Westfield's toilet in Shepherds Bush either. Standing with his hands on his hips, he stared at the cubicle wall, cursing the same symbol he had seen everywhere else. The Gate Maker.

Resigned to defeat, Bermuda slowly exited the gents, making his way back out into the shopping centre. Thousands of people wandered the centre, all with their own shopping agendas and lack of patience. Humanity at its finest, unaware of the impending extinction it faced.

There were no leads.

Nothing to tell Bermuda where to go.

Dejected, he walked to the bannister that surrounded the second floor, draping his arms over it and dropping his head. He was tired. His torso screamed in agony, the broken ribs rattling against his organs.

'I assume you will be staying.'

Bermuda smiled at the sound of Argyle's voice.

'They haven't got rid of me just yet, Big Guy.'

'I am pleased. For what it is worth, I believe you are the best chance we have of finding Barnaby.'

'Yeah?' Bermuda pushed himself back up, overshadowed by the imposing frame of his partner. 'Why's that?'

'Because it is what you do. You find people.' Bermuda scoffed. 'I know not of the reasoning for it, but that is why they call you Bermuda, is it not?'

He was right. Bermuda knew he was. He ran a frustrated hand through his hair, undoing the fine work of earlier.

'I'm out of ideas, man. I've been to every location we have for just one smidgen of a clue.'

'There is nothing. I know, I also have rechecked.'

'We have a day. A day and a half, tops.' Bermuda shook his head in disbelief. 'We got nothing.'

'I revisited Other's Town. No signs there, although word is a few Others have joined Barnaby's quest. A few fanatics.'

'Wonderful,' Bermuda sighed.

'Apparently they see it as a wise move to join him before he eviscerates this world.'

'Not a bad idea.'

Bermuda slowly turned, his feet leading him towards the exit. He could get the train back to Bushey; crack a Doombar and message Sophie. See if she wanted to spend the end of the world with him. They could hold each other as the world evaporated.

'Bermuda.'

He stopped, turning to face his partner with a look of pure dejection.

'Yeah?'

'This is my world, too. It's worth fighting for.'

'I know.' Bermuda offered a hopeful smile before turning back towards the exit. 'I know.'

Argyle watched his partner leave through the masses of consumers, assured that he wouldn't give up. Bermuda was a lot of things but he wasn't a quitter. He was stubborn and refused to be beaten.

He needed Bermuda to realise this.

He needed Bermuda to be Bermuda.

For the next hour or so, Argyle stood and watched as humanity circled around him, trading their obsession for money for their obsession with clothes.

Humanity was none the wiser.

■ ▪ |

Sophie had finished her coffee before returning to Bermuda's bedroom. She found a spare towel and took a shower, allowing the warm water to cascade over her body. She chuckled as she thought about him.

The man had been certified as insane. He was covered neck to waist in tattoos, many of them the scribblings of a mad man. He spoke of other worlds and disappearing people. Of monsters in the shadows and of warriors fighting against them. He believed her best friend had been taken by a sinister man in a top hat, harvested for her life source and stolen to another world.

Yet, lying in bed with him, with his strong arms wrapped around her, she had never felt safer.

As she washed the water through her delicate hair, she could feel her reservations about having a boyfriend being washed away. The thought of spending more time with Bermuda made her excited, the prospect of kissing him again, even making love to him, drew a large smile across her face.

She dried off and redressed, taking the time to make Bermuda's bed properly and then organise the dishes around his sink a little neater. She wasn't quite ready to do his washing just yet.

As she was on the train back to Euston, her heart fluttered as she received a text from him, a message of positivity that he wasn't to lose his job. She fired one back, a nerdy joke about his job before losing herself in her headphones.

Her music filtered out the crowds at Euston station and at London Bridge and before she knew it, she was walking through Peckham High Street, weaving in and out of the busy foot traffic and over flowing bins.

Her errands consisted of paying a cheque in at the bank and doing a quick food shop and as she meandered around the supermarket, she could feel herself smiling. As if, even though he sounded completely crazy, Bermuda had returned a measure of calm to her. For the first time since Jess had gone missing, she felt like she would see her again.

She would go home, catch up on any correspondence and demand her agent book her some more jobs.

Life could be good again.

She paid for her shopping, an uneasy feeling that a set of eyes had latched onto her caused her to scan the shop.

There was no one there.

No one was watching her.

Not that she could see.

She made her way home, responding to emails and having a lengthy call with her agent about the prospect of returning to work soon. Things were starting to feel like normal.

Why did she have such faith in Bermuda?

She knew why. It was because, despite every single warning sign that she should stay away from him, there was one quality that shone through.

He was genuine. He cared and she had seen the battle scars that dominated his body that proved it.

As she filed a few emails away, she quickly sat up from the sofa, her eyes peering into every corner of the room. Knowing full well that hearing stories of another world was exacerbating her paranoia, she couldn't help but feel there was something watching her.

She turned on the lamp, revealing nothing but a large curtain in the corner of the room. She didn't see him. How could she?

As her evening progressed, she watched the news and then did her thirty-minute ab work out. After cleaning up, she made herself a light dinner before once again snuggling on the sofa, selecting the next episode of her favourite show and praising the world for On Demand TV.

He watched her the entire time.

Her every move was noted, the graceful way in which she lifted herself from the sofa. The smoothness of her skin, such a rich and healthy colour. The contours of her well-toned muscles.

Yes, she would be perfect.

The running water clattered the dishes in the sink and Sophie hummed, testing the temperature of the water as she gazed out of the window.

London was lit up, a beautiful explosion of different shades of lightbulb. Twinkling bursts of yellow in the distance.

Smiling at the view, she slowly pulled the curtain across, blocking the outside world from her kitchen. Picking up the sponge, she slowly began to scrub the pan.

'Tap. Tap.'

She stepped back. Her kitchen was on the third floor, a good twenty feet from the ground. But it sounded like someone had drummed their fingers on the window.

She waited for a moment, leaning slightly closer to the window with every breath.

Silence.

'Come on. Don't be silly now,' she said out loud, scorning herself for allowing her paranoia to exploit her fear. She continued to scrub, the sauce from her delicious dinner now proving to be quite the adversary.

'Tap. Tap.'

She shrieked in fear. The sponge and dish clattered to the bottom of the sink and she stepped back, water dripping from her hands to the patterned tiles below. Sophie stared at the window with fear, nervously running a wet hand through her dark, silky hair.

She fondled into the pocket of her jeans for her phone, the device slipping due to the soap and crashing on the floor.

'Fuck,' she muttered, grabbing a tea towel and draying both her digits and the phone. Crouched down below the sink, she dialled the number.

'Ring. Ring.'

She nervously looked around, too scared to stand back up. It all seemed so silly. Surely, he would just laugh at her.

'Ring. Ring.'

She wrestled back control of her breathing, scolding herself for being reduced to cowering on the floor and acting the damsel in distress.

'Hello. Your through to Bermuda Jones. I can't come to phone right now, so leave a message and there is a slim chance I may listen.'

She waited for the beep, slowly pushing herself back onto her feet.

'Hey. It's Soph. Sorry; I just got a little panicked is all. I guess when you hear all those stories and what not, you think anything and everything is after you.' She giggled sheepishly. 'Anyways, I just heard a rattle against my window and went into some blind panic. I'm ok. Honest.'

She pulled back the curtain that covered the kitchen window.

That was when he launched through. Smashing the glass with minimal fuss, his long, thin, grey fingers clutched around her throat, stifling her screams as her phone crashed to the floor. Her eyes widened with fear as he smiled, showing rows of sharp, jagged teeth. He towered over her, his broad shoulders filling out the tatty suit. His jet black eyes staring through her, knowing he now had the perfect bait.

She tried to scream, yet Sophie found herself unconscious in seconds, falling limp in the arms of her captor.

Barnaby.

25

Sitting behind the wheel of his Porsche, Hugo gently squeezed the bridge of his nose. The bone shifted, still broken and shattered, and he yelled angrily, his eyes watering with pain.

'Fuck you, Bermuda!' He muttered to himself, concerned that his good looks were forever tainted. He dabbed the tears from his eyes, the faint, purple bruising around them only adding to his anger.

How could they not remove him from duty? The man was a walking liability. He lacked respect for the Otherside, for 'The Knack' and for the BTCO. He struck a fellow agent, yet they didn't punish him? He still gets to be the saviour.

'Your time will come,' Marco said, his voice inflicted with a slight lisp, only adding to his reptilian presence.

'My time is now. It has been since the day we were partnered,' Hugo sneered, his battered face contorting painfully. 'It is that rat, Bermuda, who stands in our way.'

They sat in silence, Hugo taking in the unfamiliar surroundings. The streets were narrow, lined by quaint shops, independent businesses that also acted as staples of the local community. Used to living in his penthouse in South London, surrounded by chain restaurants, he shuddered at how some lived.

It made him question Bermuda even more.

Why would he live in Bushey?

The High Street had very little beyond a couple of pubs and a few newsagents. A large church, surrounded by immaculate grounds was lodged right in the middle.

'Do you believe this will work?' Marco asked, trying to return Hugo's focus to the car.

'I don't know. He said he needed to find this Barnaby character in the next day or so, otherwise we are finished.'

'And you plan to hijack it?'

'I plan to take what is mine. I should be the one they hinge the organisation on. I should be the one who saves the world. Not him. He is nothing but an arrogant, alcoholic arsehole. No, this should be mine. And I am going to take what belongs to me.'

Hugo looked up at the building further down the road. The stolen file that sat in his lap indicated that inside, should be Bermuda.

After his speech to the Committee, Hugo ascertained that Bermuda was close. So any movement would be followed and then Hugo would sweep in. Hugo would catch this Barnaby. Then Bermuda would be gone.

'So what do we do?' Marco asked, his scaly body slightly twisted in the seat, like a coiled snake ready to strike.

Hugo caught a glimpse of himself in the mirror. The shattered remains of his nose, wrapped in plasters that divided the thick, heavy bruises around his eyes. The damage done by his nemesis.

His hatred for Bermuda was growing by the second.

'We wait.'

■ ▮ ▏

A cloud of white smoke gently wafted towards the ceiling of Bermuda's flat, hitting the whiteness before exploding to nothing. Laying on the sofa, Bermuda lifted the cigarette to his mouth again, drawing in the toxic fumes before pushing them out again.

What was he missing?

He had been banging his head against the wall of his office for hours, staring at the map of London that hung on his notice board. Random pins stuck photos and names to their last known locations, a scattergun approach that failed to reveal a pattern.

None of the stolen were linked to the other.

None of the locations special or familiar.

Barnaby was bringing about the end of the world at random.

The only thing Bermuda was sure of was that Barnaby was close to his goal. The strength the Other mustered to send him through that wall was unnerving. Eleven people already, and with the two day grace period almost up, Bermuda was staring at the ceiling, trying to make peace with his failure.

On his chest lay the photo of Chloe. His cherished possession. She would be asleep by now. Tucked up in her bed, probably surrounded by her dolls and her teddy bears. He wondered if she had a favourite, one that she wouldn't put down or give up, even when newer ones arrived. Angela and her partner Ian would say goodnight, the adoring parents that he wished he could have been.

She wouldn't know. The world would just end and she would know no different.

No one would.

Except him.

He could almost feel the darkness washing over the world, a tidal wave of destruction that would rip it apart without it realising.

'Ring. Ring.'

Bermuda started, sitting up and dropping ash all over his chest. He scraped it off, tutting as he rescued the photo, carefully placing it on the side table.

It was Sophie.

His head dropped. Just his luck, considering what had happened throughout his life, that he would meet a girl he was crazy about a few hours before the end of the world.

He couldn't bring himself to answer it, letting it ring out until it hit his voice mail. Hopefully she would leave a message; the sound of her voice would be comforting right now.

Easing himself off the sofa, Bermuda clutched his shattered side, the ribs aching as the strains of the battle began to take their toll. He could still barely see out of his eye, the swelling reducing slowly. With calm, measured steps, he ventured into the kitchen, retrieving a Doombar and cracking it open.

His office was a mess. His desk was a battlefield, with beer cans and sheets of paper battling for supremacy. An ashtray overflowed, with dead cigarettes littering the edge of the desk and surrounding carpet. The wall itself was beginning to look like a scene from a detective show, with photos and string connecting them. All of it adding up to absolutely nothing.

Bermuda dropped down onto his desk chair, his momentum knocking a few sheets of paper to the floor.

'For fuck's sake,' he muttered, ignoring the mess and fishing another cigarette from his pocket. He sparked it into life and then caught a glimpse of himself in the window.

He looked haggard and beaten.

He raised his can.

'To the end of the world.' He toasted himself, slowly shaking his head as he finished off the ale.

'Ring. Ring.'

Bermuda's phone vibrated against his thigh again, Sophie obviously eager to speak to him. Maybe he should just answer, invite her over and accept the apocalypse in the arms of the most beautiful woman he had met.

He slid the phone from his pocket.

It was his sister, Charlotte.

He silently cursed, realising he had forgotten to return her call from the other night. With a heavy sigh, he clicked accept.

'Wow, I didn't expect you to answer.' Charlotte's voice held genuine surprise.

'Sorry, Charles. I'm kinda busy, ' he lied, slowly pushing himself out of his chair and back to the kitchen for another can.

'Off saving the world?'

'Something like that.' He thought he should tell her, the end of existence that he was too simple to stop.

'Well, how are you? It's been a while.'

Bermuda caught another glimpse of his reflection, the battered mess that compiled his face gleaming off the window.

'I'm ok. Had a rough week or so with work. Got attacked by a wild beast on the Cutty Sark.'

'THAT WAS YOU?' Charlotte exclaimed, then chuckled. 'I saw it on the news. They bumped up the terror threat because of you.'

'To be fair, that's not the worst thing I have ever done.'

It was nice to hear his sister laugh. Along with Brett, she was the only other person not to give up on him. He cracked open a can and slowly walked to his living room, the stale odour of smoke in the air.

'How's George?' He asked, wishing for a day when he could meet his nephew.

'He's good. Big. Keeps telling me he wants pizza.' They chuckled.

'Even when he is in the bath. He wants pizza.'

'Such a strange child.'

'Yeah. Mum came by the other day.'

'Yeah?' Bermuda couldn't hide his disappointment.

'She is doing well. She's sixty days clean now, Frankie. She is really trying.'

Bermuda gritted his teeth, swallowing any words that would ruin the call. All he remembered was her drinking, incoherent babbling about a father who was a waste of space and angry tears of how the world let her down. The yelling and shouting. The beatings. 'There are no such thing as monsters' she used to scream, as a terrified Bermuda hid from her.

'She asked about you.'

'I'm glad she is well.'

Charlotte knew that was the end of that conversation and she hesitated, Bermuda could sense the dread.

'Angela called me.' He swung a fist at the wall, his head dropping in sadness. 'She said she saw you last week.'

'Yeah, she did.'

'She was worried.' Bermuda remained silent. 'For god's sake, Frankie, do you ever want to see your daughter again?'

'Of course I do,' Bermuda snapped. 'All I have done, every year I stayed away, it was all for their safety. Do you think it doesn't kill me, knowing someone else is raising my baby girl? Getting to tuck her in at night. It kills me every morning when I wake up and every night before I go to sleep.'

'Then change it. Be a part of her life,' Charlotte pleaded, her voice cracking with sadness.

'I can't. As long as I exist in that world, I cannot exist in this one.'

Bermuda rubbed his eyes with his fingers, begging himself not to cry. If the world only had a few more hours left, he didn't want to spend it haunted by the family he had to leave. The life he never got to have.

'That girl needs her father.'

'She needs me to stay away from her.'

'You're missing the point!' Charlotte angrily growled. 'God, you can be such an arsehole at times!'

Bermuda lifted his head. A look of realisation spread across his swollen, battle hardened face.

'What did you just say?'

'I said you can be an arsehole at times.'

'I know that. No, before?'

Bermuda slowly turned, looking towards his office.

'I said you are missing the point.'

'I gotta go.'

Bermuda hung up and dropped the phone, his eyes fixated on his office. Ignoring the pain that roared from his broken body, he shuffled quickly through the door and into the office. He frantically searched for a marker pen, sending random sheets and a number of beer cans hurling to the ground.

Snatching a black marker pen he stormed the notice board, slamming it against the large map of London and began to draw. With each line, his shoulders slumped.

Another line.

His eyes watered.

The final line.

He dropped the marker pen and stepped back, his eyes wide and pushing a tear down a face that was open mouthed. He slowly shook his head. He was so focused on the twelve sides that he ignored the points of connection.

Twelve points.

In front of him, the map now showed him everything he needed to know. Following the crude sketch of the Gate Maker symbol, he had systematically connected all of the eleven locations where Barnaby had stolen his selected.

It was never the people.

Running his hands through his hair in disbelief, he slowly approached the board, pushing through the agony as he bent down to collect the marker.

He connected the final two lines. The final convergence.

Big Ben.

That was where Barnaby would do it. The final place.

'Gotcha,' Bermuda allowed himself, tapping the landmark with his finger before heading to his bedroom. With great care, he eased off his t-shirt, swapping it for a fresh one. Jeans and shoes followed, along with the long black jacket.

He pushed his hair to the side and then collected his badge and car keys from the unit. Carefully, he opened the locked box on his dresser, the resting place of his trusty tomahawk.

Phone?

Remembering, he quickly raced to the front room, retrieving it from the carpet. He noticed he had a voice mail. As he marched to the door he played it, lifting it to his ear.

'Hey. It's Soph. Sorry, I just got a little panicked is all. I guess when you hear all those stories and what not, you think anything and everything is after you.'

He chuckled, closing the front door behind him and locking it.

'Anyways, I just heard a rattle against my window and went into some blind panic. I'm ok. Honest.'

Suddenly, the shattering of glass could be heard causing Bermuda to stop, his eyes widening with fear. Sophie screamed before being instantly silenced, the slow crunch of boot on glass. Bermuda's face scrunched into a determined snarl. He could hear the phone being lifted, someone holding it as his message came to a terrifying close. The voice of Barnaby.

'Keep up, Bermuda.'

Bermuda raced to his car.

'Keep up.'

26

He roared down the dual carriageway, weaving in amongst the traffic. Behind the wheel, Bermuda flicked through his phone, keeping one eye on the road ahead. The Spring evening had taken a turn for the worst, a shower of rain covering his windscreen in wet freckles.

Bermuda lifted the phone to his ear, shifting gear with the other hand before gripping the wheel again, the car bursting around the car in front.

'Come on. Come on.'

His mind was racing.

Barnaby had Sophie. The one thing he had strived to do ever since he had joined the BTCO was to keep those he cared about safe. For three years, he hadn't seen his daughter.

Now, within a week of meeting him, Sophie was about to be stolen, pushed through to the Otherside and bound for an eternity of emptiness.

Well done, Bermuda.

Finally, the call connected.

'Hello and welcome to Denderman Co. Please state your four digit code to proceed.'

Bermuda rolled his eyes. 'This is Agent Jones. I have located Barnaby.'

'Please state your four digit code to proceed.'

The voice was friendly and female.

'For fuck's sake, lady. I don't have the code. Just tell Ottoway that I know where Barnaby is. I'm heading to Big Ben and I need you to send Argyle.'

'I'm sorry. Please state your...'

'Just tell Argyle to meet me at Big Ben. Get him to do whatever it is he does to get there.' He hung up the phone, throwing it into the passenger seat. 'Fucking hell!'

Bermuda pushed his foot down, the engine of his car straining as it whipped through the wet night, heading as fast as he could towards London.

■ ▮ ▮

Hugo was half asleep in his car when Marco nudged him, directing his gaze towards the building. Wiping the sleep from his eyes, Hugo peered out, watching as Bermuda ran towards his car, the phone pressed against his ear.

A sense of urgency hung in the air. He dropped into the driver's seat, the lights revealing the rain. The engine erupted and within seconds, Bermuda spun a turn in the road and shot off.

'Here we go,' Hugo smirked, his Porsche waking from its slumber at the turn of a key. Within moments he was following Bermuda, eager to see where they were heading.

■ ▮ ▮

Rain had started to fall over London, the drops crashing against the side of the grand clock tower that thrust up towards the grey clouds. The clock face was an explosion of light and time, the iconic face of the Big Ben clock was fast approaching midnight.

Around the tower, the immaculate grounds were separated from the public by large, cast iron gates. Over ten feet tall and immovable, the thick, black gate kept the public a safe distance from the pristine and hallowed grounds that surrounded the magnificent structure.

A stone's throw away were the Houses of Parliament, buildings usually swarming with smart suited politicians, each one with a false smile and a hidden agenda. A cage for the snakes of the country.

Barnaby gazed out through the magnificent face of the clock, standing behind the symbol of time that rang true throughout this world. His black eyes gazed over the city before him, his revulsion at the human race resurfacing as he spied a few of them walking below.

Soon they would bow to him. A new order would reign, all under his watchful eye. The disease known as humanity would be cured, the world passed to those who truly deserved it.

Behind him, Sophie lay motionless on the ground. Her unconsciousness had lasted since her abduction; she would feel no pain as she passed through. She would become his. The only pain would be Bermuda's when he witnessed her being stripped from this world.

Over 300 feet below, a couple of pathetic Others were waiting, the preparation for Bermuda's arrival almost complete. The useless creatures had strapped all but one of his stolen to the wall. Ten of them hung from their wrists, unmoving and unaware. Empty vessels.

In the middle, Barnaby had selected the one that had brought Bermuda into play. The one that meant something to his beloved Sophie.

Jessica Lambert.

Now it was just a matter of waiting. Time was slowly becoming a commodity that Bermuda was running out of.

■ ▮ ▏

Bermuda eventually brought his car to screeching stop on the side of the street, the inevitable parking ticket not worth worrying about. Launching himself out of it and into the rain, he ran as quickly as his battered body allowed towards Westminster Bridge, the large tower of Big Ben cutting through the night sky.

The Thames crashed below him, the rain and wind picking up and causing waves to lap against the Embankment.

Bermuda continued on, his eyes scanning the area, looking for any clue that he was correct. That Barnaby was there. As he got closer, he tried to peer beyond the thick, metal fence that surrounded the magnificent clock tower, but it was too dark.

After a few minutes, he arrived at the grounds, his ribs aching as he tried his best to peer through. The darkness gave way to a blurred view, a few lights illuminating small sections of neatly cut grass and thick, stone wall.

Nothing of any substance.

'We need a closer look.'

Bermuda had never been more grateful to hear Argyle's voice. He turned, nodding his appreciation.

'If I am right, then this is it,' Bermuda said. 'We have to stop him, no matter what.'

'My duty is to protect you and the people of this world. You have my sword and my word.'

Bermuda patted him on the arm before looking for a way through the fence. Once they rounded the corner towards the House of Parliament, Bermuda moved towards the gate. Padlocked.

With a forceful shove, Bermuda leant into the gate but it barely budged. Maybe he was wrong?

He gazed up at the bright, yellow face of Big Ben, the bright light covering the rain in a vast glow, revealing it to the world. There was no way of knowing for sure.

The screech of twisted metal broke the silence, cutting through his ears like nails down a chalkboard. Turning in confusion, Bermuda shook his head in disbelief.

'Let's go,' Argyle firmly said, stepping through the twisted bars, which he had bent to the side. The sheer strength of his partner was baffling to Bermuda at times. Thick, iron bars, twisted and pushed like they were made of putty.

'How strong are you?' Bermuda asked, lightening the situation as they walked onto the wet grass that surrounded Big Ben, taking measured steps through the darkness towards the giant, wooden doors that led inside.

As they walked a few feet, Argyle stopped, protectively putting an arm across Bermuda, his head tilted, listening for clues in the downpour.

'What is it?' Bermuda asked, a hand instinctively reaching towards his tomahawk.

Suddenly, a blur leapt from the darkness, its small, clawed feet pushing against Argyle before launching back into the shadow.

Off balance, Argyle stumbled back. Bermuda turned but was instantly knocked off his feet, a slithery spine colliding with his broken ribs and sending him crashing across the grass.

Argyle flicked back onto his feet with extreme agility, his legs bent and ready for action as the dark blur raced around the shadows that framed them.

'Are you ok?' He called, scanning the edges of the darkness as Bermuda slowly pushed himself to his knees.

'I've been better.' He pushed himself to his feet. 'What was that?'

Before Argyle could respond, he launched, hauling Bermuda to the ground as the slithery shadow leapt forward again, missing them by a matter of inches. The rain pelted down on them as they hit the ground, mud smearing up Bermuda's jacket.

Argyle instantly leapt to his feet, his hand reaching and clasping the handle of his sword, the wet blade casting a glow in the moonlight.

His eyes frantically searched the darkness.

It zipped by. He could almost see it.

Bermuda slowly got to his feet, cautiously standing behind Argyle, his own search for their attacker as successful as Argyle's. He heard the footsteps scuttling, the clang of the metal fence as it lurched from the barricade.

What was it?

Bermuda, keen to get inside before the gap in the fence became public knowledge took a few steps towards the door. The mystery attacker launched itself from the shadows, its sharp, talon covered hands reaching for Bermuda's throat.

Argyle leapt across and snatched it out of the air, wrestling its slippery body as it tried to escape. Within seconds, the mighty warrior's strength dominated, the beast became still and dormant.

Bermuda turned back, hurrying over to his partner as they wrenched the beast into the glow of the street light.

Marco.

Perplexed, Bermuda approached the Neither - the creature was on their side.

'Marco? What the hell?' Bermuda asked, the Neither struggling in vain against Argyle's firm grasp around his neck.

'Fools. Both of you,' Marco sneered, his lisp dominating his speech. His skin, dark and scaly, glistened in the wetness of the night.

'Why are you here?' Argyle demanded.

No answer. He squeezed his mighty fist around his neck again.

'WHY?!'

Instantly it clicked and Bermuda looked up, his eyes wide with anger as Hugo raced towards the doors of Big Ben, about a hundred yards ahead of them.

He had been followed.

This was Hugo's revenge. He had Marco distract them, so he could apprehend Barnaby, the only reason Bermuda had been kept on by the BTCO. With Barnaby apprehended, Bermuda would be gone.

Hugo had no idea of the danger on the other side of the door.

Bermuda screamed for him to stop, even trying to run through the pain as Hugo raced towards the door. They fell on deaf ears. But before Hugo reached the massive, wooden doors, they flew open, wind whistling through and revealing a figure of sheer terror.

Barnaby had watched them, their little fracas on the lawn of Big Ben was as pathetic as he would have imagined. Bermuda and his treacherous pet, Argyle, fighting an unknown assailant whilst the clock struck midnight. With the arrival of a new day, Barnaby was ready for the final stage of his convergence. Sophie lay prone, ready to be harvested and then eradicated like the rest of her pathetic race.

Bermuda would have a front row seat.

With his power growing, Barnaby lowered himself down through the centre of the staircase, the winding spiral of three hundred and thirty-four steps. He marched through the entrance of the tower, his new found lackeys cowering at his presence.

His stolen adorned the walls like trophies, all lifeless and loose. In the centre, the blonde woman from the alleyway was ready for her death.

Bermuda would see how helpless he was when she choked. When the final breath left her before his very eyes.

It was time to welcome them in.

With a wave of his hand, the two doors ripped open, revealing the wind and wetness of the night. It whistled through, the water splashing against his grey skin, his white hair tumbling in every direction.

The man before him was not Bermuda.

Instantly, he snatched the human being by the neck, lifting him from his feet and holding him in the air.

The man was handsome, though his face was disfigured somewhat by what appeared to be a broken nose and bruises around his eyes. His accent was strange. Not like Bermuda's.

There was fear in his eyes.

He was useless.

'Please, monsieur,' the man started to plead.

Barnaby clicked his jaw a few times, his jet black, pearl-like eyes alive with murder.

He flashed his jagged teeth and with a flick of the wrist, Barnaby snapped Hugo's neck, dropping his lifeless body to the ground in the doorway of one of London's most famous landmarks.

Racing through the rain, Bermuda screamed in anger at the death of his comrade, something that brought joy to Barnaby as he walked back into the structure, leaving the door wide open.

He was inviting Bermuda and Argyle in for the final moments of the human race.

Bermuda dropped to his knees, reaching out for Hugo. He grabbed him by the scruff of his jacket, shaking the body and willing it back to life.

'Come on, you bastard. Don't fucking die.'

He knew the words were useless. Bruising and swelling had already surfaced across the snapped neck, the spinal cord severed from the brain.

Hugo was dead.

Rain crashed down around them, slapping against the concrete as Bermuda gritted his teeth with fury. The man may have been as antagonistic as they come, but he was a good agent.

He didn't deserve to die.

Argyle and Marco slowly approached, their rain soaked scuffle ending when they heard Bermuda's cry of anguish. With a sense of dread they approached, Marco slithering next to Bermuda, his pained eyes staring at his dead partner.

'I'm sorry, Marco,' Bermuda muttered.

Marco just stared at the body, the man he had spent the last eight years with lay motionless. Slowly, Marco hissed his bitter words.

'All he wanted was your recognition.'

'I know. I never asked for this,' Bermuda said, gently patting the Neither on the back as he got to his feet. Marco hung his head, the rain crashing against the scales that covered his body.

'Don't let it be in vain.'

Bermuda nodded and turned towards the large doors, the wind

hurtling through as the clock tower welcomed them. Argyle gently rested a hand on Marco's back, urging him to return to the BTCO and request help, to ensure Hugo's body would be properly taken care of.

Marco took a few more moments, saying a silent goodbye to his fallen partner before slithering off into the shadows as Argyle suggested. With powerful, purposeful strides, Argyle approached the tower, joining Bermuda.

'Let's do this.'

Argyle's voice echoed with bass, the warrior ready for battle. With a vengeful scowl painted across his face, Bermuda led the way, the two of them crossing the threshold and into the famous tower.

The doors slammed shut behind them.

27

Their footsteps rebounded off the high, concrete walls encasing each step with its own echo. The walls were lined with a thin, wooden skirting that rain around the entire room like a bow around a neatly wrapped present.

The floor itself was wet and slippery, the rain that managed to infiltrate only adding to the cold, dereliction of the mighty tower.

Bermuda looked around; the bare walls were unnerving, and the most famous clock in the world was surprisingly hollow on the inside.

Argyle walked with calm, measured steps, one hand reaching high behind his neck, his fingers dancing a few inches from the handle of his blade. Ready for anything.

Towards the far wall was a thick, wooden door with a small window that revealed only darkness. Splashed across the frame in white letters, was 'Clock Tower'.

'Here we go,' Bermuda said, more to himself than to Argyle.

Creaking on large hinges, the door slowly opened, revealing a wooden floor that disappeared a few feet further into darkness.

The crunching of mechanised cogs was extremely loud, drowning out any second thoughts that could have possibly infiltrated Bermuda's mind.

There were none. Barnaby had Sophie. He had just killed Hugo and was going to end the human race. Bermuda needed to stop him.

Nudging slowly ahead of Argyle, Bermuda cautiously stepped into the darkness, his hand under his coat, ready to draw his weapon at any moment. Pain slipped away from him, replaced by a steely determination to save the world.

Beyond the cranking of the clock's mechanics, Bermuda heard a shuffling, the sound of beastly claws dragging across the wood. Something was in the room with them.

Argyle clearly heard it too, his hand clasping the handle of his mighty blade, his body ready for action. His voice full of menace.

'Show yourself or face death.'

Bermuda was impressed, fearing for any creature that defied his partner.

The lights suddenly burst into life, the large room they were in bathed in a sharp glow. Large, rusty cogs slowly circled each other, the mechanised motors shifting in different directions as the clockwork tower continued its job as being a large time piece.

There was no sign of Barnaby.

It was what framed the wall that caused Bermuda the most distress.

With their hands wrapped in thin, course rope, ten humans hung from the wall, their arms outstretched, their eyes lifeless. Vincent had mentioned there was still hope for them, that they were not dead, just lost. Their bodies, empty and void of life that could still be returned to them. Bermuda knew how, but retrieving the latch stone from Barnaby was another challenge entirely.

Proudly displayed, a punishing proof of just how powerful Barnaby had become.

'Bermuda.'

Argyle hauled Bermuda's attention away from the prizes that aligned the wall, his eyes widening in shock. It was Jessica.

Recognising her from the photo, she again stood lifeless, her feet precariously planted on a small, shaking wooden stall. Around her neck, a noose, ready to catch, tighten and remove her from existence.

Argyle slowly approached, sword ready as three Others, thin and gaunt with sharp, pointy features, surrounded the human, ready to end her.

Argyle took one more step.

They kicked the stool.

Jessica dropped, the cable wrapped around her neck caught tight, instantly cutting off her air supply. She began to choke. Argyle reached for his blade, but was set upon instantly by two of the Others, their speed jolting and confusing, their movements hard to gauge as they dodged his wild, swinging arms.

Bermuda ran towards her, grabbing her legs and lifting her upwards, causing the rope to slacken and return air to her body. The redness of her face began to fade, Bermuda trying his best to keep her alive.

A blade plunged into his shoulder.

Roaring with agony, he stumbled forward, releasing Jessica who dropped and swung again. Her timer began again as Bermuda fell to his knees, the ripping of his flesh only outdone by the searing pain of being connected to the Otherside.

The Other circled him as he reached for the blade, slowly pulling the sharp, other worldly weapon out of his shoulder, the link trying hard to reconnect and force its way back in again.

Just as he was about to remove it, the Other slashed his face with a clawed hand, blood splattering across the wooden slats.

Argyle struggled on the floor, the two Others holding him down by his mighty arms, using their weight to pin him in place. With slow, synchronised movements, they began to drag him across the jagged, wooden boards. Arching his head back, he saw the destination as the mechanical cogs that twisted and turned a few feet away.

Somewhere in the tower, Barnaby was ready to steal Sophie from the world.

The ten stolen hung from the wall, unaware of what was going on.

Swinging from the ceiling, Jess's final breaths were leaving her body.

Bermuda slowly pushed himself up to all fours, only to receive a vicious kick to his shattered ribs, taking him off the ground and slamming him into the concrete wall. His breath shot out of his body, the impact cracking a few more ribs.

Jess slowly began to fade, the final breath imminent.

A ferocious cough and Bermuda spat blood onto the wood, his hand once again reaching for the blade that was lodged into his shoulder.

The Other slowly approached, baring its teeth as it sized him up.

Bermuda yanked at the blade, his roar of anguish bouncing off the walls like a rubber ball.

The Other leapt.

He pulled the blade from his shoulder, blood flicking against the pale concrete.

The Other collided with him, sending them both rolling across the floor. After a few moments of silence, Bermuda pushed the Other to the side, the blade sticking out of its neck, dark blood spurting like a fountain.

It died painfully.

Bermuda slowly stumbled to his feet, dropping again to one knee as the Otherside clawed at his wound, trying it's hardest to converge with him.

Jess's struggle for life was starting to fade.

Bermuda spun his body to face her, his fingers clasping the handle of his tomahawk. Using all of his strength, he launched it upwards, the blade slicing through the cable and dropping Jess to the floor. The remaining cable was slowly swallowed by the mechanics that it swung from.

With blood oozing from his shoulder, a few more broken ribs and pain shooting from the cuts across his face, Bermuda quickly checked her, exhaling in relief as he found a pulse.

Argyle struggled, trying his best to draw himself away as the cogs clashed together a metre away from his head. Soon he would become part of the rotary system that powered Big Ben, a grisly demise. The two Others held him tight, one of them sneering at him as they dragged him to his death.

It suddenly howled in agony.

Bermuda stepped back, the blade that had stabbed the neck of his attacker now pierced the foot of Argyle's, pinning it to the floor. It temporarily let go of Argyle, which was all the Neither needed.

With a free hand, he caught the pain stricken Other with a ferocious right that sent it straight to the floor. Panicked, the other attacker tried to flee, only for Argyle to catch its ankle, dragging it to the floor. A few punches later and it too was unconscious.

A beaten and battered Bermuda helped Argyle to his feet.

'Thank you,' Argyle offered, concerned for Bermuda.

'Don't mention it.' Bermuda scurried towards the door to the stairwell. 'I have to stop Barnaby.'

Just as he approached the door, it burst open, knocking him

onto his back. Spinning around, his eyes widened with horror as the goliath muscled in. It was a Gorgoma, a feral Other similar to the one they battled in the Cutty Sark.

As big and as menacing, this one was more proportionate to a human, its arms not as long but still tipped with razor sharp claws. Its eyes, black and furious, locked onto Bermuda, who slowly crawled back.

Argyle stepped forward, his hand on his sword.

'Go,' he commanded, drawing his blade. 'I have this under control.'

Not needing a second invitation, Bermuda slunk to the side of the room, following the display of lifeless humans until he came back to the door. He slowly and silently slipped through, looking up at the spiralling stairs that disappeared into darkness. His heart sank at the task ahead.

He slowly began his ascent.

Argyle walked slowly into the middle of the chamber, the cogs coming together every few seconds. Three Others lay dead or indisposed on the floor. Eleven human bodies were motionless. Before him, the Gorgoma circled, brandishing its claws as it prepared for battle.

Saying a silent prayer, Argyle swung his sword into position before charging forward, meeting the giant beast head on. It swung its hefty arm forward, four blades slicing through the air. Argyle ducked the swipe before slicing it across its spine, the skin splitting between its sharp, numerous spikes.

It roared, disconnecting its pelvis and spinning unnaturally to face Argyle again. It backed Argyle towards the wall before launching a beastly foot into his chest, shaking his armour and sending Argyle flying into the brickwork which cracked on impact.

The giant beast growled, dragging its claws across the floor as it stalked Argyle. Slowly pushing himself to his feet, Argyle touched fingers to his temple, recoiling in anger at the appearance of blood. With his sword still in his hand, he drew it to his side, approaching the beast, the two of them making eye contact as they circled the room.

Death was the only way to finish this battle.

They both silently agreed before charging once more.

■ ▌ |

A hundred steps high and Bermuda held his side, collapsing against the dusty, concrete wall beside him. The steps were endless, each one mocking him for his life as a smoker. Each step he took sapped more energy. Each foot hitting the concrete sent a wave of pain lapping over his shattered rib cage.

The pressure to quit was overbearing, mocking him with the idea he could save the world.

Somewhere below him, Argyle was risking his life to battle that monster, willing to die to save the world.

Somewhere above was the creature that wanted to destroy it.

Barnaby had Sophie and was ready to complete his convergence.

With a grunt of anguish, Bermuda pushed himself off of the wall and began to climb the dusty steps, ignoring every pain that rattled through his body.

■ ▌ |

Argyle flew through the air, colliding with the harsh concrete between two, lifeless humans. Slamming into the concrete, he dropped to the floor, his spine another throw closer to breaking point.

Blood trickled from his eyebrow, another large gash across his neck also trickled as the pool of dark blood gathered around him. The floor shook as the Gorgoma approached, its large, merciless hands grabbing the back of his armour and dragging him across the jagged, wooden floor.

His collection of splinters was astounding.

Somewhere in the room was his sword, the behemoth that clutched him had smashed it from his hands, before subjecting Argyle to a ferocious mauling with his sharp, razor like claws.

Now, dragged effortlessly across the floor, Argyle mused on his fate. Would he die here? He refused. Shunting the idea from his mind, he used his remaining strength to roll backwards, pushing his leg free from the mighty grip of the beast. Expertly rolling away, he launched onto both feet, his eyes alive with anticipation.

The Gorgoma roared, its mighty voice shaking the walls around them. It began to bound towards Argyle, the room shaking and the mechanical cogs behind it were drowned out. As it approached, Argyle ran towards the beast, ready to meet it head on. Inches before they collided, Argyle shot the Retriever into the throat of the beast, the alien metal piercing its neck and latching to the bone.

It was locked in.

Argyle leapt over the beast, landing on both feet before leaping again, this time over the cogs, the jagged, metal plates that systematically turned to keep the clock working.

He began to pull.

With blood gushing from its neck wound, the Gorgoma tried to fight, pulling back against the unbreakable cable that hung from his wound. Argyle began to reel it in, shifting his entire bodyweight to haul in the beast.

Slowly it began to move.

Roaring and frantically flailing its mighty claws, it tried to resist. Argyle, blood pouring from his wounds, refused to budge, yelling loudly as he pushed himself through the pain barrier. Very slowly, the arm of the Gorgoma became lodged in the cogs, the metal slowly turning and crushing its bones to paste, the shriek of agony was one tainted with an acceptance of its fate.

Once the arm disappeared so did the shoulder, closely followed by the skull.

After a few harsh minutes, Argyle recalled the Retriever, the blood trickling from the gauntlet that clung to his wrist. With slow, heavy steps, he collected his sword before venturing towards the staircase.

The ten humans hung from the wall, oblivious to the battle they just witnessed. Jessica was motionless, clutching to life by the thinnest of threads.

The cogs of Big Ben continued to turn, caked in the blood of the Other as it gushed from metal slabs.

Argyle pushed open the door and tackled the first step, hoping beyond hope that he wasn't too late.

28

Sweat poured from Bermuda as he clambered up stair three hundred. Peering over the banister, he imagined how it would feel to soar down to the ground below.

He had to push on.

With his hand pressed against the wall for support, he continued, each step more laborious than the last, each one pushing his body to breaking point. Blood slid from the cuts across his face, merging with the sweat that dripped from his chin.

Step by step, he finally clambered over the final stair and a small, concrete landing awaited him. As he shuffled towards the wooden door before him, he made an empty promise to quit smoking.

With more strength than he believed he could muster, he pushed open the door. The brightness of the clock face almost blinded him, the magnificent timepiece illuminating all four walls. Each one was dissected by two, thick hands, showing the time to be fifteen minutes past midnight. The face itself was a myriad of glass panels, curved and slotted together to create the most recognisable clock in the world.

In the centre of the room, hanging from a sturdy clasp attached to the roof, was Big Ben itself. The giant, chrome bell hung dormant, the power and volume it could generate was not something Bermuda was keen on testing.

Underneath the bell, the floor was barricaded off, a wooden bannister that surrounded a large square gap that led to a three hundred foot drop to the floor below.

That was when he saw her.

Sophie. Lying motionless on the floor.

He raced towards her, ignoring the pain that swaddled him like a strait jacket. He took a few steps through the door when a hard fist caught him in the side of the head, sending him sprawling across the floorboards. His brain shook, rocked by the impact.

Barnaby stepped into view, his measured steps echoing through the chamber.

'Welcome, Bermuda.'

Bermuda pushed himself up, shaking free of the dizziness and checking his jaw wasn't broken.

'Let her go,' he demanded, struggling to his feet. Barnaby smirked.

'Now, now. She is the final piece. The last drop. Look at her Bermuda, look at how beautiful she is. Tell me, what would you do to save her?'

Bermuda managed to stand, wobbling slightly and slowly circling. Barnaby kept his back to him, approaching Sophie with calculating steps.

Rain crashed against the four faces of the tower.

'I'd kill you.' Barnaby turned, raising an eyebrow. Bermuda shrugged. 'You asked.'

'Quite.' Barnaby stopped as he arrived, his feet a mere few centimetres from her motionless head. Her hair cascaded freely across the wood. 'She is so peaceful. So blissfully unaware of her significance to me.'

Bermuda took a few more steps, his feet bleeding from the mammoth staircase. He looked down at Sophie, cursing himself for including her in a war she never knew existed. She was here because of him.

'If you need to take someone, take me,' Bermuda offered, surprised by his sincerity. 'This is a fight that she is not a part of.'

Barnaby began to chuckle, his laughter like broken glass shattering. It made the hairs on Bermuda's neck leap upwards.

'Oh Bermuda. That is good.' He chuckled more, slowly turning. 'However, this is all about her. And you!'

Suddenly, a burst of speed and a black and grey blur exploded towards Bermuda. Unable to move quickly enough, Barnaby caught Bermuda with another firm right, the punch sending Bermuda sprawling to the ground. He spat, a puddle of blood circling one of his teeth. Barnaby moved quickly, another burst of acceleration that Bermuda could barely detect.

He was thoroughly overpowered.

Barnaby took one more gaze at the peaceful Sophie, she was so perfect. The pain it would cause Bermuda was so delicious. Without a regard for where his adversary was, Barnaby stepped forward, his menacing frame a silhouette in the bright lights of the clock face. A large, top hat wearing shadow. He reached a thin, grey hand into his blazer, beyond the latch stone that held his connection.

He withdrew the Gate Maker.

Jagged, crude and with twelve sides, he held it in his hands, summoning the power to once again combine the worlds. Create an illegal opening. A doorway.

Bermuda slowly sat up, blood dripping from his lips. Suddenly, a burst of light flew from the glass, as Barnaby placed the device against it. The whole room shook, Bermuda reached a hand to cover his eyes as the room was bathed in a tremendous glow. The floor trembled beneath him and slowly, in the face of the clock, a doorway forged. Burnt into the gigantic, round glass, an archway crudely burnt its way into existence, the portal between worlds a dusty, purple colour.

The Otherside.

It called to him.

'Can't you see, Bermuda? I will be the dawning of a new era. A second chance for this world.' Barnaby gazed into the doorway, his black eyes reflecting the purple energy as it danced before him. 'I will be the god that your race has feared.'

He slowly turned, the jet black eyes latching onto Bermuda like two hooks.

'I will be your extinction.'

With a sudden surge of power, Barnaby turned and threw his arm out, his hand open and palm facing Sophie, as if urging her to move. Sure enough, with the pull of the portal and the increase in power, Sophie slowly began to lift, a force more powerful than gravity hoisting her off the wood. Bermuda began to panic, watching as she lifted completely off the floor, suspended in the air like a marionette.

'For god's sake, let her go,' Bermuda pleaded, struggling to his feet, the air in the room alive, a gale force wind trapped within the four walls. With forceful steps, he pushed against the onslaught, his eyes watering as the wind force rose.

Sophie hung in the air, her mind elsewhere as Barnaby stared at her. Slowly turning his head, his black, cavernous eyes met Bermuda's. A sickening smile spread across his scarred face.

'This world belongs to me now.'

Slowly, Sophie began to move towards the doorway, an unseen

force wrapping its cold grasp around her and began to reel her in. Bermuda broke through the pressure, racing towards Sophie as fast as he could, one last, valiant attempt to save her.

Barnaby whipped across the room, colliding shoulder first into Bermuda's chest and knocking him across the floor. He rolled to a stop, precariously close to the opening that lead to certain death.

His chest was broken and his pain threshold decimated but Bermuda once again pushed himself up, blood dripping from his face and instantly, Barnaby approached him.

'Resist,' Barnaby commanded.

Bermuda responded, cracking a firm fist against the crooked jaw of his nemesis. It had little effect and a severe uppercut sent Bermuda hurtling across the room again, his brain almost shaken loose from its cranial confinement.

He lay for a moment, the acceptance of being beaten to death trying its best to dissuade him from getting back to his feet. His blurred vision focused on Sophie, her slow journey to extinction playing out in front of him.

Again, he clambered to his feet. Broken, bruised and bloody, Bermuda stood a few feet from the demonic force before him. Barnaby looked him up and down.

'There is no happy ending, Bermuda.' His words were heavy, laced with satisfaction. 'You will die here, tonight. Your entire world will.'

Bermuda thought of Chloe.

His beautiful daughter, the innocence which bathed her world and the experiences she was yet to have.

'Then I'll die trying to save it.'

Bermuda launched himself forward, catching Barnaby in the centre of his stone-like face with his fist, the impact shattering a bone or two in Bermuda's hand. He stumbled forward, his hands planted against Barnaby's chest to steady himself. Furious, Barnaby struck him in the stomach with venom, the impact crushing his intestines.

Dropping to his knees, Bermuda wasn't sure how much he had left.

Barnaby circled him, like a shark smelling blood in the water. Carefully sliding a hand to the bottom of his spine, he reached a long, thin hand and clasped the handle. Unable to move through pain, Bermuda heard the blade slide from its latch, the jagged sword would soon be his end.

He couldn't fight anymore.

He watched as Sophie drew ever nearer to a world that would destroy her.

He wished he could save her.

With both hands clutching the handle, Barnaby rested it slowly to the back of Bermuda's neck, the razor sharp, jagged metal slicing through a few strands of hair.

He could feel the coldness of the blade.

He took one more glance at Sophie as Barnaby lifted the blade, closing his eyes and accepting his failure.

The world would end tonight.

Barnaby swung the blade down as hard as he could.

Argyle's blade caught it a mere foot from Bermuda's neck, knocking it backwards and sending Barnaby off balance. Having raced up the stairs and seeing his partner about to be executed, Argyle had leapt across the room, his blade deflecting death and saving Bermuda once again.

Scowling and spitting venom, Barnaby regained his composure, snarling in Argyle's direction as they circled each other, their blades drawn.

To the death.

The silent promise to each other was made and Barnaby launched at Argyle, the blade slicing the air to the side of his head, Argyle weaving to the side before deflecting the next swing with his own sword. The mighty clash echoed around them, the two swordsmen taking calculated swipes, both blocking and deflecting.

After a few more wild swipes, Barnaby lunged towards Argyle who side stepped, before striking his adversary with the handle of his blade. Barnaby stumbled back, angered as blood seeped from the wound under his eye. He dabbed at it with his treacherous fingers, the blood thick and black, like oil.

'These scars belong to you, Argyle,' he snapped, pointing to the permanent damage that stretched across his face.

Argyle silently stood, sword drawn, ready to continue the battle. Both men stepped towards each other, their swords clattering as they swung with the intent to kill.

■ ■ l

Opening his eyes to find his head still attached, Bermuda quickly backed away from the two swordsmen, their blades swinging in a whirlwind of skill and murderous intent.

Sophie was a few feet from leaving the world and despite the agonising state of his body, Bermuda launched himself towards her, wrapping his arms around her waist and desperately trying to halt her course.

She continued to move, the pull too strong for the human spirit. A few feet now, she was almost gone. Literally sliding through his fingers. He couldn't stop her.

Taking a deep breath, he limped to the Doorway itself, the smoky, purple portal calling to him, beckoning him through with mystical fingers.

He turned his back on it, facing Sophie who's waist was inches from him.

'This is gonna hurt,' he muttered to himself, before throwing his arms out to the sides, his fingers latching onto the edges of the doorway, jagged glass cutting into this fingers.

The Otherside latched onto his back, one strike, like being whipped by fine cable wiring, slicing the skin on his back.

Sophie pushed into him. Bermuda dug his feet in, his fingers dripping blood as his knuckles turned white, refusing to lose. To let the Otherside take her.

She pushed him backwards, his back tipping over the threshold and The Otherside gratefully embraced him. It collided with him, he could feel it ripping the skin from his back, the ink covered skin slowly disintegrating as the world tried to claim him. Claim them both.

With a roar of agony, he gritted his teeth, his eyes watering as the pain caused him to shake.

The first layer of skin was burning away.

Soon the rest of him.

He refused to let go.

The world could have him, but not her. Not her.

The roar of anguish echoed through the room and Barnaby turned, his face distorting with fury as he saw Bermuda's defiance. Ducking a blow from Argyle, Barnaby caught the warrior with a firm punch to the kidney before swinging his sword wildly in the hope of decapitation.

Argyle ducked, launching forward and hooking his arm under Barnaby's, flipping him over onto his spine. Taking a few steps back, Argyle heard another cry of agony from Bermuda, his eyes frantically searching for him.

Stood in the doorway, he was refusing to let Sophie through.

His world was trying it's best to dismantle him, the screams of anguish were testament to that.

Bermuda needed him.

Suddenly, the blade shot through Argyles armour and through the left side of his chest. It pierced through the armour, blood spraying out like a wet firework.

His grey eyes opened wide, the life draining from them as Barnaby sneered behind him, his hands planted firmly around the handle.

Argyle slowly went limp, feeling the life draining from his body as he reached out a hand towards Bermuda.

He knew Bermuda could see it, the fear in his eyes evident as Barnaby slowly twisted the sword, the blade slicing through tendons that held his chest in place.

Instantly, Barnaby span him around and then launched a vicious kick to his chest.

Argyle slid effortlessly off the blade and clattered through the wooden barrier, plummeting three hundred feet to the concrete death below.

Bermuda tried to scream, his final hopes disappearing with his partner as he fell to his death.

Argyle was gone.

29

With the crooked, glass edges covered in his blood, Bermuda gripped them tighter. Behind him, The Otherside was lashing at his back, fragments of his skin slowly scraping away - the connection between himself and a world that wasn't his, was growing.

Pressed against him, the woman he was falling for was trying her best to get through, the unstoppable force dragging her to an undeserved end. His refusal, her final chance.

Tears fell down Bermuda's cheek as he watched Argyle slide from Barnaby's blade, his limp body falling through the gap and hurtling towards the earth. A warrior who had given everything, including his life, to preserve his own.

Now he was dead.

The world would soon follow.

Broken splinters of wood whipped up into the air, the blast of wind from the open portal causing mayhem within the four walls. Each one ablaze with the lights of the clock face.

Barnaby slowly turned, the light ricocheting off his eyes, like two shiny, black marbles.

They focused on Bermuda.

With slow, measured steps, Barnaby's boots slammed against the wood, each one bringing the end of the world ever closer.

Outside, the rain lashed against the clock tower, its drumming echoing like a backing track to the chaos. Barnaby grinned, his broken smile mocking Bermuda as he clung to existence.

'Your futile attempt at survival is admirable,' Barnaby mused, impressed as he slowly approached. Between them, Sophie hung in the air, still pressing her entire bodyweight against Bermuda, trying her best to pass through.

Barnaby slowly swung his sword, the blood stained blade cutting the air like a knife through butter.

'Just let go, Bermuda. Just allow the inevitable to take its course. You will die a hero, a man willing to sacrifice himself. A man who tried.'

Bermuda gritted his teeth, the glass digging further into the joints of his fingers. His ribs cried for mercy, the majority of them shattered. His face was decorated with blood, the finger marks of another world slashed across it. His back was merging with the world, its force trying to pull him through the doorway and merge with him completely. His skin was slowly ebbing away.

The pain was unbearable.

He would not let go.

'The pathetic animals that you call a race will know no different. They will all perish, wiped from this canvas and a new world will be created.' Barnaby gazed towards the clock face, peering out and over the land he would soon conquer. 'So just let go.'

Bermuda groaned slightly, the grip around Sophie tightening as he felt the tendons in his shoulder strain as she lurched nearer to the portal. He felt a sharp, burning sensation between his shoulder blades.

It would soon claim him.

'Tell me, Bermuda. Before this whole display of defiance comes to an end.' Barnaby balanced the tip of the blade against the floorboards, leaning both hands on the handle nonchalantly. 'What exactly are you fighting for?'

Bermuda took deep breaths, trying his best to manage the pain. A finger slipped, his grip shaking but he held still.

Blood trickled down the frame of the recently created doorway.

'You are willing to sacrifice yourself for a world that wouldn't even know that you did?'

Barnaby shook his head, failing to comprehend the fight in Bermuda. He slowly raised the blade, approaching the doorway and the obstacle delaying his convergence. His eye's twinkled with excitement, his final effort to consume the world building to a satisfactory crescendo.

'Very well.'

Barnaby swung the sword up, spinning it expertly, the jagged blade cutting through the wind that stormed through the top of the clock tower. Outside, the rain slashed the glass, a Spring storm erupting over the city of London.

Bermuda clutched the glass.

Slowly, the crude blade rested near his arm, Barnaby slowly teasing up and down his arm, the pressure of Sophie pressing against him causing his muscles to stretch and his arms to shake.

Blood trickled down the cracked glass.

His back roared, his exposed flesh slowly disintegrating.

'Where, oh where, should we make the cut?'

Barnaby spoke with a mocking swagger, his misshapen teeth contorted into a crude smile. His jet black eyes hooked on Bermuda.

'Hmmm.' Barnaby mused, still waving his sword. 'Above or below the elbow, that is the question.'

Bermuda gritted his teeth, refusing to look at the sharp instrument that would soon remove his limb and resign the human race to a premature end. As he shook through fear he recalled the entire case. The disappearance of Jess that brought Sophie into his life, the woman he was refusing to lose to the world that had ruined his own.

The attacks. The pain.

Hugo dead.

Argyle gone.

Sophie next.

Furious, he arched his back, expelling his anger with one, long roar of anguish. The motionless body of Sophie hung before him, pressing against him and begging his will to break. Wishing for him to let her pass through. Let her be stolen.

Barnaby rested the blade on Bermuda's arm, a decision close to fruition.

'Above or below the elbow?' He offered, knowing it was a loaded question. Bermuda refused to answer. Defiant to the end.

Spinning the sword above his head, Barnaby tightened his grip. Bermuda gritted his teeth, bracing himself.

'Hey Barnaby,' Bermuda's words were straining against his pain threshold. 'I have a question.'

Barnaby hesitated, loosening the sword slightly as his marble-like eyes flickered with curiosity. Holding the sides of the doorway, Bermuda readjusted himself, the strain reaching its limit.

'Go on,' Barnaby humoured.

'What do you do when something finally loses its power?'

The question hit Barnaby with a slap of confusion. Bermuda had just relayed his own question back to him, the dots refusing to connect. Bermuda loosened the fingers of his right hand, all of them coated in a thick, scarlet.

A chain dropped, hanging from his bloody digits.

It was Barnaby's latch stone.

Every essence he had stolen trapped inside.

Frantically, Barnaby reached inside his blazer, his elongated fingers searching in vain. Bermuda had taken it, when Barnaby had toyed with him.

Barnaby roared with anger, his voice ripping through the wildness of the room, his fury engulfing everything in a venomous explosion of aggression.

He lifted the sword as Bermuda dropped the stone to the floor.

Bermuda raised a boot and stamped down.

The latch stone shattered.

A sword pierced through Barnaby's spine, shooting out of the centre of his chest. His eyes quickly went vacant, his own blade falling from lifeless hands as he slowly went limp.

Dark, navy blood oozed from his mouth and dripped down the blade to the handle.

A handle that was gripped firmly in the hand of Argyle.

■ ▌ ▏

Plummeting towards his death, Argyle thought of the what the world would become. The vulgarity of Barnaby's imagination, the tyranny with which he would rule.

He had escaped that himself when he left The Otherside, the BTCO a saving grace in a world that accepted him as much as it could.

In Bermuda he had found more than just a partner and someone to dedicate his life to protecting. He had found a friend.

A friend who was fighting to save the world on his own and protect a family he never got to see.

He would not die.

Not in this tower.

A hundred feet from the floor he slowly turned, the pain of a severed pectoral muscle burning through his armour. Facing back up, he shot out his right arm, the Retriever flying back up through the tower he was falling through.

It shot into the Big Ben bell, piercing the famous, metal and latching on.

Twenty feet from death, Argyle started retrieving, his shoulder wrenched from its socket as he started to climb, the room lined with lifeless humans and carpeted with fallen Others disappeared as he shot back up to the battle.

To finish the fight.

He had slowly scrambled through the hole, silently and slowly recalling his hook as he saw Barnaby approach Bermuda, his dear friend nearing the end of his battle.

Gritting his teeth and willing himself to silence, Argyle wrenched his shoulder back into place, tendons snapping as it reset.

The left side of his chest hung from his body, disconnected and aching.

He reached down, collecting his sword as he approached Barnaby, who lifted his own sword, ready to amputate his partner.

He saw the gleaming of the stone.

Slowly approaching, he waited for Bermuda to break it, the power of Barnaby slipping away as the humanity left him, his convergence reversing and rendering him nothing more than what he was.

Just another Other.

Not a god. Not a second coming.

Just an Other.

Argyle felt a measure of victory as he plunged his sword through Barnaby's spine, his flesh ripping easily and the battle coming to an end.

He looked at Bermuda, the strain on his face told him the fight was over.

He reached an arm into Barnaby's blazer, rummaging around as he flopped lifeless on the end of his blade. He removed The Gate Maker, the crude key that unlocked all of this mayhem.

Bermuda released his grip, his sliced hands wrapping around Sophie as he pushed away from the doorway, The Otherside severing its connection as he ripped his back free.

Blood splattered down to the floor.

Instantly, Argyle tossed Barnaby's body through the portal, back to the world he had run from. Holding the Gate Maker, he retrieved the lock from his pocket, the two instantly attracting to each other like magnets. With a mind of its own, the lock latched onto it, the mechanisms clipping to each other and solidifying.

It followed Barnaby through the portal.

Instantly it closed and Sophie dropped to the ground, Bermuda catching her and collapsing next to her, his back causing his eyes to water, the rawness of his wounds felt like he was being slowly roasted alive.

Suddenly, with an earth shaking crash, the doorway shattered, blowing a massive hole in the clock face of Big Ben.

Joining the rain on its plunge to earth, the shards of glass twinkled in the night sky like fireflies, scattering the grounds of Westminster below. The wind swirled around the inside of the tower, splashing both Argyle and Bermuda with rain.

Bermuda sat up and faced it, allowing the water to collide with his face.

It was over.

He looked up at his partner, appreciating what they had been through. Argyle's face was dripping blood from the wound above his eye, his chest was splattered with blood and his shoulder was beginning to swell.

Bermuda's face was slashed; claw marks drew red lines from ear-to-ear. His back was bleeding, a layer of skin removed. His hands were dripping with blood, the slashes across his palms were deep and painful.

Sophie lay motionless beside him, and he hoped that the rain splashing her face would soon bring her back to consciousness.

Looking out over the city, Argyle and Bermuda shared the silence. The world would never know what had happened. How close it had come to being wiped clean.

Argyle looked at Bermuda, finally smiling before speaking.

'I bet you ten pounds that Ottoway blames you for the glass.'

Bermuda chuckled, nodding his agreement.

It didn't matter.

Stories would be concocted as to what happened, the reasons behind the hole in the clock. They would lie to the world, keep it safe and secure in its own naivety. The world would never thank Argyle or Bermuda for what they had done.

It didn't matter, Bermuda told himself. There was only one thing that did.

It was over.

30

Rain clattered against Sophie's face as she began to stir, the coldness of the wind slithering around her like an anaconda. Her vision was blurry, her blinking doing little to alleviate the sensation of not being quite there.

She felt heavy, as if she only recently suffered at the hands of gravity.

She was floating. Her dream felt so real, as if she was being transported to a new world.

Now she was on a cold floor, her head resting against something soft. Her face, wet and cold as the rain whistled through. Where was she?

Bermuda had been sitting for fifteen minutes at the top of Big Ben, looking out through the hole that had been ripped through the famous face of the clock. Sophie had been lying in his arms, her head resting against his thigh as he quietly contemplated the severity of what had happened.

The sense of relief that the world was still intact.

She now stirred, moving gently and battling the confusion of time spent in the void between worlds. She would return to him, he knew that much. It was just safer for her to arrive there by herself.

He would sit for as long as it took, a cigarette burning in his hand that dropped lazily to his side.

Sure enough, after a few minutes of bewilderment, she spoke.

'Bermuda?'

He smiled down at her, his face recently wiped clear of blood but the cuts remaining fresh and prominent.

'Hey.' He flashed a grin, lifting the cigarette and exhaling deeply. 'Welcome back.'

Suddenly a penny dropped, her eyes widening with terror as she sat up, drawing her knee's in and hastily looking from corner to corner.

'It's ok,' Bermuda reassured her.

'He's here. The top hat,' she murmured, shaking slightly. 'Those black eyes.'

'Hey!' Bermuda's sternness got her attention. 'It's over.'

She looked into his eyes, confirming she was worth the fight. All the pain he had gone through, the shattered ribs, the slashed face and chest, the sliced up hands.

All of it worth it.

Her face shimmered in the moonlight, the water sending a wet gleam dancing across her cheekbones. Her dark eyes were slowly relaxing and she leant forward, wrapping her arms around Bermuda's neck and hugging him powerfully.

He winced, accepting the pain.

They were finally safe.

Time stopped as they embraced and Bermuda allowed his tiredness to wash over him as he held her, his eyes heavy as he slowly rocked to the timing of her breathing. She pushed her cheek against his, slowly withdrawing so their lips brushed and she kissed him.

Only gently and for a few seconds.

It was a thank you.

The gratitude for not giving up on her. For going to the ends of the earth to keep her safe.

'Guess what?' He asked her, her eyebrows raising with intrigue. 'I found her.'

It took a second, then Sophie stood up instantly.

'What? Where?'

Bermuda struggled to his feet, the evening's battle taking its toll as she steadied him.

'Downstairs. Argyle is with her and the others.'

Sophie raced towards the door, the number of steps between her and her friend was irrelevant. She descended as fast as she could, each step taking her closer to a feeling of normality.

Her world had been turned upside down, literally. She had learnt truths about her world that she should never have had to, exposed to the Otherside and the very real danger that rested on the edges of her existence.

Now she would be able to return to normal.

Step by step.

She burst through the door, her eyes scanning the room and the people who were seated on the floor, their worlds altered as they tried to grasp the time they had lost.

They had all been stolen against their knowledge.

Each one had a vacancy in their eyes, as if they had experienced a dream and thought it real. As if they had seen something move in the shadow but know there was nothing there.

She saw them all, a young boy who was crying gently, afraid of the people around him and the strange realisation that he wasn't at home. The last thing he remembered was counting to ten against a tree.

An overweight American was reassuring everyone that they would be ok, that he was going to call the cops. The last thing he remembered was reading something about a boat.

A young man puffed on a cigarette, wondering how he went from looking at engagement rings to being trapped in a huge tower, waking up and finding himself tied to the concrete wall.

That was when she saw her, the girl who remembered only being on a bus, then walking towards her home.

Jess.

Sophie ran towards her friend, the two of them throwing their arms around each other and holding as tightly as possible.

She was back.

Bermuda had found her.

They both began to cry, their happiness pouring out through tears as the rest of the Stolen returned to the world, the wailing of police sirens reassuring them all that they would be ok.

No one saw Argyle, the battered warrior, as he returned from the stairwell, helping his friend and partner Bermuda down the last couple of steps. He had previously been detaching them from the shackles that held them to the wall, gently placing them on the floor for them to adjust to reality in their own time.

The police raced in, radioing through with excitement that eleven reportedly missing people had been held captive against their will. They arrested Bermuda, despite Sophie's protests. He reassured her and said to let it happen, that it would be fine.

Reluctantly, she relented, watching angrily as he was roughly pulled out of the tower, a gathering crowd watching as he was plonked into a police car.

The rain was flashing blue in the night sky.

Bermuda rested his head against the window and begged for sleep, happy that the world was safe.

It was over.

Slowly but surely, each of the Stolen was tended to, the police taking statements and arranging safe transportation for them, a few ambulances joining the parade of emergency vehicles to administer safety checks.

There were no signs of any injury.

As the Stolen were placed into the squad cars and taken home, Bermuda was awoken by his car door opening and him falling face first onto the gravel, his hands bound between his back.

'Fucking hell!' He bellowed, as the young police officer helped him up, apologizing as he uncuffed him.

'Your language is truly atrocious at times.'

Ottoway stood before him, his rotund body wrapped in a waterproof jacket, an umbrella keeping him dry.

Bermuda was soaked through.

'Hello, sir.'

'Bermuda.' He turned to the hulking warrior beside him. 'Argyle.'

'Sir.'

Argyle joined Bermuda, who slowly sat on the hood of the police car, the blue lights bursting every few seconds, lighting the raindrops up like fireworks.

'I have been told your wounds will heal.' Ottoway's words were matter-of-fact. Bermuda shrugged, patting his jacket for his cigarettes.

'That's no skin off my back,' he quipped, the red rawness of his back having been bandaged by the medical staff as he awaited his trip to the station. The skin was gone, as was the entire back of his jacket.

'Well, let's review shall we,' Ottoway demanded, waving away the plume of smoke that was shot his way.

'You owe me a new coat,' Bermuda pointed out. 'And a new rib cage.'

'You were under direct orders to maintain a level of calm, to ensure that we acted with complete secrecy and discretion and would reduce any evidence of The Otherside, including any damage to public buildings.'

'I know.' Bermuda's words danced through the smoke.

'You ignored your orders, desecrating one of the most famous buildings in the world, causing untold damage to it at a cost we dare not speculate. At the same time, you endangered yourself and your partner.'

Bermuda sheepishly looked at Argyle, a ten pound debt agreed between them.

Ottoway broke into a smile.

'And you saved the world.'

Bermuda and Argyle both turned, looking at their superior with surprise, the rain trickling off the edge of his umbrella. Behind him, police cars were loaded with people looking to be returned home.

'Sorry?' Bermuda asked, flicking his cigarette and immediately searching for mints.

'You saved the world. Well done.' Ottoway offered a warm smile as he addressed Argyle. 'Argyle, bring him back to HQ for treatment.'

'I'm ok,' Bermuda interjected, trying and failing to stand unsupported.

'You look like hell,' Ottoway commented. 'You need rest and to recover.'

Bermuda nodded, his boss gently patting his arm with gratitude. Bermuda looked

'Sir, about Hugo.'

Ottoway cut him off abruptly.

'What happened to Hugo was unfortunate. But Marco has explained what happened and it was not your fault at all. So don't carry it.'

With a reluctant nod of the head, Bermuda accepted Ottoway's words. Ottoway gave them both one final look before he turned and disappeared as easily as he arrived, the police ignoring his presence under strict orders. Bermuda sat for a moment, the pain trying to bear hug him to submission.

'Bermuda?'

Her voice cut through the rain and he turned, her beauty twinkling in the raindrops. Sophie approached him as he slid off the bonnet of the car.

'Hey.'

'They are going to drive me and Jess home now. I just thought I'd come and say goodbye.'

'Goodbye?' Bermuda winced, not knowing if it was through his crushed ribs or heartbreak.

'I like you, Bermuda. I think I really like you.' She was struggling, her voice creaking and tears forming. 'But I can't fall for you. To see the world the way you do, to know what you know. It's too dangerous.'

'Don't say that,' he said, refusing to stay alone in the world.

'I can't stay with you.'

'Then I'll leave. I'll walk away from it.'

'No you won't.' She smiled, gently pressing her palm against his bruised cheek. 'The world needs you, Bermuda.'

He closed his eyes, gently pressing his face against her hand. He knew she was right, a begrudging acceptance spreading through him.

Just another reason to detest his curse.

He had found a wonderful woman who wanted to be with him, who felt the same as he did. She was the most beautiful woman he had ever seen and when they kissed, he had felt more than he ever had before.

She was perfect for him.

But she could never be with him.

A single tear rolled down his cheek before he opened his eyes. Hers were red, a few tears leaping to freedom.

'Goodbye Sophie.'

She stepped in and hugged him, carefully wrapping her arms around his broken body.

'Goodbye Bermuda.' She shook gently in the cold. 'Thank you.'

He gently rubbed her back before releasing her, watching her walk between the police cars, the rain around her bursting with sudden shots of blue. She entered the car, her friend Jess beside her, and they slowly rolled towards the main road, the tyres crunching over the gravel.

They rounded the corner.

Sophie was gone.

Crestfallen, he slumped back against the car, the rain crashing against him as the world returned to normal. Next to him, Argyle stood, arms folded and patiently waiting to follow his orders.

'Well, Argyle. At least I will always have you.'

Epilogue

It was five days before Bermuda eventually made his way home. Vincent had led the medical staff in treating Bermuda, applying their advanced medical knowledge and experience to treat his back, their concoction of drugs and expertise numbing the pain and setting Bermuda on a fast road to recovery.

He slept for two whole days, safe in the knowledge that Argyle never left his side. His partner healed within a day, his chest reattaching, summoning his Otherworldly ability for recuperation.

In private, Vincent had warned Bermuda that he believed his attachment to The Otherside had only worsened his link, the wound on his back healing at an inhuman pace. Promising to keep it between the two of them, Vincent agreed to look into a way of severing the link. A way to keep Bermuda from converging.

After four days he was up and walking around, annoying Ottoway with his continued insistence of smoking within the confines of the BTCO HQ.

The fifth day he was brought a black suit and tie and attended the procession for Hugo's funeral, standing quietly whilst a number of obituaries were read and his body was sentenced to an ashy eternity in an urn.

After a week of being cooped up several floors below ground, Bermuda, with a replacement coat, was allowed to return home. The BTCO even paid his parking ticket.

'Well, it's good that you are on the mend.'

Brett held up his pint, Bermuda gratefully accepting the cheers. They clinked their glasses together before taking a large gulp of Doombar.

'God that tastes good,' Bermuda stated, wiping his lips. The swelling had gone from his face, as had the bruising. His back was healing well and his ribs were slowly making their way back together.

The Royal Oak was fairly empty for a Sunday afternoon; a family were discussing holidays over a Sunday lunch whilst a young couple spoke in hushed whispers over their bottle of wine.

Paul, the always accommodating landlord, had given them a pint on the house on account of Bermuda's injuries.

Life was continuing as normal.

No one had any idea of what had happened. The credit for saving the world would never come. Bermuda was happy to drink to no one ever needing to know.

'So, what now?' Brett asked, shiftily looking towards the door.

'What on earth are you doing?'

'I'm, err....'

'If you are looking for Argyle, he is right here.' He pointed to the empty chair next to him.

'Is he?' Brett said excitedly. 'Can I touch him?'

Bermuda looked up, Argyle slowly shaking his head.

'I wouldn't.'

'Fair enough.' Brett shrugged, his fingers quickly rolling a cigarette. 'Smoke?'

Bermuda shook his head, happy with his five day old decision to quit. Reflecting upon that night in Big Ben, Argyle found it astonishing that Bermuda's biggest revelation was he struggled to race up the stairs.

They sat in silence as Brett walked to the outside, the Spring sun bringing with it a blanket of warmth.

He sipped his drink and thought of Sophie, the beautiful dimple in her cheek when she smiled. The flicker of her eyelash when he said something she wouldn't comprehend.

He missed her.

Suddenly, the door to the pub opened and Brett burst in, his face highly animated.

'Hey, BJ.' Bermuda rolled his eyes. 'Come and give us a hand, will ya?'

'A hand, with what?'

'Some woman's car has broken down.' Brett exited again, much to Bermuda's anger. He tutted loudly, taking a large swig to finish his pint before following, leaving Argyle to guard the table.

He pushed open the door, already working on his excuses.

'I'm sorry, I don't know what my friend has told you but I'm really not the right perso....'

Bermuda stopped mid-sentence.

It was Angela.

His ex-wife stood ten feet from him, her car parked on the small ring road that framed the quaint green that the Royal Oak sat on. She smiled at him.

'Hi, thanks for helping. Your friend said you would be able to have a look.'

Bermuda looked at them both in confusion. Brett nodded towards the vehicle.

'You check the backseat, yeah? I'll check the engine.'

Suddenly it dropped and Bermuda suddenly began to shake. A lump swelled in his throat that he battled to swallow as Brett and Angela walked to the front of the car, pretending to examine the damage.

The backseat.

He took a step forward and felt his heart slamming against his chest, doing its upmost to re-shatter his ribcage.

He opened the door.

'Hello.'

Chloe's voice was angelic, her large blue eyes looking up at him and wrenching at every heart string. He smiled, a few tears rolling down his cheek as he squatted down beside her, hidden from both worlds.

Just him and his daughter.

His Chloe.

After a few moments and failed attempts, he spoke, his voice cracking under the weight of his emotions.

'How are you?'

'I'm fine.' She spoke with such youthful exuberance, a wonderful innocence to her words. She smiled at him.

'Hey.' He pointed. 'Where have your teeth gone.'

'They fell out!' She exclaimed, the two gaps reappearing as she smiled.

Bermuda felt himself choking, the love he felt for this child was overbearing.

'Are you sad?' She asked, every word genuine.

He shook his head, wiping away tears that he knew would be endless.

'I'm actually really happy.'

'Me too.' She showed him the gaps again.

'Yeah? Why's that?'

The next sentence stopped him dead. The words shook him, he thought his heart would burst.

'Because Mummy says that you are my Daddy.'

Words escaped him. More tears burst forward as he looked at her, lost in the splendour of her beauty.

'Are you?'

He nodded. She reached out and dabbed his tears. He reached in and hugged her, feeling her delicate arms wrap around his neck, her golden locks cascading over his shoulder.

'I love you, kitten,' he whispered, nuzzling into the side of her head.

'I love you too, Daddy.'

He held her close for a few more seconds, the fear of the Otherside witnessing this moment was growing as they ticked by. Eventually he let go, straightening her jacket and checking her seatbelt.

'Now you be good for Mummy and Ian, ok?' She nodded.

'Bye, Daddy.'

He smiled one more time before stepping away, closing the door and wiping his eyes. He exhaled powerfully, regretting his decision to quit smoking almost instantly.

The bonnet slammed shut and Angela walked towards the driver's side of the car. She glanced over the roof at her ex-husband.

He mouthed 'thank you'.

With her lip quivering and eyes watering she nodded, hurrying into the car and pulling away, a curious five-year-old looking backwards through the back window at her father.

Bermuda cried as they slowly rounded the end of the green before disappearing back to their lives.

'I'll give you a minute,' Brett offered, walking back towards the pub.

'Thank you,' Bermuda called out after him, knowing full well what his friend had done for him.

After a few moments, Bermuda strode back into the pub, his eyes red but now tear free, the magnitude of the meeting bearing heavy on him. Every night and every morning, he had looked at the photo of his Chloe, wishing for a world where he was more than just a myth to her. A broken fragment of memory, gone before she even knew him.

Every day he would dream of seeing her again, holding her close to him and letting her know that he would never let anything hurt her.

When he stood in that doorway, refusing to let Barnaby steal Sophie and destroy the world, it was her face that kept him holding on.

His Chloe.

He approached the bar, ordering three pints of Doombar which Paul gratefully poured. He even commented on how Bermuda was smiling, as if he 'had slept with a coat hanger in his mouth'.

Clasping three pint glasses in his hand with complete control, Bermuda re-joined the table, sliding one of the pints across to his grateful friend.

Argyle raised an eyebrow.

'You know I can't drink that, right?'

'Who said it was for you?

Smiling, Bermuda lifted the two glasses, clinking them together. 'Cheers.'

The End

Born and raised in North West London and now residing in Hertfordshire, Robert Enright has been writing for over 10 years. His debut novel – ONE BY ONE – was self-published on Amazon in March 2015, receiving critical acclaim and was nominated for Books Go Social Book of the Year 2015. The violent, revenge thriller gave Rob a path into crime fiction, but the constantly embraced geek within him went a different way.

Follow Robert on Twitter

https://twitter.com/REnright_Author

Acknowledgements

WOW. I can't believe that this is the second novel and I have a number of people to thank for their support and patience with me whilst we arrived here.

First off, I want to thank Sophie Holland, my lovely lady, who has put up with a whole year's worth of crazy ideas and spooky stories until I arrived at this book. You have my love and gratitude always!

I want to thank Daniel Carter and Saira Donaldson for their constant pep-talks and for not letting my head drop!

My brother, Anthony Enright, who continually inspires me with his drive and ambition and keeping me focused.

My entire family: Mum, Dad, Jane, Dave, Tracy, Kevin, Charlotte and Jack. You are all incredible and your love and support goes further than you know.

A whole heap of people who are nothing but supportive, such as Ben Entwistle, Sam Matthews, Neil Stevens, Nick Leete, Matthew Hannon, Johnny Denham, Josh Cooper, Karen Jones, Francesca Brown, Alice O'Dowd, Karlene Smith, Brett Archer, Elaine Hunter, Rob Thorpe, Kylie Edwards, Matt McGuire, the Newsome's and to anyone I may have forgotten when writing this. You guys have been amazing.

I also want to thank Louise Hunter for making me believe I could make it as a writer and for giving more exposure than I ever dreamed off. Also shout-outs to David McCaffrey, Paddy Magrane and Leigh Russell. Exceptionally talented people who I am honoured to know and consider friends.

A thank you to Matthew Smith at Urbane Publications for signing me, believing in this idea and pushing me to create the best book I could. For just taking a punt on me and having me realise a dream is beyond amazing.

And finally, a thank you to you, the reader, for giving me a reason to write.